Reckless Nights in Rome

A Ludlow Hall Story – Book 1: Bronte and Nico

By CC MacKenzie

Reckless Nights in Rome - Copyright

By CC MacKenzie
Copyright © C C MacKenzie 2015
CC MacKenzie has asserted her right to be identified
as the author of this work.
All rights reserved. No part of the publication may be
reproduced, stored in any retrieval system, or transmitted in any
form or by means, electronic, mechanical, photocopying,
imaging, recording, or otherwise, without the prior permission of
the publishers.
ISBN 9781909331143
This book is a work of fiction. Names, characters, businesses,
organisations, places and events other than those clearly in the
public domain, are either the product of the author's imagination
or are used fictitiously. Any resemblance to actual persons, living
or dead, events or locales is entirely coincidental.
Published by More Press

Cover Design by *Gabrielle Prendergast*

Chapter One

"Don't be such a bloody tease, Bronte. You know you fancy me. And I have it on very good authority that it's been a while since you got laid. How about it, love? The rooms in this place cost a fucking fortune. If we go up now we can get our money's worth."

In something like dazed bewilderment Bronte simply stared at the man sitting across the table, a table set with crisp white linen and heavy cutlery of solid silver. Then she wondered if there was a blue moon in the night sky. Maybe the stars were in some sort of weird alignment because Anthony was clearly out of his tiny mind. And it wasn't the first time he'd alluded to someone who was a 'good authority' on Bronte Ludlow, someone who seemed to know a hell of a lot about her. Little things. Personal things.

Bronte was beginning to get a very bad feeling about this.

Right from the start, when her best friend Rosie Gordon had been approached out of the blue by the sister of an old school friend and told Rosie that her brother had had a crush on Bronte and would love to meet her, she'd suspected something hinky. And against her better judgement, she'd listened to Rosie when she'd told her to *'Go for it. He might be a really nice guy.'*

Yeah right.

No way could Anthony be classed as a *really nice guy*.

Anything but.

At the moment, Bronte was classing him as a repellent little creep. A creep who couldn't hold his alcohol. As soon as they'd arrived at the Hall for their blind date, he'd downed a couple of Cranberry Kamikaze's (a vodka drink which was called that for a very good reason) before he'd hit the red wine. Anthony was now on his second bottle of Chateauneuf du Pape. With a mottled flush on his jowls and the randy gleam in his beady eyes, her blind date was looking more than a little hot under the collar.

Now those eyes made her flesh crawl as they slid over her black off the shoulder sweater to linger on her breasts. Breasts that were supported by chicken fillets inserted into a black strapless Wonder bra. Now Bronte wondered why she'd bothered. And the way he now licked his fat lip seriously gave her the creeps.

"Since I met you for the first time two hours ago, trust me, sex with you is never going to be on tonight or any other night's agenda," she said in a tone that would melt solid steel. Her brow creased. "And I have to admit that I'm very confused, Anthony, about why you would think I fancy you? Who is the *good authority* you mention?"

His response was another lick of his lips and a lewd wink.

Bronte's response was to get to her feet because she was out of here.

However, his hand shot out, grabbed her wrist and squeezed hard.

It hurt.

Fear might have her heart beating too hard against her ribcage, but she wouldn't give him the satisfaction of flinching or making a squeak.

Bronte was in trouble.

And by the predatory look in his eyes, he knew she knew it.

"The name's Tony. Use it."

Her eyes met his and what Bronte saw there made her shiver and her heartbeat roar in her ears.

"I'm going to the ladies room... Tony. Let me go."

He squeezed harder and all the time his beady and bloodshot eyes stayed on hers.

"I know *all* about you, darlin'. I know you like to say no when you mean yes."

Now Bronte wondered if he was on drugs or maybe he lived in his own parallel universe, because there was something very wrong with the man.

"You're hurting me," she said through clenched teeth. "You have two seconds to release me before I scream."

When he ignored her and squeezed even harder, she grabbed his thumb and bent it back.

He released her, but now his face was puce.

"You're nothing but a bitch of a cock-tease."

Charming.

"And you're nothing but an obnoxious thug. If you don't watch your mouth, I'll report you to security and trust me, they'll sort you out."

He sat back in his chair, spread his legs to show her the bulge between his legs and what she was missing.

Yuck.

"You'd never make a drama here. You've too much pride. You worry too much about what other people think, what they'd say. How the mighty have fallen, eh? When you lived here you never gave me the time of day. Now you're slumming it with the rest of us plebs. Don't be too long in the Ladies room I'm not going anywhere, darlin', and neither are you."

Bronte blinked.

After everything she'd said and after everything he'd done, he still thought she was going to sleep with him?

Jeez, the man was certifiable.

Bronte picked up her bag and walked on legs that were not quite steady straight to the cloakroom to grab her coat. When she turned to leave, she found Anthony leaning back against the bar and watching her like a raptor. The bar was situated in a spot right between her and the exit.

Now he raised his glass of wine as if to say *I'm waiting* and drank deeply.

Crap.

Bronte made a beeline for the Ladies restrooms, entered, and locked the door behind her.

She chewed on her bottom lip.

Now she had to admit that she'd been beyond stupid to meet with a man she'd never met and decided right there and then that this was her first, and her last, blind date.

Her cell phone was tucked in her bag, she could quite easily call Rosie for help.

However, if she did that Rosie would send the cavalry, which meant Rosie would call Alexander.

The very *last* thing Bronte needed was her brother sticking his oar into this mess.

She'd have to endure yet another lecture.

Plus, she'd never hear the end of it.

God, the horrible nerves in her stomach were going crazy.

Something like panic rose into her throat as she scanned the room, eyed the high narrow window.

Trapped.

Now what the hell was she going to do?

Nico Ferranti played to win.

Winning was in his blood. Along with a certain raw intelligence that had served him well in the backstreets of Rome. The scent he inhaled now might be the heady aroma of Bentley leather, but he never forgot the stink of human garbage or the unique burn of an empty belly.

He was a bastard. His maternal grandfather might have rescued him from one hell, but his hatred of his late daughter's illegitimate son had thrust the young Nico into another type of hell. One of cold disdain, a lack of affection and a certain controlled bullying that should have destroyed him. Instead it had only made him harder and stronger.

Illiterate at ten, with both hands he'd grabbed the opportunity of a Jesuit education. By the time he was sixteen, he'd gained straight A's in every subject and was fluent in four languages.

Although he hadn't exactly danced on his grandfather's grave when he turned twenty-two, he'd shed no tears. And even found it in his heart to be grateful when the old bastard left him the legacy of four hotels.

Now, twelve years later, he was seriously wealthy. Not that he saw wealth as an achievement, but with real money came responsibilities and many pitfalls for the unwary.

Tonight his Bentley growled to a halt in the car park of Ludlow Hall. A gust of wind slapped the car, splattering sleet onto the windscreen. Switching off the headlights, Nico relaxed for the first time in three days as he sat back and studied the building.

January in England did nothing to dull the pleasure of his latest love and she was a beauty. Built in the seventeenth century for a trade Baron, Ludlow Hall with its one hundred and forty rooms, was built along the graceful lines of a bygone era and looked magnificent. The contractors had done an outstanding job bringing the renovations in early and more importantly, on budget.

Along with his business partner, Alexander Ludlow, Nico ran eight Ferranti Hotels and Spas right across the world. And he wanted his guests relaxed and happy. The watchwords in his business were quality and class and Ludlow Hall oozed both along with an old world charm. But what underpinned the whole was sheer luxury. The food and service were outstanding in a Ferranti hotel. The rooms ran from luxurious to sumptuous. And Ludlow Hall was set in fifteen hundred acres of fabulous countryside and catered for everyone including intimate romantic breaks, clay pigeon shooting and fishing.

But the spa was at the heart of it.

The great and the good loved to escape from the city to indulge themselves and their latest passions. They could come for a day to be pampered, oiled and treated. Or spend a week detoxing from indulgence or experience mind and body balance for burnout. A Ferranti Hotel and Spa catered for all.

Nico rubbed gritty eyes. He'd been travelling for thirty hours straight. His brain needed to crash and his stomach craved sustenance. With a yawn, he decided to do both, after he bid a quick hello to Alexander.

Nico's tired brain mulled over the main reasons for his visit.

Alexander's parents, Lord and Lady Ludlow had been killed in a head-on collision with a drunk driver. Two years later, the tragedy still shook the neighborhood and the family.

And Alexander was suffering. He'd thrown himself into work to cope with his loss. Nico could understand it even if he'd never had a family himself. The Ludlow family had been a close-knit unit comprised of their late parents, Alexander and his sister Bronte. But recently, something had happened to blow the sibling's relationship apart.

It wasn't bereavement or the sale of Ludlow Hall that had caused the rift, Nico was sure of it. Although he knew the sale had stirred up a goddamn hornet's nest. Bronte in particular had taken it hard and refused to have anything to do with the renovations. So she'd de-camped to The Dower House.

Whether Alexander and his sister got along or not was none of Nico's business, but he was worried, his friend appeared close to burnout.

It had taken time, but he'd managed to sweet-talk Alexander to carry out a spot inspection of three hotels, saying he had concerns about the management, which wasn't quite true. All of Nico Ferranti's hotels ran like clockwork. But he wasn't above using underhand methods to get his own way and to ensure Alexander took a break. The deal was that Nico would run Ludlow Hall in Alexander's absence. Since he rarely got the chance to get his hands dirty these days, Nico was looking forward to enjoying a bit of down-time. He'd arrived a day earlier than expected in order to attend the first society wedding to be held at the Hall tomorrow. The high public profile of the couple meant the press pack were out in force.

Meanwhile his mind considered his next challenges, The Dower House and the issue of the elusive Bronte Ludlow, both of which occupied far too much of his thoughts these days. His four offers for The Dower House and its eighteen acres of land had been more than generous. The purchase of the property would complete the estate. However, things were not going according to plan. Alexander's sister wasn't having any of it. Bronte's initial rejection of his offer was a one word reply. No. Three subsequent written offers, she'd returned to sender.

He'd managed to speak to her by phone, once. The conversation, her part of it anyway, had been short, sharp and to the point. His hands gripped the steering wheel as the memory of how she'd spoken to him, the icy tone and her clipped voice in particular had pressed a hot button. The Honorable Bronte

Ludlow had been nothing short of... obnoxious.

She wasn't, Bronte said, interested in selling her home to a man who had far too much money and no soul. She was, Bronte said, perfectly content with living in a house built on land her family had lived on for generations. The Dower House was her home, was it not? Why didn't he bugger off and find something else to do instead of harassing her?

Impudent little witch.

The unfairness of it still stung since Alexander had approached Nico in the first instance to buy the Hall.

Nico knew Bronte must be desperate for money since their parents had left their children nothing but debts and death duties. The way Nico saw it, he was offering the girl a wonderful opportunity to make a fresh start. Then he thought that maybe he should leave her to stew in her own juice. But he wanted The Dower House and since Nico Ferranti always got what he wanted, that was the end of the matter.

Fingertips tapping the steering wheel, he frowned as he mulled the tricky situation over.

Maybe Alexander could help him convince his sister to sell?

The idea held a certain appeal.

But then he changed his mind.

No, he decided, the man had enough on his plate and he didn't want to cause more trouble between Alexander and his stubborn sister.

Bronte would sell once he'd found the right button to push. And in Nico's vast experience with women, that button, usually, was money. But by her behavior, Nico knew that nothing would be as easy as simply offering the woman more money. He was beginning to realize that Ms. Bronte Ludlow was a piece of work.

Mulling over the issue, he was staring unseeing through the window, when a movement on the ground floor of Ludlow Hall caught his eye.

The small window to the ladies restroom swung open.

Nico flicked a switch and the passenger window slid down a couple of inches.

He narrowed his eyes and watched events unfold.

A girl tossed what looked like a black puffa jacket out of the window, followed by a red handbag the size of Utah. She was blonde, her hair tied back in a slick tail that reached down her back. Her long and lean body, also dressed in black, squeezed out of the opening. Her leg swung over the ledge and her booted foot stretched down searching for a toehold. Her foot found a drainpipe and she eased her body cautiously over the ledge. Then the heel of her other foot caught in the window ledge, leaving her at a dangerous angle.

If she fell at that angle, the drop was well over six feet, she'd probably break something.

Nico shook his head in disbelief.

What the hell was she doing?

A thief?

Maybe.

He considered the expensive cars in the car park, pursed his lips and decided that whatever she was doing, she was up to no good. Back in the days when he'd been a street rat, he'd slipped out of plenty of windows of less reputable establishments.

Now his eyes narrowed again on the girl balanced precariously on the edge of potential disaster. She had a lean build. Boyish. Nico permitted his gaze to linger on the taut little bottom, those endless legs. And he put the tightness in his belly and his thighs and everything in between, down to the fact it had been a while since he'd been with a woman. She was slick; he'd give her that, and probably a pro.

He checked his limited edition Breitling.

Just after nine thirty.

Yep, she'd timed it well. Most guests were in the bars or restaurants.

Exhaustion warred with irritation as he opened the door, got out, closed the car door with a soft click and stepped forward.

Bronte's scream pierced the night when strong hands gripped her waist, lifting her as if she weighed nothing and dumped her unceremoniously on her feet. Terror hitched her breath as her hands fisted, ready to fight. Over the frantic beat of a heart going crazy against her ribs and the roaring in her ears, the scent of an evocative cologne spun around her heightened senses. And she realized, with something like a heady relief, it wasn't Anthony who had a firm grip on her waist.

The hands released her.

She spun around too fast, struggled to find her balance, and found herself pulled against a brick wall in a shirt.

"Thank you," she gasped. "A fall from that height wouldn't have been pretty."

Trembling with cold and adrenaline coursing through her system, Bronte blinked up to look into the face of a tall and very dark man. A man with tremendous shoulders. He wore a suit, white shirt and tie and an overcoat in black cashmere. Since the lights of the car park were behind him, she couldn't get a good look at his face.

Bronte gave a tug on her arm. "You can let me go now." The gesture was completely futile, since his hand tightened on her arm like a vice.

"Not a chance, sweetheart." The deep voice was silky and tinged with a hard edge of suspicion. She couldn't quite place his accent. "I think the police might be very interested in what you have stashed in your bag, don't you?"

His strong hand felt too hot as it seemed to burn through her cashmere sweater.

For reasons Bronte didn't immediately comprehend, the knots in her belly wound tighter.

Understanding and logic now rose through the residue of panic as she realized how her behavior might appear to him. He thought she was a thief?

The idea made her peer harder into his shadowed features.

She gave another tug of her arm.

Understanding dawned that he had absolutely no intention of releasing her.

Nerves fluttered madly in her stomach making her frown up at him.

"Honestly, this is really not what you think it is."

She caught a flash of white teeth.

It wasn't a smile.

He bent to pick up her jacket and the bag.

"No? What is this?"

Bronte felt like saying, *What the hell does it look like?*

Then decided she'd better not push her luck, because she had a feeling her saviour was not a man to mess with.

"A Mulberry Piccadilly," she said, looking up into the darkened face.

No sign of the teeth or of a sense of humor either.

"Expensive," he drawled in a way that made her teeth ache. "On the large side. You could fit a small car in it. Plenty of space for purloined items." His tone was ice over steel.

After the night she'd had, *this* was all she needed.

Bronte spluttered on a laugh. "Purloined? Seriously? Why don't you just say what you mean? You think I'm a thief."

The idea was so ridiculous Bronte couldn't help but throw her head back and roar with laughter.

And of course once she started, she couldn't stop.

The result, she knew, of too much stress and the deep mortification of being caught red-handed running away from a date that had gone very wrong.

Bent from the waist, she tried to catch her breath, her eyes streaming.

"*Dio*, I fail to see humor in the situation." The guy sounded seriously annoyed now, which set her off again. "If you are not stealing, why use the window when there is a perfectly good door?" He gave her arm a little shake. And she realized his deep voice held an Italian accent.

Incredibly, an illicit little thrill slid up her spine.

Cold fingertips wiped her freezing cheeks as Bronte took a couple of deep breaths. With big eyes she stared up into his face and deliberately pumped up the volume of her smile. She heard his breath catch. Yep, the smile worked with most men and seemed to work with Mr. Italiano, too. Feeling more confident, even though her breath was unsteady, she poured charm into her voice.

"Honestly, it's a long story. And terribly embarrassing."

She shivered and his grip on her arm tightened.

"Let us go in where it is warm. You can tell me all about it."

He turned and her heart took a stumble as she got her first good look at his face.

Wow.

Bronte Ludlow had seen plenty of good-looking men in her life. But she'd never seen anyone who looked like this. His hair was jet black and swept back from a strong, glorious face. Eyes, dark and broody, considered her with a mix of annoyance and curiosity. At the moment that amazing face wore a do-not-mess-with-me expression. She couldn't tear her eyes from his hard mouth, a mouth with an incredibly sensual bottom lip.

Long dormant ovaries, flared triumphantly to life.

Mouth dry, her smile slipped as Mr. Italiano helped her on with her jacket.

She grabbed her bag, gave it a tug.

"Thank you, there's no need for... Hey!"

He won the short battle for her bag and tucked it under his arm.

Then Bronte flinched as he held her wrist in a grip that was too tight.

It hurt.

Earlier in the evening another man's touch had not only hurt her, it had repulsed her, too.

But this man's fingers on her skin appeared to have the opposite effect.

She had no idea what cologne he wore, but he smelt fabulous; all peppery, citrusy, fresh and healthy male.

"I insist." His voice was cool now, the tone hard.

He headed for the entrance to Ludlow Hall, towing her behind him.

Her heart fell.

Oh God, she was in so much trouble.

Bronte's feet picked up the beat of her speeding heart as she struggled to keep up with his long stride. When Alexander found out what she'd been doing here tonight, he was going to go absolutely mental.

"Look, you're making a big, big mistake." Her voice, the way it went too high now, mortified her.

The man's response was a stony look that assured her he was a man who never made mistakes.

They entered a side entrance to the hotel and immediately the scent of hot food, the hum of voices and soft music hit them. The place was full she realized; grateful no one appeared to be paying any notice to this little scene.

As she was being marched along the corridor, Bronte managed to take a good long look at him. He looked... expensive. She happened to know that his tie was Armani. And since she had a thing for shoes, Bronte recognized outrageously expensive footwear when she saw them. Italian. Now she studied his face. He had the slashing bone structure and the skin tone of a Latin. That fact along with his accent made her already unsteady heart roar in her ears as the penny finally dropped.

Crappity crap, crap.

Surely not?

It couldn't be, could it?

He stopped dead, knocked on a door with the sign 'Alexander Ludlow, General Manager.'

And to Bronte's eternal shame, she whimpered.

Her captor's response was a hard look as he opened the door and thrust her in before him.

Chapter Two

Alexander Ludlow glanced up from his desk and stood.

He beamed a smile at the man.

Then his green eyes sharpened as he noted the firm grip on her wrist.

"Nico, how are you? Good trip?"

Her brother stepped forward and shook *Nico's* hand.

Bloody hell.

Her luck, Bronte decided as her throat went bone dry, was running bad tonight.

This must be the infamous Nico Ferranti.

Since her brother had brought his business partner into their lives, Bronte hadn't had a decent night's sleep. She'd managed to avoid Nico Ferranti when he'd done one of his flashy helicopter visits. There was a long list of reasons why she couldn't stand the Italian. Not least of which was the fact that Nico Ferranti had torn the heart out of her home. How he'd got the restructuring and refurbishing of Ludlow Hall past the local planning authority, was a mystery. By some miracle the planners and English Heritage were eating out of his hand. He'd brought in specialists in listed buildings. Legions of construction workers, architects and interior designers had descended on her old home like locusts.

These days, it looked like a plush decadent hideaway for the über-wealthy instead of a building rich in heritage that had been part of her birthright. And on a point of principal, she'd refused to have anything to do with the renovations, too. Her brother seemed to view the man as some kind of hero. However, Bronte saw Nico Ferranti as nothing more than a smooth operator with his eye on the main chance.

She simply couldn't bear watching the destruction of her

family's past, present and future, and moved to The Dower House.

But Ludlow Hall wasn't enough for Nico Ferranti.

Now he was sniffing around The Dower house and the land that surrounded it, too.

She'd very politely rejected his first very generous offer.

Insulted that the man would even think that she could be bribed to give up her heritage by the likes of him, she'd ignored the other offers, even the last one, which had been totally outrageous. Money might talk to him, but to Bronte Ludlow money meant nothing. He'd phoned her once. And as soon as he'd given her his name, she'd let him have an earful. The memory of how she'd stood her ground against a person she regarded as nothing less than an infidel made Bronte stiffen her spine and lift her chin.

Alexander turned to regard her with a hard stare.

A stare that broke her heart.

These days there wasn't a lot of love lost between them.

But Bronte refused to show Alexander how much he'd hurt her by selling their heritage down the river. Her brother must have seen something in her face because he folded his arms and leaned back against his desk.

"Long time no see. Color me surprised. I thought you said you'd never set foot in the Hall ever again?"

The silky tone and the delivery, cranked Bronte's fast fraying temper.

She huffed out a breath, and gave another useless tug on her wrist. The last thing she needed tonight was another futile argument with her brother. They'd both said everything that needed to be said. And they both disagreed with the choices the other had made.

Now she wished she'd spent the night at home in her pj's with a big mug of hot chocolate.

This evening was turning into a complete and utter nightmare.

"It's none of your business why I'm here. Please ask your friend to let..."

Nico rudely interrupted her,

"She nearly broke her neck climbing out of the Ladies restroom window. She tossed her jacket out first, followed by this." He held up her bag.

Then he released her and with a quick flip emptied the contents onto Alexander's desk.

Stunned, Bronte's jaw dropped.

Who the *hell* did he think he was?

And then her eyes bugged out of her head as certain personal belongings rolled across the shiny desk.

Heat scorched a path up her neck and into her cheeks.

Feminine hygiene products along with an assortment of lipsticks, coins, her purse, her Smartphone, pens, a hairbrush, and a large pack of Percy Pigs candy (it was no secret she had the sweet tooth of a five year old) tumbled over the desk.

"How *dare* you?" Bronte's voice rose.

Then her eyes went like saucers as she spotted something else.

Something that made her cheeks go nuclear.

Something she just knew she would never, ever live down.

Closing her eyes, Bronte swore an oath to kill Rosemary Margaret Gordon because nestled in the middle of the detritus on her brother's desk of polished oak was a box of fruit flavored *extra large* condoms... with twenty-five per cent extra.

Alexander's shocked laugh brought a hot lump to her throat as she glared at him.

He lifted the condom box, read the label.

"Well, well, well. It seems my sister is getting down and dirty with a well-endowed guy." His tone told her that if he had his way she'd be locked in a room until she was forty. "For the ultimate in pleasure and sensual experience," he read. Bronte closed her eyes. She would never hear the end of this, never. "At least you're practising safe sex."

"I am not practising safe sex! Um, I mean..."

Her eyes slid to Nico.

A Nico who was studying her through narrowed grey eyes, his mouth tight. He had a half bored, half reflective expression on his face. An expression tinged with a contempt that brought even more heated mortification soaring into her cheeks.

Shame battled with annoyance that she should feel hurt by his attitude, his obvious disapproval.

What the hell did she care what Nico Ferranti thought of her?

But now his physical presence seemed to overwhelm the room as he took off his coat and made himself nice and comfortable on a wide couch of tan leather.

He loosened his silk tie and undid the top button of his shirt.

One foot shod in a Dolce & Gabbana loafer rested on his knee.

Like a King surveying his domain, Nico leaned back and those dark eyes took their own sweet time studying her from head to toe and back again.

Bastard.

Bronte couldn't help it, she gave as good as she got; her gaze cruised over narrow hips and a washboard flat stomach, before returning to his face. Sleek black hair was brushed back from his high forehead. It almost reached his collar, throwing his cheekbones into sharp relief. That hard jaw saved him from looking too beautiful, thank goodness, but nothing in her, admittedly limited, experience with men thus far, had ever caught at her lungs the way this man did.

He simply stared at her, those amazing eyes all seeing, all knowing.

His brows rose with an insolent query and Bronte realized with a surge of mortification that she was staring.

"I might have known Rosie Gordon was at the bottom of this," Alexander said now, his long suffering tone diverting Bronte's attention from the fallen angel on the couch. Her brother read the sticky label sellotaped to the side of the box. "It says, *Just in case you get lucky, love, Rosie.*" Alexander tossed the box of condoms on his desk. His vivid green eyes pinned her to the spot. "I'll probably be sorry I asked this, but why were you climbing out of a window?"

Good question.

Now she wondered if she'd lost her frigging mind.

Why on earth had she listened to Rosie?

Why?

Hadn't she told Rosie a blind date with a friend of a friend's brother was not a good idea?

So what if Rosie'd told Bronte she was worried that her best friend hadn't had a date in over eighteen months.

Who the hell was counting?

Who the hell cared?

If she told Alexander the whole sordid story of her date, he would, she knew, staring at the determined look in his eyes, go ballistic.

Now that she had time to have a close look at him, she thought Alexander looked too tired these days and she was sure he'd lost weight. Bronte ignored the niggle of guilt that perhaps she was the one responsible for him appearing a little frazzled around the edges. She ordered herself not to cause a horrible scene in front of the enemy, Nico Ferranti, and to play it nice and cool.

"I was trying to avoid a scene precisely like this one," she replied. Turning to Nico still sitting on the couch and watching her like a hawk, Bronte jerked her chin in his direction. "Unfortunately, *he* stuck his big nose in or I would be long gone."

Nico rubbed his nose, his eyes narrowing into slits as he stared at her.

Alexander nodded.

"Strangely enough, that makes perfect sense. I put money on it that Rosie Gordon is at the bottom of whatever trouble you're in." Irritation with Alexander that he was right, along with the silent witness boring holes through her, merely added fuel to Bronte's fire. "I had a date. Not that it's any of your business."

At her tone, Alexander ran his tongue along the top of his teeth.

A bad sign.

So much for playing it nice and cool.

"Who was he?"

"Anthony."

Her brother's green eyes drilled into hers and Bronte fought not to squirm, especially since Nico appeared to be riveted by the scene.

Bastard.

"Does *Anthony* have a surname?" Alexander asked in a silky tone.

The jumpy nerves in Bronte's stomach nudged her temper.

"I have no idea. Tonight was the first time I met him."

Alexander's eyes stayed on hers.

"Tell me you didn't meet him on the internet," he said in a tone that made it sound as if internet dating was the equivalent of selling her soul to the great Satan.

For God's sake, this whole situation was turning into something like farce.

Who did he think he was, her keeper?

It was so typical of Alexander to jump to conclusions these days.

And why was he interrogating her like this in front of Nico bloody Ferranti?

"I didn't, but there's nothing wrong with internet dating, as long as it's done safely. Rosie knows his sister."

Her brother stalked behind his desk.

"I bloody *knew* it."

Alexander sat and swung his leather business chair around to face Nico.

"When they were three, Rosie stuck a crayon up Bronte's nose, which meant a trip to A&E. When they were ten they fell from a barn roof. Rosie ended up with a broken leg and Bronte a broken arm. They were lucky not to be killed. At boarding school, the pair of them attempted to drink a bottle of neat vodka. You should have seen my sister. Think of Bambi, pissed. I could go on, but we don't have all night."

Pushed beyond endurance and refusing to rise to the deep laugh from the man on the couch, or her ridiculous response to it, Bronte thrust her belongings into her favourite bag.

All the while she eyed her brother and Nico with a deep loathing burning fiercely in her heart.

"Neither of you have any right to find what happened to me tonight funny."

Her brother's eyes flashed green fire.

"Trust me, I'm not finding it funny. I'm merely sharing past experiences."

Stung, Bronte glared at him.

Enough was enough.

"You've no right to ridicule me in front of a complete stranger," she yelled.

Alexander's face flushed with annoyance.

The look in his eyes warned her to back off.

"He wouldn't be a stranger to you, Bronte, if you learned some manners. Nico was there when we needed him most."

Here we go again with Saint Nico, she fumed. According to her brother, Nico Ferranti could do no wrong. Maybe the man should be beatified by the Pope in Rome.

"What happened to putting family first?" she flung back.

Then she sucked in a breath as Alexander's face went pale, as he flinched as if from a blow. Too late, Bronte remembered that they weren't family. Not anymore. Not since their parent's funeral when they'd found out she was not, after all, a Ludlow. Remembering the awful day they'd learned the truth in a letter addressed to Bronte, a letter written by her mother and by the man who'd brought her up as his own, a man she'd adored, a man she learned in the cruellest way was not her natural father. And that was the day she'd lost her brother, too. Alexander refused to listen to her when he'd sold off the family home. But much worse, he refused to support her in her quest to find out more about her past and approach her real father. A man who had no idea she even existed. Alexander wanted to remember the good times with their parents and he'd made it crystal clear he had no interest in digging up dirt, as he'd called it. The dirt he referred to was the event in the past when their parents had separated for a short time, when Alexander was six, and Bronte's mother had met another man. Her brother simply couldn't cope with the fact that the people he'd loved and looked up to most in the world, in the end had feet of clay. And he most certainly didn't want his sister to bring a complete stranger into the family. A stranger who would stir up a hornet's nest of gossip and innuendo about the two people Alexander had loved most in the world. He'd forbidden her to contact her father. And he'd forbidden her to discuss it.

Recognising the hurt in Alexander's face, in his eyes, broke Bronte's heart all over again.

Didn't he understand that she was hurting and that she was missing their parents, too?

That even now, two years later, she often went to pick up the phone to call them and remembered, too late, that her wonderful mother, and a father who'd been her rock through thick and thin, had gone? Didn't he understand that she felt anchorless, as if she didn't know who she was anymore? Didn't he understand that she needed closure?

And she knew that if their parents could see them now, at each other's throats like this, arguing over every petty little thing, they would be utterly devastated.

Why did every single conversation between them these days end in a fight?

Why?

The ache in her heart caught her throat.

"Your good friend Nico grabbed me in the dark and scared the life out of me."

Bronte was too far gone to care that she was stretching the truth.

Alexander's brows flew into his hairline.

"You're overreacting."

A red mist hazed in front of her eyes and Bronte blew.

"Am I? Am I really? You sold your heritage to a shark." Once the dam broke, Bronte couldn't stop it. "And I will not take responsibility for Anthony's behavior, either. Get off my back. Stop treating me like an imbecile just because you're not coping and find it too hard to deal with..."

Alexander silenced her with a finger stab.

Once upon a time Alexander and her had been so close.

They'd looked out for each other.

They didn't look out for each other now.

She'd not only lost her mother and the man she'd called father.

She'd lost her home.

She'd lost her fiancé.

She'd lost her future.

And she'd lost her brother, too.

Tears flooded Bronte's throat as the room swam.

Dear God, she couldn't cope with this.

Alexander simply refused to listen to her or take her feelings into account.

Nico Ferranti coughed and stood.

"I feel responsible for your disagreement. I made a mistake, Bronte, and I apologize," he said in a deep voice, his Italian accent a throaty growl that made the fine hair on the back of her neck stand on end.

Chest heaving, Bronte couldn't look at him and kept her burning eyes on Alexander.

Her brother merely nodded, looking sad and terribly tired.

She desperately wanted to run to her big brother and put her arms around him.

But Bronte refused to feel guilty for something that was completely out of her control.

"You weren't to know, Nico." Alexander glanced at her face and bit his lip. "Be nice, Bronte, and shake his hand."

She'd rather shake hands with an Emperor scorpion, but the way her brother's brows rose, Bronte knew she had no choice. With a reluctance that brought a twitch to Nico's lips and almost made her snarl, she placed her small hand in his.

His hand was warm and smooth and strong. And for some reason she felt... safe... secure.

Which was a weird feeling to have, since the man was determined to make her homeless.

"A pleasure, Miss. Ludlow."

The purr in his voice as he lifted her hand to his mouth made her breath hitch.

His lips touched her fingers, whisper soft, and sent an unwanted slow and steady pulse of awareness through her system. Bronte had been taught from the cradle that if she couldn't say something nice, say nothing. So she kept her mouth firmly shut.

She slanted him a look as he released her hand and caught him surveying her from top to toe. His eyes held a gleam which made her deeply ashamed of the way she'd very nearly washed the family's dirty little secrets in public.

Those eyes, a cool grey now, settled for a couple of beats too long on her mouth.

His pupils dilated in a way that seriously annoyed her.

She'd seen that look on a man's face before.

It appeared Nico liked the way she looked.

And the purely female part right at the heart of her reacted.

Seriously unimpressed, her hackles rose.

Bronte wasn't, and never had been, a tiny and feminine girly girl. She had no breasts and no bum. She might be slender, but she was five foot ten inches tall. However, it was also true that her looks had brought her nothing but trouble throughout her life. *How* she looked appeared to send out all the wrong signals to a certain type of man. Her ash-blonde hair was baby fine. Her slight frame gave her an air of fragility and her green eyes appeared to be too big for her face. For some reason her looks sent the signal that she had the intellectual capacity of a turnip. None of it was helped by the fact that she looked seventeen instead of twenty-six. Her mother had found her insecurity hilarious and used to say Bronte would be thankful when she was forty; but because of how she looked, she'd had to fight extra hard to attain the success she now enjoyed.

Although Bronte had to admit that jumping out of a window and running away from a bully like a pathetic coward could hardly be considered the behavior of an adult. But these days, she simply couldn't cope with a drama acted out in public. Escape had appeared a logical option. And look what a great idea that had turned out to be?

Her eyes narrowed into slits as the Italian's lips twitched as if he was reading her mind and trying too hard not to laugh and Bronte's hand itched again.

Of course she'd known it was just a matter of time before she'd need to deal with Nico Ferranti face to face. But Bronte had wanted their meeting to be on her turf and on her own terms, not with her off balance and at a disadvantage.

Deciding she'd had more than enough of men for one night, she picked up her belongings and headed for the door. "I'm leaving."

"Hold it." Alexander's tone held an edge that brought her to a dead stop. "Just what the hell did Anthony do to you that made you jump out of a window?"

Before she turned to face her brother, Bronte took a deep breath, too aware of Nico's eyes on her. Those eyes were darker, more watchful now, and they never left her face.

"We had a misunderstanding," she said with something of an understatement.

"And?"

"He's nursing his thumb."

Her response made Alexander frown and Nico's mouth tighten.

Bronte wondered what they'd do if she told them she'd been called a bitch of a cock tease.

A knock at the door brought their attention to a harassed looking young waitress.

"Sir, sorry to disturb you, security needs you. We have a young man shouting for your sister." She cast a speculative look at Bronte. "He's had too much to drink and is making a scene."

"I'm coming." Alexander turned to Bronte and shook his head. "Stay here, I'll take you home."

Could this evening possibly get any worse or any more embarrassing?

The throaty cough beside her told her that, yes, it could.

"Please, allow me." Nico smiled at her brother, before giving Bronte his full attention. "I am the one who made the mistake. I will take you home."

Those dark eyes held a challenge and an intensity that made her pulse thrum.

Alexander nodded, and with a sharp glance at Bronte that promised this was not the end of the matter, he left to deal with Anthony.

Now she was alone with him, Bronte shot Nico a defiant look as he stood over her.

His long finger tapped her chin while his eyes stayed on hers.

"One day someone will take you up on the invitation of that chin. You should be careful."

Who the hell asked for his opinion?

Her eyes locked with his in a silent battle of wills.

"Thank you for those unasked for words of wisdom. I'm perfectly capable of making my own way home."

Eyes cold now and filled with disapproval, Nico pulled on his heavy coat.

"It will be my pleasure," he said in a tone that suggested it was anything but.

He moved to open the door.

Bronte sailed past him.

And she ordered herself to ignore his hand at the small of her back.

Sheer willpower prevented her from stepping away.

She wouldn't give him the satisfaction.

As they walked down the hall, Nico placed himself between her and the bar lounge as Anthony's voice, raised in anger, made her cringe with mortification.

Leading the way to the car park, the tall Italian didn't say a single word.

The weather had deteriorated, sleet turning to snow as the temperature and Bronte's mood plummeted. Zipping up her black quilted jacket, she thrust her hands into the pockets, all the while wishing the night was over.

But then her step hitched when they reached his car.

She might have known it.

It was wrong of her, Bronte knew, but she couldn't seem to

help herself.

Thrilled, she turned to him.

"Well, well, a Bentley Continental GT," she said, contempt dripping from every word. "Get you, a babe magnet. Very sexy. Very pretty." She paused for two beats. "Very... you."

Chapter Three

Nico refused to rise to the bait.

Exhaustion nibbling at his temper made his tone hard as he opened the passenger door.

"Get in."

Bronte ignored him and purred low in her throat, which did strange things to his libido.

Now she was brushing snow from the bonnet with her fingertips, emerald eyes sparkled into his with a mix of challenge and ill humor.

"Very shiny. Very smooth. You have the need for speed in all things, I hear."

He wasn't in the mood for this.

"Were you never spanked as a child?"

Bronte's mouth fell open.

Did he seriously just say that?

"I ask," Nico continued in a voice as smooth as silk, "because every child needs discipline. I was and I learnt a great deal from the experience, most of it positive."

Good God, the man was a neanderthal and look what happened to them.

In all of her twenty-six years, Bronte had never struck another person, but she wanted to belt the man standing right in front of her, hard.

She'd never in her whole life met a man who could drive her up the wall so far so fast.

Nico Ferranti was... obnoxious.

Who the hell was he to comment on her upbringing?

"You are incredibly stubborn, Bronte," he went on relentlessly. "Your refusal to unbend and cause a rift with Alexander over the fate of Ludlow Hall is a case in point. There was no need for it. Believe me, a spanking is the least you deserve."

Stung, her cold face flushed.

She'd never had a stranger judge her behavior like this.

And she didn't care for it.

It didn't matter that he had a point about her argument with her brother about Ludlow Hall, Nico Ferranti needed put in his place.

And fast.

She merely raised an arched brow.

Nico read the temper flashing in those fabulous eyes the color of glittering emeralds.

And wondered why the hell he found the fact that he'd annoyed her so arousing.

"So we've moved on from manhandling to physical violence have we?"

Snow settled on the shoulders of her jacket and the wind whipped color into those smooth cheeks as she shivered.

Nico sent up a prayer for patience.

"Get in."

Someone listened, because this time she slid in without a murmur.

He closed the door, stalked around to the driver's side and told himself to keep calm.

As he clicked his seatbelt into place Bronte gave a little shimmy of her shoulders and another deep purr in her throat that had him catch his breath.

"Hmm, it smells terribly expensive in here. If you bottled the scent of Bentley leather, you would make another fortune. Your many businesses must be doing well."

He rolled his tongue over his bottom teeth. "You are trying to make me angry, Bronte, and I am wondering why."

She merely crossed endless legs, making herself comfortable.

Nico wondered what was wrong with him that he found the move incredibly sexy.

"It's not a mystery. I don't like you."

"You do not know me."

"I don't like your type."

"You judged me before you met me?"

"Not fair, is it?" she shot back, her eyes shining with ill humor.

Baffled, he stared at her. "I have no idea what you are talking about."

Her nostrils flared and that chin lifted. "Bronte Ludlow is a spoilt prima donna who was born with a silver spoon in her mouth. Alexander is worried sick about her. It is one drama after another."

At any other time her droll mimic of his accent might have been highly entertaining. The conversation was one he recalled having on his Smartphone with his architect and good friend. With a frown, Nico recalled ducking into a cavernous loft space at Ludlow Hall to have the conversation in private.

Bronte continued, "I was in a storeroom, packing personal possessions. I didn't see you, but I heard every word, Mr. Ferranti."

Nico remembered that at the time of the conversation, Alexander had been beside himself. "I was concerned about your brother, Bronte."

She continued as if he hadn't spoken. "What particular drama were you referring to?"

Nico couldn't really blame her for being angry, so he made a clean breast of it.

"You had broken your engagement." He frowned into those beautiful eyes, green, feline and filled to the brim with utter loathing for him. "Apparently, the man was a bastard."

"Yes, the world appears to be full of them."

He received the message loud and clear, the little witch.

With the flick of a wrist, he turned on the engine.

"Ooh, it sounds like a grumpy tiger," she squealed in a high, girly voice. A low growl escaped from his throat and she grinned. "Yeah, exactly like that."

Nico closed his eyes and sent up another prayer.

As the Bentley cruised out of Ludlow Hall, Nico glanced over to his reluctant passenger as she stared moodily into the road ahead, a road lit by the car's powerful headlights.

Her behavior was a disgrace.

Something about him appeared to bring out the bitch in her.

His lips twitched as he observed her scowl horribly into the darkness.

When he'd lifted her from the window and his hands spanned her tiny waist, he'd recognized the stirring in his loins for what it was. Lust. He was attracted to Alexander's sister. Now there was a can of worms that had disaster labelled all over it. Bronte Ludlow was stunningly beautiful, with a smart mouth and an outrageous personality. God knew, she would be a handful for any man. The thought made him smile. It had been a long time since a woman had stirred his interest or presented such a challenge. These days he didn't need to work very hard to capture a woman and he wondered if that was why he'd been in the middle of a lengthy dry spell.

In a silent rhythm, the windscreen wipers batted fat snowflakes.

Clearing his throat, he gave into temptation and lifted his hand to smooth her glossy pony tail.

He caught her eye. "Stop worrying."

Those green eyes went all sulky and so did her exquisite mouth.

"Excuse me?"

A sizzle of awareness warmed his blood.

Not many people used that tone with him and got away with it.

He stroked her hair again. "You look as if I am going to eat you."

He loved the way she narrowed her eyes, loved the way she flared her nostrils.

Staring determinedly into the road ahead, she told him, "Self-delusion is a curse, isn't it? You are not the centre of the known universe, Mr. Ferranti. In fact, I do my level best not to think of you."

He laughed.

And was delighted to see it brought a reluctant twitch to her lips.

He kept his voice soft and the tone teasing.

"Why have we never met?"

She flicked him a cool look. "Just my good luck, I suppose."

The girl had courage, he'd give her that.

"The kitten has sharp claws."

His eyes were on the road as he swung the car into the entrance to the long driveway of The Dower House.

"I'm twenty-six years old, hardly a kitten, Mr. Ferranti." Her arctic tone only whetted his appetite.

He brought the car to a halt.

Subtle night lights lit the grounds and entrance porch.

He turned to her and absently toyed with her ponytail.

It felt all soft and silky.

"You do not look it. Your coloring is quite different from your brother."

The look in Nico's dark eyes reminded Bronte of a starving cat staring at a mouse hole.

"I take after my mother." With a dark look, she flicked her hair out of his hand. Alexander's hair was a rich chestnut, although they shared eye color and, Bronte thought as a sharp blade pierced her heart, the same mother. But this was neither the time nor the place to think of that. It appeared Nico Ferranti had a problem respecting personal space, too, she realized, as he leaned towards her, his eyes keen on her face.

"Yes, she was a beautiful woman, almost as beautiful as her daughter."

The genuine regret in his voice brought a lump to Bronte's throat as he took her hand.

Grief, still horribly fresh, coursed through her.

She closed her eyes tight and fought for control.

"I am sorry," Nico said, his thumb stroking her knuckles. "I did not mean to upset you. I know you were close."

Bronte opened her eyes and stared straight ahead into the

night.

The one thing she simply could not tolerate from him, or anyone else, was pity.

Nico gently squeezed her hand and she nodded, closing her eyes again to steady herself. There was no way she could permit this man to get under her skin. Again, he was playing with her hair and she resisted the crazy urge to crawl into his lap, bury her face into his neck and stay there. As ever, she was allowing her emotions to rule instead of using her head.

The only thing Nico Ferranti wanted was her home and she'd better not forget it.

She turned and gave him a level look, not in the mood for games.

"Flirting, Mr. Ferranti? Let's stop tap dancing around the subject, shall we?" And she caught the surprise in his eyes before he hooded his lids. He had amazing lashes she mused, long and thick.

Cool now, his eyes met hers.

He drew back to study her face.

"Nico, it is my name, please use it." The tone made it a command rather than a request and, unfortunately for him, reminded her of her date earlier in the evening. A man who'd commanded her to call him Tony. Her gaze searched Nico's and all she saw was a man determined to get his own way, no matter what. Ah yes, the gloves were off Bronte realized, ignoring the increasing flutter of nerves in her stomach.

Here was the real man.

Bronte recognized raw male power when she saw it and the force of a strong will when she felt it. Nico would be a formidable adversary. Well, she was no pushover either. Exasperation with him made her tone hard.

"The Dower House is not for sale, Mr. Ferranti."

She caught the quick flash in those eyes before his hand lifted and his finger tipped up her chin. Her gasp of alarm narrowed his eyes, the finger moving down to trace the hectic pulse in her neck.

His smile reminded her forcibly of a great white shark.

For the first time, Bronte realized she may have overstepped the mark. Her throat tightened, saliva dried in her mouth as she pushed his hand away.

"Everything and everyone has a price," he told her.

Struck speechless by his arrogance, she stared at him. Was it not enough for him to turn her home into a hotel? Now he wanted the only link she had left to her family? Nico Ferranti, she decided, needed a major boot in the ass.

Bronte was a woman who rarely lost her temper, although you wouldn't know it by her lack of control this evening. A hot stinging sensation in her eyes along with the tight feeling in her chest warned her she was ready to blow.

She made a fist and he gripped her wrist.

"Let go of me." She spat the words and stared at him with wide eyes.

Too late, Nico realized he held a hissing cat by the tail.

Bronte's emerald eyes flashed and her full bottom lip trembled with outrage.

He must be more tired than he thought. Crossing three time zones had obviously influenced his ability to control himself. True, she'd gotten to him by calling him 'Mr. Ferranti' in such a precise tone. Although why it annoyed him so much, he couldn't say.

When he'd plucked her from certain injury and held her close, the unique scent of neroli mingled with warm female, along with the impact of those big eyes and her smile, had thrown him.

He must be tired he decided, because no woman had ever affected him in this way.

The combination of the condoms she'd carried and her embarrassment intrigued him, too. She had an air of refinement and exuded pure class. He couldn't imagine someone with her style would need a blind date or even consider a fling with one. Which just went to show that looks could be deceptive.

But when that chin and those eyes had issued a direct challenge, it would take a stronger man than him to resist.

Bronte's soft wide mouth was sheer temptation and the urge to take swept over him. Only the cloud of vulnerability in her eyes held him back. She was no coward. No woman of his acquaintance would dare speak to him the way Bronte did. And then he remembered that she had been through enough this evening at the hands of another.

He fought to keep his tone level, his voice soothing without taking his eyes off hers.

"What happened to you this evening, Bronte?"

Her brows drew together at his change of subject.

His thumb rubbed the hectic pulse under the soft skin of her wrist and she winced in pain.

With a frown, he pulled up the sleeves of her jacket and sweater and switched on the interior lights.

The livid marks had him catch his breath.

Had he put those fingerprints on her skin?

Never.

Furious, his eyes captured hers. "Your date did this?"

The angry expression on her face vanished to be replaced by one of genuine distress.

Now she blinked up at him like a miserable owlet. It made him want to hold her tight, to offer comfort, to protect. An alarm rang loud and clear in his mind. Bronte Ludlow was not his concern. She didn't need him to protect her. After all, she had a brother to watch over her.

Nico released her as if she'd burned him and leaned back.

Rubbing her wrist, Bronte's eyes now glittered into his.

"He put his hands where they weren't wanted and paid the price. You would do well to remember that, Mr. Ferranti."

The girl, Nico realized with admiration, didn't know when to give in.

"I believe you run a wedding cake business?"

Her brow rose.

"Why? Thinking of getting married?"

Nico had to laugh, not only at the statement, but the acid tone it was delivered.

Marriage and babies and everything a lasting relationship

entailed was not in his long term plan.

"No. I am not the marrying kind," he admitted. "I understand your company is supplying the cake for the society wedding tomorrow?"

"Yes, I run a cake business. A little hobby of mine. I fit it in between peeling the grapes I eat with my silver spoon." Nico almost smiled when she frowned in a way he was beginning to find adorable. She continued, "What has that got to do with anything?"

He wasn't above using subtle intimidation in business or in his personal life.

"If you want to keep the Ludlow Hall contract, I suggest you mind your manners, Ms. Ludlow."

Stunning emerald eyes glinted into his.

Nico found himself taken aback by her reaction.

Was that a smirk on her beautiful face?

"Are you threatening me, Mr. Ferranti?" Shoulders back, she looked down her nose as if he was a bad smell. It was a unique experience and Nico found he did not care for it.

Seriously annoyed now, he leaned forward and was small enough to feel satisfaction when she retreated against the door. He almost touched a finger to the frantic pulse in her neck, and then changed his mind.

After a decent night's sleep, he would deal with Bronte Ludlow tomorrow.

His eyes held hers.

"Alexander will be in Europe for four weeks and you will deal with me. I don't care if you are his sister. I expect only the best from my contractors."

Giving him a look that would melt solid steel, Bronte opened the door and got out.

Then she leaned into the car and sent him a smile that did not reach her eyes.

"I look forward to working with you, Mr. Ferranti," she said in a silky voice before closing the car door.

As he drove back to Ludlow Hall, Nico knew he had not come out the winner of his skirmish with the beautiful Bronte

Ludlow this evening. And he put it down to a lack of sleep. However, he wasn't too tired to make sure that Alexander dealt with Anthony in a proper and fitting manner. Nico was looking forward to meeting the man who'd put his mark on Bronte. He didn't stop to ask himself why it was any business of his, or why he should care.

The car swept into the car park of Ludlow Hall.

Life, Nico realized with a wry smile as he thought of Bronte, had just become a lot more interesting.

Chapter Four

"I've never been so embarrassed in my entire life."

Bronte glared at Rosie.

When she'd got to the part in her story where she'd got stuck in the toilet window, Rosie couldn't stop crying with laughter.

Her best friend wiped her eyes with the back of her fingers.

"God, I wish I'd seen it. I can't believe you jumped out a window and just left him there." She leaned her hip on the edge of the kitchen table, tore off a piece of kitchen roll and dabbed her cheeks. "Is my mascara running?"

After a bad night, she was not in the mood for humor and now Bronte gave her best friend a dark look.

"Your mascara is fine. What on earth possessed you to set me up with that awful man?"

"Sorry, sorry, I thought he was a nice guy. His sister's lovely. She told me Anthony's had a thing for you for years."

Bronte shook her head.

"I don't understand why he thought I had the hots for him," she said, completely bewildered. It was something that continued to bug her. Even though she hadn't encouraged him, the man had been utterly convinced she'd been prepared to go to bed with him. She simply could not understand it. But then remembering Anthony's hair trigger temper, perhaps he was delusional?

Still mulling over the previous night's events, Bronte checked the temperatures on her industrial ovens, and glanced up at the vast white-board on the wall that held their schedule for the day.

Three trainee pastry chefs laughed and joked in the adjacent kitchen. The sound mingled with an iPod rocking Coldplay and the clang of pots and pans.

"I wouldn't worry about it," Rosie said. "Put it down to experience."

Bronte glanced over at her best friend.

A best friend who was still dabbing her face.

She frowned.

"It's not funny. Nico Ferranti looked at me as if I was a slapper."

Rosie tied a white chef's bandana over dark curls tied in a knot at her neck, topped up their mugs with coffee.

She sent Bronte a sly look.

"I bet it made Alexander laugh. You didn't tell him I put them in your bag did you?"

With a little smile that didn't reach her eyes, Bronte folded her arms and sent her a bland look.

"My brother may not be Sherlock Holmes, but he deduced who was responsible by the note sellotaped to the box."

"Ouch, okay." Rosie pursed her lips and widened her brown eyes. "So how was he, still brooding and as miserable as sin?"

Bronte winced remembering how tired Alexander had appeared.

"Worse, he had that long suffering, kicked dog look on his face."

"Hmm, it's not often Alexander Ludlow's vulnerable. I'd make the most of it if I were you."

Sinking into a chair, Bronte pressed fingertips to her temple and puffed out a long breath.

Her eyes met Rosie's.

"I need to do the right thing. I can't leave it any longer. The trouble is I don't know what to do for the best. Alexander's not budging an inch. He thinks that by contacting my natural father, I'm somehow blackening the family name, which is utter nonsense. And how the hell do I tell a perfect stranger that I'm the daughter he never even knew existed?" She closed her eyes. "God, my life is such a mess."

The ache in her gut, a constant companion these days, burned like acid. No matter how many times she went over and over the reality of her situation, she was hurting Alexander. He wanted her to forget about a man who'd had nothing to do with her upbringing and to let the dead lie in peace.

Rosie gave her a quick hug. "Whatever you do, it's your decision. And I know you'll make the one that is right for you. You know I'll back you all the way whatever you decide."

"And now I have bloody Nico Ferranti to deal with," Bronte whined in a tone that made her friend make a face.

Rosie caught her eye and gave her a cheeky smile.

"What's Nico Ferranti like?"

While Bronte considered her response, Rosie checked the cool-room temperature and wheeled out a stainless steel trolley which held four separate tiers of snowy white wedding cakes ready for assembly and finishing touches.

"He's... big."

How do you describe power and sheer physical presence? Bronte wondered as she stood. How do you describe a man who was too good-looking and oozed sex appeal? How could she describe the hum in her blood when his hands gripped her waist? How could she explain the overwhelming desire to give him a black eye?

She slid four trays of mini muffins into each oven and set the timer.

"I need more information." Rosie sent her a quizzical look.

Knowing her friend wouldn't let the subject drop until she had all the details, Bronte gave in.

"He's well over six foot, wide shouldered, long legs. You know... big." Her cheeks grew warm when Rosie raised her brows, leaned back against a table and folded her arms. "Okay, he smells fabulous. He's got hot Latin looks. And he says Brrrronte in an Italian accent."

Rosie stood as she cocked her head.

"Wait a minute. I know that face."

"What face?"

"That face you're wearing." She smacked her hands on the table and leaned over. Eyes the color of warm chocolate peered into Bronte's. "Do I detect a spark of life in the empty expanse of your libido?" Rosie's eyes went big with a silent question. Then she turned, sliding a tray of fondant snowdrops and winter roses into a narrow container. "And don't huff and puff like that.

This is very good news."

Bronte, not admitting to anything that might incriminate her, checked her watch.

"I feel a break coming on. We're ahead of schedule." Hot air from the ovens filled her huge kitchen with the sublime scent of warm toffee. "You can test a muffin. They're looking good."

"How many more to go?" Rosie sniffed.

"Four batches of four trays."

"What kind of icing?"

"White chocolate fudge."

"You should set up a business."

"Har har, you're a riot this morning."

"So spill." Rosie blew on a muffin from the first batch, her brown eyes sparkling. "He drove you home, then what?"

Good question.

Then what?

The sound of Adele rocking the adjacent kitchen lifted Bronte's heart and made her smile as she lifted her mug and took a sip of her coffee. She stared unseeing through wide French doors into her garden, the grass silver with frost. Ice glistened on a bird bath. The mortgage she'd taken out for the re-modelling of the kitchen and new equipment, along with expenses and salaries didn't leave much left over, but financially *Sweet Sensation* was doing well. Rosie had taken a huge gamble on Bronte's vision. Her best friend had sold her much loved cottage and given the business a much needed cash boost. Working in partnership with Rosie and realizing their dreams was nothing short of a blessing. More than just money was invested into this business. The girls had invested their hearts, their souls.

No matter how hard things got, Bronte would never let Rosie down and she'd fight tooth and nail to never, ever give up The Dower House, the land and *Sweet Sensation*. Never.

"He wants to buy my home and the land," she said now.

The previous night's conversation returned to her. She'd made it more than clear to Nico Ferranti that the Dower House was not for sale at any price, end of debate. That should be the end of the matter. So why did she feel a curl of anxiety in her stomach? It was how his jaw clenched, she realized, and how those heavily lashed eyes had narrowed as his fingers tapped the steering wheel. Yes, she mused, Mr. Ferranti was not accustomed to hearing, or accepting, the word no. The memory of his touch on her wrist made her mouth dry.

And she decided not to worry Rosie with his threat to tear up their contract with Ludlow Hall. There was no point in worrying her friend for no reason. If he did tear up the contract, he would alienate Alexander. And Bronte had finally realized last night that the friendship between the two men was a deep one. Nico Ferranti would never risk that friendship with her brother, which meant the Italian was full of hot air. However, more to the point, *Sweet Sensation* didn't need Ludlow Hall for business; they'd been a huge success before the Hall opened. Since money was the language Nico understood, she would show the big gorilla just how valuable her company was to his bottom line.

"What did you tell him?" Rosie wanted to know in a sharp tone that Bronte knew meant business. Her best friend might be small, but she was mightily ferocious in her defence of what was hers and the people she cared deeply about.

Yep, Rosemary Margaret Gordon made a very bad enemy.

"To bugger off," Bronte said.

Rosie took her hand and squeezed her fingers.

Bronte squeezed them back.

Her best friend was dearer to her than any sister.

"I know there have been times since the accident..." Rosie began. "When you've wondered if all the hard work has been worth it."

Still holding hands, Bronte's eyes met Rosie's.

"I've never regretted starting this business. It's kept me sane, and hey, for the last six months we've been in the black."

Rosie patted her hand, sat back and grinned like a fool.

"It was Oliver and Lucy's wedding that did it. The glossy magazine spread of the super model and her super husband as they cut the cake was awesomesauce." With a satisfied smile, Rosie popped the rest of her muffin into her mouth.

"We did it, cheers," Bronte told her as they clinked coffee

mugs.

The sound of the front door bell made them jump.

Rosie checked the time and sprang up.

"I'll get it. I'm expecting a delivery."

Nico pushed his hands further into the fleece-lined pockets of his battered shearling jacket and admired his surroundings.

With its sweeping driveway and ocean of manicured lawns, The Dower House was a miniature version of Ludlow Hall and could have been plucked right out of a fairy story. His mind raced with thoughts and plans for the future. The house was secluded, with plenty of space for guests, an office, and was the perfect base for him.

Even though Bronte had been the last thing on Nico's mind as he tumbled into sleep and the first thing on his mind when he awoke, the conversation with her the previous evening and a good night's sleep had energized him this morning.

Nico shook his head, frankly amazed at himself that she'd had such an effect on him.

He liked women, a lot.

He particularly liked them tall, dark and stacked.

He liked experienced professional types who knew the score and were too busy for a long-term commitment.

This *thing* he appeared to have for his best friend's sister might not be such a good idea.

He chewed on his bottom lip as he mulled over the scene at Ludlow Hall the night before. In Nico's opinion, Alexander's reaction to his sister's dating habits was over the top. But he would do nothing to jeopardise their friendship and business relationship.

As for Bronte herself, she had a refinement that sang to him. Her vulnerability also appeared to bring out the protector in him. Who'd have thought it? Anthony, he thought with a grim smile, would think twice about hurting another woman.

Nico couldn't forget the feel of Bronte, the tingle of awareness that still warmed his system and how small her waist had been between his hands. He smiled remembering her embarrassment at being caught in the act. Naughty too, with those big eyes full of pretend innocence.

The light floral scent of Bronte still lingered in his car. It was warm, sweet and feminine. How could he have missed her on his previous visits?

The thought brought his mind back to the task in hand – The Dower House.

The plans he had for the place warmed his heart as he tugged the brass bell pull.

Then he admitted that he'd been clumsy in the way he'd handled her the night before and threatening her like that. What had he been thinking? Again, he shook his head and told himself to focus on the task at hand and not on the woman.

The door opened.

A curvy, dark-haired, dark-eyed female poked her head out and looked him up and down with bright-eyed interest. By her clothes Nico surmised she was a cook.

He smiled and opened his mouth.

"Deliveries are received at the back. Follow the road all the way round," she told him and closed the door in his face.

Bemused, he looked down at his ancient boots and jeans. Yep, he could easily be mistaken for a driver. It was a misunderstanding anyone could make. Nico wound a black cashmere scarf around his neck, strolled back to his car and followed instructions.

The road led to a courtyard and a large coach house converted into four garages.

A snazzy mini cooper convertible in shiny black was parked next to the frosty lawn. Two gleaming black vans with *'Sweet Sensation'* painted in gold on their sides, stood with their rear doors open.

A couple of young girls, dressed in chef whites, were busy loading shelves and wheeling trolleys carrying white cardboard boxes.

The dark haired girl who had opened the front door widened her eyes when she saw his car.

She was trying, Nico realized as he got out, not to laugh.

"I'm so sorry. I thought you were a delivery. Can I help you?"

Her brown eyes sparkled into his.

"I am Nico Ferranti for Bronte Ludlow." He frowned as her eyes cooled and the smile slipped.

"Of course you are."

"Please, call me Nico, and you are?" He held out his hand wondering what in the world he had done to offend her.

She took his hand.

"Rosie Gordon, Bronte's business partner. How do you do?" she said, with a distinct lack of enthusiasm that tickled his sense of humor.

Curious and surprised at the set-up, he looked around.

"Is Bronte available?"

"Sure, follow me." Rosie led him through a narrow hallway, a busy compact kitchen and into a larger space with a beautiful vaulted ceiling.

Nico didn't have a particularly sweet tooth, but the scent of fresh baking, toffee and chocolate made his mouth water. More than seventy per cent of the room, he realised studying the space, was a recent addition and constructed of heavy oak beams and glass.

Acres of stainless steel food preparation areas, fridges, cold stores and ovens gleamed in the fragile winter sun.

Then his eyes found her.

Wearing chef whites, Bronte stood at a central island, hands rock steady as she decorated the bottom tier of one of the most spectacular wedding cakes he'd ever seen. Not that he took much notice of such things, but this cake was incredible. In cream and pale pink, it towered above her. Constructed of six octagonal pieces he assumed would be dismantled and re-assembled in-situ. The black framed designer glasses she wore he found terribly erotic for some strange reason. And Nico immediately wondered what the hell was wrong with him.

Rosie pulled him to the side, out of Bronte's line of vision.

They watched as Bronte worked with a single-minded focus, an attention to detail and determination that totally threw him. An iPod plugged into her ears, she spun the cake wheel with one hand and piped icing in a steady rhythm with the other. A foot encased in a white rubber clog tapped to the tune in her ears. The pink tip of her tongue rubbed her top lip. And Nico had the sensation of blood rushing from his head to pool low in his belly.

She was stunning.

His expert eye estimated her height at five foot nine inches tall, one hundred and twenty pounds, maybe less with a lean figure that was almost boyish. The face was beautiful in the clear light of day with creamy, flawless skin and high cheekbones. Her ash-blonde hair ran down her back in a slippery tail and she had a chef's cap pulled low on her forehead.

The urge to pull her into his arms and taste that soft, seductive mouth shocked him. He'd attempted to justify his physical reaction to her last night as the effect of jetlag. Obviously, he was deluding himself.

"She's nearly finished," Rosie whispered. "If you interrupt her she'll hand you your head in your hands." Surprised, Nico looked down at her and realized she was absolutely serious.

Bronte finished with an expert flourish that made him smile. Then boogied her hips in a way that electrified his groin and Nico ordered himself to get a grip.

She turned and saw him.

He almost missed the flash of awareness in her eyes before they cooled to chips of emerald ice, and he managed not to wince. He couldn't deny the pang of disappointment in his chest.

And couldn't deny that she looked gorgeous.

Bronte unplugged her ears and tucked her glasses into the top pocket of her jacket. Pulling off latex gloves, she gave him what he thought of as her polite customer smile. The look in her eye told him she wasn't in the mood for a discussion, her dislike of him clear by the stiff body language. It appeared that between last night and this morning, Ms. Ludlow had erected implacable defences.

The air crackled with the toxic mix of arousal and heightened awareness from him and a deep loathing from her.

With a jolt, he realized Bronte Ludlow wished him straight to hell.

Nico imagined most men would back off and get the message. Unfortunately for her, he was not most men.

"What can I do for you, Mr. Ferranti? Have you decided that you're in the market for a wedding cake after all?" Her voice was firm, polite and precise.

But the hint of nerves intrigued him.

"It is fantastic, Bronte."

He meant every word, and her eyes widened at the compliment.

Nico stepped into her, took her hand, and testing, rubbed his thumb along her knuckles.

The move brought a surprised flush to her cheeks and he pressed home his advantage.

"You are very talented. I had no idea."

And the little leap in her pulse under his fingertips made his day.

Her eyes flicked to Rosie before meeting his.

The blush in her cheeks intrigued him, too.

She cleared her throat.

"As you can see we're very busy this morning. Saturday tends to be hectic." She gave a tug of her hand.

He held it a second longer than was strictly necessary and read the beginning of wariness in her eyes. She smelt of sugar, sweet vanilla and neroli. It was an alluring, sensuous mix. A mix which spun around his heightened senses.

Nico had a feeling Bronte Ludlow would taste even better.

Chapter Five

Bronte took a deep breath and ordered her erratic pulse to calm down.

The Nico Ferranti who held her hand today was very different from the one she'd met last night. Today he wore jeans, the seams white with wear, with as much style as his expensive suit. The worn boots and battered leather jacket, along with the tousled hair almost made her swallow her tongue. While the I-need-a-shave look had her hormones flashing on red alert. Mr. GQ had morphed into Mr. Hot and Sexy.

His eyes, the color of a stormy sky, held and trapped hers.

From a great distance she heard Rosie say something she didn't quite catch.

Bronte turned to her friend.

"I'm sorry?"

"I said would you like a coffee, Nico, and perhaps a little taste of something?" Rosie said, adding under her breath, "except Bronte."

Nico blinked and gave Rosie a perfunctory smile, since his attention was fully focused on Bronte.

"If it is no trouble. I realize I have interrupted your work."

Bronte couldn't tear her eyes from his.

The intensity of his gaze was rather unnerving.

Her mouth went bone dry.

Why couldn't she breathe?

"Take Nico into the sitting room and I'll bring it in." Rosie instructed, and then gave Bronte a poke in the back along with a firm little push.

"I need to tell you, Bronte, that you are full of surprises."

The way his voice went deep when he purred her name did strange things to her legs. It made them weak and it also made the jumpy nerves in her belly tighten too hard.

Bronte debated how to respond to the remark as Nico shrugged off his jacket, turning in a circle as he took in the room with a calculating gleam in his eye that she took great exception to. The black sweater in fine cashmere accentuated his wide shoulders and narrow waist. He tossed his jacket, chose a corner of the sofa and settled himself comfortably.

Too comfortably, she decided.

However, Nico Ferranti might have arrived uninvited, but he was on her turf now. It didn't matter that her hormones went crazy every time he so much as looked at her. She was a normal woman with a pulse and not dead, so her attraction to him was perfectly normal. He was a man made of flesh and blood and bone. He might be looking at her like a big black cat eyeing a cornered mouse, but she'd be damned if she was going to simply curl up, give in and let him take everything he wanted from her. Just because he owned Ludlow Hall, didn't mean she was going to hand him The Dower House on a plate. The man had an agenda and she'd be wise not to forget it.

Her mouth hardened.

His cock-of-the-walk attitude brought Bronte's hackles up, too.

Those amazing eyes pinned hers. She shivered at how dark and intent his gaze was as he studied her.

Seriously annoyed that he could affect her like this, Bronte narrowed her eyes.

"What, surprised that I work hard to make a living?" she asked tartly.

Nico opened his mouth to respond and paused as the door opened.

Rosie's eyes went wide as she picked up the charged atmosphere in the room. Her gaze flicked from one to the other as she placed the tray on a table. Then she did a spectacular eye roll behind Nico's back as she left.

What on earth was Rosie thinking, Bronte fumed, bringing Nico Ferranti right into the house today of all days? They were on a very tight schedule. She didn't have time for coffee and cakes. And why on earth had Rosie used the priceless Limoges coffee set?

Bronte decided that soon, very soon, she was going to strangle her friend.

However, none of those thoughts showed in her face as she sat opposite her nemesis.

She lifted the coffee pot, poured and handed Nico a cup of black coffee in a fragile porcelain cup, watching him carefully as he added cream and stirred. A part of her brain noticed he had lovely hands, with long fingers and short nails.

"You are never going to let me forget that, are you?" he asked, those eyes, sparkling with humor now, never left her face.

Bronte merely shrugged and fought not to smile back.

He was too smooth she decided.

Too charming and she'd been burned once before by a slick operator.

She took a deep breath, noticed the way his dark eyes sharpened, but she held her nerve and kept her voice steady and firm.

"The house, Mr. Ferranti, is *not* for sale."

Those stunning emerald eyes issued a direct challenge.

A challenge that had Nico smile to himself as he relaxed back on the sofa and studied the exquisite woman opposite him. *Dio*, she was absolutely gorgeous, and it was not just her looks that had him tied up in knots, it was the whole package, too. It was the way her eyes shot daggers into his. The way she held herself, shoulders back, chin up. Bless her, she had no idea who she was dealing with.

Now she placed her coffee on the table, sat back and crossed long legs dressed in blue and white checked cotton trousers. Slender fingers clasped her knee. Back straight, her eyes met his unflinchingly. She was sexy and proud and beautiful. And he had to admit that Bronte Ludlow was not in his usual style, her cool beauty was a definite departure for him.

The hard and worsening ache in his groin was an interesting development, too.

His mind racing, Nico took a sip of excellent coffee.

The issue with the *Sweet Sensation* being run from The Dower

House was not an overwhelming obstacle. Although, he seemed to remember a clause in a covenant which he would have his lawyers' research. However, it appeared dealing with Bronte on a personal level and acquiring the The Dower House, too, would require creative thinking on his part. So for the moment he would back off as far as the house was concerned and see where this attraction led.

He wanted Bronte, he wanted the house and he would not alienate Alexander. Taking another sip of coffee, Nico decided there was nothing like a challenge.

He kept his voice low, the tone friendly as he studied her pale face carefully.

She was a woman, he judged, who liked straight talking.

So Nico decided to be nothing but honest with her.

"Bronte, I need to tell you that I find myself in a unique situation."

She frowned, those emerald eyes appeared confused now.

Her full mouth looked terribly vulnerable.

"I don't understand. I thought you were here about the house."

She looked so cute and earnest, his mouth watered.

Nico sent her a friendly grin and watched the heat flooding her face with interest. It appeared that Miss. Ludlow might be attracted to him. That attraction didn't surprise him, since in his vast experience, most women felt the same way. He wasn't being arrogant, just honest. Plus, he knew how to show a woman a good time in bed. After all, he was Italian.

"I am here about the house, amongst other things."

The frantic pulse in her neck told him she might be frightened and Nico found himself admiring her again. Most people found him intimidating, but Bronte refused to give into it. When her chin rose it didn't annoy him as it had done the night before. Instead, it aroused.

Without taking his eyes from her face, he picked up his jacket, removed a crisp envelope from the pocket and placed it on the table between them.

Bronte didn't even glance at it.

"Just what the hell is your problem? Do you think offering more and more money is the answer?" she demanded.

Actually, he wasn't offering her more money. But he knew she'd assume he was. She'd played right into his hands and now he had her exactly where he wanted her. How he kept a straight face as temper warred with good manners in her face, he'd never know.

Nico decided he'd be magnanimous in accepting her heartfelt apology. If he was lucky, he might even be rewarded with a kiss.

Rising, she walked to a magnificent sandstone fireplace. She reached up on tip-toes to place her palms on a mantle groaning under the weight of family photos in a variety of silver frames.

"This is my home. These stones are rooted deep into the soil." She turned to him with a determined look in her vivid eyes. And Nico thought he'd never seen a woman look so magnificent in his life. "This house anchors me to a land my family have lived in for generations. It's all I have left of them."

Then it appeared as if she'd run out energy as her fingertips rubbed her brow in a sad, tired gesture that he found curiously moving. Nico was aware of a click in the region of his heart and an emotion he didn't want to identify.

Now he frowned into his coffee.

"Do you always get what you want, Mr. Ferranti?" she asked him in a soft voice.

He stared at her.

To answer yes would be the simple truth. But he had the feeling the truth would upset her further and Nico found, surprisingly, he didn't want to do that.

So he simply shrugged and spread his hands in a gesture that said '*Of course I do.*'

Bronte's eyes narrowed into emerald slits and she folded her arms.

"Last night you threatened to break the contract our business has with Ludlow Hall. Today you've come into my home, uninvited by the way. And now you refuse to take no for an answer. Just who the hell do you think you are, the Cosa Nostra?"

The remark was targeted to insult and she hit the bull's eye. Nico Ferranti was Italian. The words were more than a hard slap in the face. They offended his integrity, his honor and his hard won reputation for fairness.

Unwelcome heat surged into his cheeks as an unpleasant notion wormed its way into his brain. She knew nothing of his father, his brother or the extended family he refused to acknowledge. No one did. His past was carefully buried in Italy. How could Bronte have discovered it?

Suspicion narrowed his eyes as Nico observed alarm flare in hers. He could read her like a book. There was no guile or hidden agenda in those bright emerald eyes. Relief warred with dismay that he'd been provoked so easily by a rank amateur. He'd made enemies, plenty of them. A man in his position didn't rise to the top without stepping on a few toes. But none of them had managed to get under his skin or under his guard the way Bronte did.

Taking great care, Nico placed the delicate cup and saucer on the table.

With a firm grip on a temper that appeared to be too close to the surface, his eyes lasered into hers. Color drained from her cheeks leaving her too pale. Now she sank to the sofa and all the while her eyes never left his face.

Good, at last he had managed to assert his authority and get through to her.

He stood.

Pain, the memory of old hurts, old sufferings, swam through his system as he slung on his jacket. His eyes never left hers. Nico realized he'd alarmed her and couldn't be sorry for it. She had crossed a line with him. Bronte Ludlow needed her bottom paddled for her rudeness. That soft mouth trembled as the hectic pulse in her neck matched his own.

The need to devour those lips, to take, both thrilled and appalled him in equal measure. But Nico was honest enough to admit that his anger came as much from his physical and emotional response to Bronte as the words she'd used to insult him. No one ever spoke to him in that tone or challenged him the way she did. She'd thrown him completely off balance. It was a sensation with which he found he simply could not cope.

Therefore Nico took refuge in stiff formality.

He didn't attempt to hide the bite to his tone or keep the anger from his voice.

"I have asked you twice before to use my name. I will not ask you a third time." He gave a quick bow of his head. "I apologize for disturbing you, Bronte."

Without a backward glance, he walked out.

Chapter Six

Appalled by what had happened and with her heart hammering against her ribs, roaring in her ears, Bronte stared at the door.

Why did she feel as if she was in the wrong?

Vulnerability.

She'd seen vulnerability in his eyes, quickly hidden, but it had been there. And she'd upset, angered him, and why should that make her feel small? He was the one who'd come into her home - uninvited. *He* was the one who'd used that arrogant tone and supercilious attitude with her. She had every right to defend herself. If he was upset and angry with her, then too bad. After all, he was an adult. He'd get over it. If it meant that he'd forget all about the Dower House then it was worth it.

Irritated with herself, she was always such a wuss with disagreements and scenes. Now she was just as irritated with Nico because he'd turned her into a first-class bitch. She'd never been good with confrontations, they actually made her feel sick.

Bronte picked up the thick expensive envelope, almost tossing it into the fire before she stopped herself.

Her name was written in black ink in a strong, fluid hand.

Masculine.

Dominant.

A pain in the ass.

Ripping the envelope open, she pulled out the stiff cream and gold embossed card.

Then sank to the sofa as she read.

Mr. Nico Ferranti would be delighted and honored if Miss Bronte Ludlow would accept an invitation, to accompany him to a Ball to celebrate the Grand opening of Ludlow Hall next Saturday evening.

Dismayed, she read it again.

Shitty, shit, shit.

Bronte stared at it in a mounting frustration, tapping the card on her palm before dropping it on the table. He'd set her up. Set her up knowing she'd assume the letter he'd handed her was yet another offer for The Dower House.

Great, she'd just jumped down his throat over an invitation to the Grand Opening of Ludlow Hall.

And now she would need to apologize.

By late afternoon Bronte was in the grand hall of Ludlow Hall and had managed to put Nico bloody Ferranti out of her mind.

At least that's what she told herself. The hot lump of guilt in her stomach was a niggling reminder of the horrible scene in her sitting room earlier in the day. Yes, she'd been unpleasant, but he'd deserved it. Now she forced herself to clear her mind as she put the finishing touches to the spectacular wedding cake. And tried desperately to forget all about an Italian, who was so damned sexy, he should have a warning label tattooed to his smooth forehead.

The wedding ceremony itself was being held in the old chapel in the grounds of Ludlow Hall and she had mixed feelings not only about being here herself, but also about the entire business. Today was the first time she'd really seen inside her old home since Nico Ferranti had sprinkled pots money around like fairy dust. Honesty had her admit that Ludlow Hall looked fabulous, but she missed her previous life and the people in it too much, to enjoy how the house looked now. When she'd lived there with her parents, money had always been tight with not much left over to indulge in the *pretty things* as her mother had called soft furnishings.

Today the grand hall was filled with round tables and chairs covered in pristine white cotton. Heavy brocade curtains in deep jewel colors spilled onto the floor from windows that arched almost to the ceiling. Glittering chandeliers, dripping with clear crystals bathed the room in light. The effect was one of quiet good taste edged with luxury. Pink and cream wild roses spilled out of tall centre-pieces on the tables, swept over the arches and wound around staircase balustrades. Nico's expert team obviously knew how to put together the perfect scene for a glitzy society wedding.

She checked the soft pink roses were still fresh between each tier of the cake and nearly jumped out of her skin when a deep voice spoke too close behind her.

"It is a work of art. You are not a guest? I understand you are a friend of the groom."

Turning to the harsh unsmiling face of Nico Ferranti, for a moment Bronte lost the power of speech. He wore a dark bespoke suit which hugged those enormous shoulders and lean, muscular thighs. Along with a snowy white shirt and a silk tie the precise color of his eyes. Heavy silver cufflinks peeped out from the cuffs. His jet hair was brushed back from his face, immaculate, merely enhancing the smooth skin, the plains and valleys of his brows and cheekbones. Eyes, almost black with what looked like possession, swept over her face and settled for a couple of beats too long on her mouth.

When his dark brow rose, Bronte felt the heat of mortification rush into her cheeks as she realized she'd been openly staring at him, again. Add in the fact he smelt amazing and dressed in all his finery, Nico Ferranti was quite the package.

He was standing too close, and judging by her body's reaction to him, too dangerous.

Rubbing suddenly damp palms down the front of her crisp white apron, Bronte felt like Cinderella at the Ball minus the gown and glass slippers.

Her hormones buzzed like bees in her system. She studied his expressionless mask and found it difficult to swallow. He was still angry with her. It was ridiculous to be so nervous of him. What on earth could he do to her in the middle of a room full of staff?

"We have a rule, never to mix business with pleasure. It's not a good idea. But we will attend the party this evening and have a drink with the happy couple. Rosie loves to burn up the dance floor." Mortified, Bronte realized she was babbling like a complete fool. And ordered herself to get a grip.

Unable to meet his eyes she focused instead on his chin, which was a mistake since just above it was that amazing mouth with the sensual bottom lip. It was important to Bronte to apologize for her behavior this morning. She'd deliberately insulted him. There was nothing worse than being in the wrong and waiting too long to eat humble pie. Even if it choked her.

"Look," she said now. "I want to apologize for my behavior..."

But before Bronte could launch into her carefully rehearsed speech, Nico reached out to take her hand, rubbing his finger over the back of her knuckles as his eyes caught and held hers.

"Please, do not worry. I should have made it clear the letter was an invitation to the Ball and not another offer for The Dower House. But in my defence, I could not resist bringing the spark to your eyes. But then you threw me a curve I was not expecting. You are not only fierce in the defence of your home, but you are quite beautiful when you are angry."

She was?

Then she wondered if it was an Italian thing the way he always wanted to touch her, because she seriously wished he wouldn't since it kept her off balance and scrambled her brain cells.

A commotion at the entrance to the grand hall alerted them to the presence of a tiny flower girl with black curls, flushed cheeks and over excited eyes.

A pink circlet of flowers hung at a crazy angle on her head.

Spotting the wedding cake, she let out a yell and headed straight for it.

Bronte moved fast to intercept, and with a laugh scooped the little girl up in her arms and spun her round to delighted squeals and giggles.

"Oh, no you don't, Melissa Jane Lucas. You can have cake after the wedding ceremony." She gave the child a big kiss on her rosy cheek. Melissa dimpled adorably so Bronte indulged herself with a soft kiss on the small nose and adjusted the circlet of flowers on her dark head. "And don't you look like a princess? Are those new shoes?"

Three year old Melissa dressed in pink silk taffeta with huge puffed sleeves and skirt that made her look like an irresistible fairy, batted big blue eyes. She arched a foot that wore butter soft ballet pumps in white leather, nodded and stuck a thumb in her mouth.

Someone, Bronte realized with a tender smile, had missed her nap.

"There you are." The pregnant sister of the groom, looking flushed, plucked Melissa out of her arms and air-kissed Bronte's cheek. "Thank you. I'm going to enter this one for the sprint in the Olympics. Gosh the cake looks fabulous, darling. You are so clever."

Melissa's mother stared at Nico with a look in her eye that was pure female checking out an attractive male. With a roll of her eyes at Bronte, she rushed off with Melissa gazing longingly at the cake over her shoulder.

For a big man, Nico moved fast.

His breath sent a frisson of awareness from her neck to her toes.

The firm hand at her waist and deep voice in her ear made her tremble in reaction.

"Good with children too. I'm impressed."

The words might have been like a cold dagger to the heart, the pain of it making her eyes sting, but it was the low suggestive purr in his throat that scorched her cheeks. Her feelings were too raw, too near the surface, as his breath fanned her ear, the scent of him making her head spin. Logically she knew it wasn't his fault that his words had upset her. After all, Nico Ferranti had no idea that she may never be able to have a child.

Emotions all over the place, instinctively Bronte moved away from him and out of his reach.

The hot expression in his eyes cooled as his eyes narrowed into hers.

And the realization that she'd annoyed him, again, made the nerves in her stomach wind even tighter.

Without even trying, the man tied her every coherent thought in knots.

"It's all part of the job," she said now.

Then she took another careful step back, cleared her throat and smoothed the table cloth with a hand that was far from steady.

He took a step forward.

It cost her, but Bronte forced herself to stand utterly still.

"Have dinner with me tonight," he said, without taking his eyes off her face.

It wasn't a request.

As a result of her stomach clutching, her chin lifted with sheer bravado.

"No... thank you."

Dark eyes explored her face as his hand reached out to cup her face, the pad of his thumb slowly caressing her jaw in a way that made her tremble.

He studied her mouth as if it was the last Belgian chocolate in the box.

Attraction flooded her system and his pupils dilated as his eyes stayed on hers.

She couldn't look away.

"Scared, Bronte?" His husky voice deepened his Italian accent.

Terrified actually.

Her pulse was going crazy under his thumb, but she refused to give in.

"Now you're being ridiculous."

Her eyes flew to his and she knew immediately she'd made a mistake.

A big mistake.

Why couldn't she breathe?

Bravado leaked away to be replaced by a dark longing, a response to the soft seduction of his touch, his accent.

"Prove it," Nico demanded softly.

Stormy eyes challenged hers and she studied him for a long moment.

Taking a breath, she stepped out of his touch and her face burned where his fingers had lingered.

"I'm attending the party this evening, or had you forgotten?"

"What time did you rise this morning?" he wanted to know.

She blinked.

What had that got to do with anything?

"Six o'clock."

"Then you need to eat. We have a new chef, what do you say? I've been invited to the party this evening, too. We can have a few dances with the band, have dinner and return later for the disco. We appear to have got off on the wrong foot, Bronte. This way we can have a chance to get to know one another."

He took her hand and rubbed his thumb across her knuckles, again the sensation sent shock waves through her system.

That voice went dark and low. "Please, *cara*."

She recognized that his plea was sincere.

She recognized that she was going slowly and completely out of her tiny mind.

Bronte hissed out a breath as her hormones fizzed.

Temptation whispered in her ear, it would save her heating up a pizza. The new chef in the restaurant at Ludlow Hall was supposed to be brilliant, too. Perhaps they could get to know one another and perhaps he would realize how much her home meant to her.

Almost swaying on her feet, she wondered if this devastating and exciting sensation was the elusive sexual chemistry that Rosie was always going on about. For the first time in months, Bronte felt truly alive.

"What time do you want to eat?" She asked, immediately telling herself she was a fool.

He didn't attempt to hide how pleased he was to have won.

The smile transformed his face showcasing dimples and Bronte's hormones did a delirious little shimmy through her system. She'd always been a sucker for dimples. Obviously she'd lost her mind because there was no way in hell she could possibly resist him when he looked at her like that.

"Eight thirty." He placed a hand on her arm as she moved away. "What made you change your mind?"

Good question.

She turned, sent him a small smile.

"You said, please."

Chapter Seven

"You must wear the ivory silk, it'll knock him dead," Rosie advised her.

She was sprawled on Bronte's monster of a sleigh bed built of solid mahogany. Glossy black curls cascaded down the back of a silk bustier in a vivid fire engine red the exact shade of Rosie's lipstick.

"According to an expert on weddings... my late mother," Bronte said seriously, "A wedding guest should never wear white or cream." She eyed her friend's wondrous figure with sheer envy. "I hate you. I do. Look at those breasts."

Rosie stood, stuck out her breasts and gazed with pride at perfect creamy globes.

"Chicken fillets, honey. Plus I'm boned, lifted and separated."

Bronte stood in white lacy panties and peered wistfully down the neck of her T-shirt, remembering her ex-fiancé's withering comments on her lack of 'a rack.' Jonathon never held back when it came to listing her many flaws.

"Mine look like poached eggs."

Rosie grinned and picked up another dress from the pile on the bed, a black floaty number in pure silk.

"Your boobs are pert, they don't sag. I could never wear a sexy backless number like this, but then you'd look good in a bin liner. Bitch."

Used to her friend's thought processes, Rosie always wanted what she didn't have, namely poker straight hair, five more inches and to be lean and mean.

Bronte ignored the comment and ran a critical eye over the black dress.

"The problem with that one is underwear. Even a thong leaves a line." She took it from Rosie, held it up against her and frowned into the mirror. It was gorgeous, an impulse buy, never worn.

Rosie lifted the flowing skirt of Bronte's dress.

"It's lined and floor length. Don't wear panties. Who's to know?"

"I'd know," Bronte said.

Nevertheless and in spite of her many misgivings, she stripped off her T-shirt and stepped into the cool silk.

From the front the dress wasn't particularly revealing.

But from the back the dress was quite a different proposition.

A spaghetti strap hooked over each shoulder leaving her back naked.

It was a dress made for sin.

She had no idea what she'd been thinking when she bought it.

"Hmm, I can see panty line. Take them off," Rosie said.

After a couple of beats, Bronte shimmied out of her tiny panties.

Turning around, she checked out the back in the full length mirror.

The dress sat snugly above the dimple of her buttocks.

"I don't know about this, Rosie." She bit down hard on her bottom lip. "I feel naked."

Worse, she felt vulnerable, torn between adoring the dress and being scared to death.

Wearing this to dinner with a man like Nico Ferranti was asking for trouble.

Especially after the way he'd been looking at her this afternoon.

And yet was she going to deny herself the chance to flirt with a man who set her hormones on fire?

Rosie lifted a brow and shook her head, hands on her hips.

"You know, I don't get you at times."

Bronte met her friend's eyes in the mirror and raised a brow. "You don't?"

Rosie's expression was quizzical.

"It's been almost two years since you've had sex."

Here we go again.

Bronte suppressed a long suffering sigh.

Keen to avoid a debate about her lack of a love life, she released newly shampooed hair and rubbed her scalp.

Then she picked up a hair brush and turned to Rosie who'd plonked herself on the bed.

"You, Missy, are obsessed with sex. And your point is?"

"I'm only obsessed with sex because I'm not getting any," Rosie muttered, then added before Bronte could interrupt, "Anyway, I'm not talking about me. My point is an incredible man looked as if he could swallow you whole this morning. And you lost the ability to remember your own name."

It was nothing but the truth.

Bronte sat on the bed with a bump.

Perhaps the whole dinner thing was a bad idea?

Even though the physical attraction couldn't be denied, she didn't need all these conflicting emotions or the complications having an affair with a man like Nico might bring into her life. Something like panic rising in her gut had her pick up her bag and rummage around for her Smartphone.

"I'll tell him I'm ill, a migraine." Bronte rose, paced back and forth as her friend watched her with big eyes and an even bigger grin. "No, I'll leave a message with Alexander to tell him I'm unwell and I can't make it."

"Bronte Ludlow, you're running away from a man like Nico? Why are you scared of him?" Rosie asked.

Good question.

Why was she scared of Nico?

Bronte kept pacing.

"It's just that, around him, my skin sort of feels too tight for my body."

Rosie scowled.

"You mean he creeps you out?"

Bronte shook her head, her brows knitted as she tapped her cell phone on the palm of her hand.

"No, just the opposite. There's a strong connection. Too strong. I don't like how it makes me feel."

"For goodness sake, woman, get a grip. It's only dinner with the man. It's not as if Nico Ferranti is in the market for a wife. He's the king of love them and leave them. He's never been engaged and he's never been married."

Bronte stopped dead and simply stared at her best friend.

"And how do you know all this?"

"Google is my friend," Rosie said, without embarrassment or shame.

"You searched him on the internet?"

"Of course I searched him on the internet. My best friend is being chased by a lovely Latin. I want to know all about him."

"You need to stop sniffing out men for me, I mean it."

"I do not sniff out men for you." Ignoring Bronte's snort of derision, Rosie continued, "Well, okay, I'll admit to keeping a weather eye open for a likely candidate. But you snagged this one all on your own. Go, Bronte!"

"You watch too many American sitcoms."

"They're the best. You would've done the same for me." Rosie told her, and then thought for a moment. "Or maybe not. You have nothing to worry about, my dear Bronte. Nico is not a keeper. Therefore the man is perfect for you."

"I'm not sure. He only wants one thing."

Thinking about the one thing made her legs turn noodly.

Bronte sank onto the bed.

Rosie held up her hands in a 'whatever' sign.

"Yeah. Trust me on this. It's not only bricks and mortar the Italian stallion is after." Rosie caught Bronte's hand and looked into her eyes. "You've worked like a dog, we both have. And now you *deserve* to have a little fun. All work and no play makes Bronte a very dull girl. I put good money on it, Nico Ferranti is a fully paid up member of the screaming orgasm club. You could do with a couple of screaming orgasms to exorcise that low life scumbag, Jonathan, from your psyche. He might have broken your heart, but you had a very narrow escape there, my girl." Rosie leaned back, raised her eyebrows. "What's with the face?"

Bronte wrinkled her nose.

"We're getting ahead of ourselves, my dear Rosie. It's the idea that I somehow *deserve* Nico."

Her friend blinked.

"You don't *deserve* to be happy or have fun?"

"I am happy. I'm a single, healthy female who is mature enough to have a physical relationship with a hot man when she feels like it," she said in a prim tone that made her friend grin.

As soon as the words were uttered, Bronte knew deep in her heart they were a lie.

She'd never been able to detach her emotions from any form of intimacy.

But it was time for her to get real.

Jonathan's words came back to haunt her.

She needed to be more responsive to a man instead of just lying there, he'd told her.

How was it his fault if Bronte couldn't satisfy him as a man and Annabel could?

Yes, those words had hurt.

A lot.

But what had thrown Bronte completely was the fact that she hadn't been as upset as she should have been when Jonathan had dumped her immediately after her parents had died.

Honesty made her wonder if she'd agreed to marry him just to keep her parents happy?

And if true, how pathetic was that?

Her parents had adored the Honorable Jonathan Whitfield. Since he was from the 'right' background he'd been perfect for her, they'd said.

But the horrible truth was that Bronte Ludlow was not the right lineage or pedigree for Jonathan now, was she?

Bitterness grabbed her by the throat and squeezed her lungs.

She was a cuckoo placed, through lies and a ruthless deceit, into the wrong nest.

With the stubborn determination she'd been born with, Bronte decided not to think about all that now. Avoiding her fears went against the grain of her honest nature. But her whole world had tilted on its axis and until she found her feet again Bronte refused to think about the truth she had another father in the world.

A man, she'd learned of in the cruellest way, who had no idea he had a daughter.

Her eyes stung.

What on earth was she worrying about?

Nico was an infamous playboy.

And here she was acting like a simpering virgin.

Perhaps she should take a leaf out of her dead mother's book and toss her knickers in his lap.

Rosie frowned now, dark eyes scanning her face.

"I've upset you, haven't I?"

Bronte blinked, brought herself back into the moment and rested her aching head on Rosie's shoulder.

"No, I hear what you're saying. You're right. I need to live life the way I want to these days."

After all, it wasn't as if she was promiscuous, she'd only ever known one man.

And at twenty-six wasn't that simply pitiful?

Rosie leaned back on her elbows on the bed and took a long hard look at her.

"You're still struggling with what that bastard Jonathan did to you, aren't you?"

Bronte shook her head.

"I'm struggling with the fact that during our relationship I wasn't honest with myself or with him. I would have settled for a marriage that was fundamentally flawed. No matter how hard I try, I just can't get past that fact. What the hell was I thinking?"

She gave a sad smile as Rosie continued to stare.

"Hmm, but you didn't marry him. I don't understand why you keep beating yourself up over it." Rosie's anxious brown eyes stayed on hers. "What's going on with you?"

Bronte wished she knew.

"I don't know what's going on. These days, I just don't feel like *me*," she said.

Rosie rolled to her side and leaned on her elbow, her dark head rested on her hand.

"Okay, I get that. Life's certainly been throwing you a few curves recently. And deep in your heart you want for yourself what your parents had. I don't know how many times I've heard you say it."

Bronte avoided her friend's eye and plucked at her dress.

Right there was the hard truth she'd been avoiding for far too long.

"My whole life my parents lived a lie. I trusted them, Rosie. I *believed* in them and they *lied* to me." Her eyes met Rosie's and by her friend's wide-eyed expression of disbelief, Bronte knew she wasn't getting her feelings through to her.

Rosie shook her dark head, her brown eyes filled to the brim with worry and concern.

"Your parents utterly adored you. I was there, too, and I saw how much they loved each other. You're smart enough to know that every marriage, even what appears as a happy marriage, has its ups and downs, Bronte. Whatever happened nearly twenty-eight years ago, they got past it and found a deep and abiding love with each other. You need to get past it, too."

Bronte stabbed a finger at Rosie.

"You see, that's just it. I can't get past it. So, rather than living in a past I can't change, or living in a future that hasn't happened yet, I've decided to live in the moment." She gave Rosie's fingers a squeeze. "And it's working for me, I'm happy living here." She lifted a determined chin as Rosie chuckled. "And if Nico Ferranti is as attracted to me as you seem to think he is, and he wants a no strings fling, then that's fine with me."

Yeah, right, a little voice whispered in her ear.

Eyes twinkling, Rosie grinned.

That was the trouble with having a friend that had known her since they were three years old. Bronte couldn't pull the wool over Rosie's eyes.

"How long did you practise that little speech?"

"All day."

Brown eyes filled with an unconditional love and affection, Rosie slung an arm around Bronte's shoulders. "Why don't you wait and see what happens. Go with the flow. And," she added with a truly wicked chuckle, "you have a plentiful supply of condoms, since I've put a box in your evening bag."

"You're a disgrace."
"No, we were girl guides, always be prepared, dib dib dib."

Chapter Eight

Nico knew the precise moment Bronte entered the grand hall.

The air changed, became electrified.

He had to admit the sensation was a new experience for him.

And he was honest enough to accept that he wasn't quite sure how he felt about it.

He stood in a quiet corner, where he could keep an eye on the quality of service. He couldn't see her, but he knew with every fibre of his being she had arrived.

If he'd been a romantic he would have said that the change in the atmosphere, a frisson of energy, was a connection between them through time and space. Since he knew for certain he didn't have a romantic bone in his body, Nico went with his instincts and his entirely physical reaction. Blood pooled low in his belly. His muscles in his thighs, his gut and everywhere between went rock hard.

The music from the live band vibrated through the floor and connected with the hot rhythm of the blood coursing through his veins.

Again, Nico wondered what it was about this woman that affected him on such a visceral level. He struggled to understand it. It was as though common sense and logic had simply deserted him.

He'd had more than his fair share of incredible women. Along with Alexander Ludlow, Nico Ferranti had cut a swathe through the capitals of Europe on a search and destroy mission to see who could bed the most promising beauties. He wasn't embarrassed about it. At the time they'd been young, working hard, no-one and nothing could touch them and they did no harm.

Naturally, Nico took care of the business end of sex personally.

After the way he'd been brought into the world, he'd been very careful to ensure that there were no little surprises in store for him.

Fond memories of wild nights and even wilder days made him smile.

Ahh, those were the days.

But thinking about them tonight, the memories almost embarrassed him.

Nico didn't view Bronte in the same way as he'd viewed those other women who'd given him pleasure.

No.

He didn't see her as a conquest.

If anyone had asked him how he saw her he would be hard pressed to answer. Logic did not play any part in his feelings. With Bronte, there was a connection he'd never experienced before.

Amused with himself and not a little irritated, Nico now wondered if he wasn't going too far, too fast.

But then he saw her.

His breath caught in his throat.

Lei e cosi bella.

She was beautiful.

The black silk gown clung to small breasts and narrow hips. As she swung the silver curtain of her hair to one side, she turned and he got a full view of her back, naked, with skin as smooth-as-silk.

His tongue felt thick in his mouth.

A young man, his color high, dragged a laughing and protesting Bronte onto the dance floor. He spun her around, held her back against him thrusting his pelvis in time to the hot beat of the music.

The up-lights shone through her dress.

Nico couldn't believe what he was seeing.

Dio mio, she was naked.

What the *hell* was she thinking going out dressed like that?

Eyes narrowing, his mouth a tight line, he stalked through the tables towards the dance floor and her.

By the time he reached Bronte, three things had struck him.

The girl had absolutely no idea that the lights made her dress virtually see through. And she was having the time of her life. The truth hit Nico hard. He would die a happy man to have her smile at him just once, just like that.

The music proceeded into a slow romantic number.

With a firm hand he tapped the young man on the shoulder.

A young man who took one look at his face and relinquished her.

Bronte slid into his arms and it didn't surprise Nico how good she felt there.

Weeping violins filled the air. *Cristo*, she smelled amazing. Flowers and warm and willing woman. He placed his hands on her narrow hips and she raised her brows as she stared up into his face.

Her palms rested reluctantly on his chest as she leaned away, her back stiff.

"You are a woman who appears to attract drunken young men."

He made the observation with a wry smile.

Her breath hitched as he placed her hands around his neck and pulled her close, hip to hip.

Emerald eyes studied him, they held caution and a shy wariness he found incredibly arousing.

Clearing her throat she said, "He's harmless."

Those big eyes stared into his and he couldn't help it.

With a soft murmur, Nico buried his face in her hair and inhaled her scent as he swept feather light fingertips from her shoulders to the small indentation above her buttocks. He enjoyed himself and took his sweet time, delighting in the feel of her soft, silky, fragrant skin. Her sensitive shudder told him she felt it, too. The power of their attraction both thrilled and dismayed him. What would it be like to explore her, he wondered, how would she feel under him? How would her body feel as it held his in her tight and slick heat?

Raising his head, his heart took a stumble as those emerald eyes, drowsy now with desire, stared into his.

Bronte's soft bottom lip quivered as her breath hitched.

Something was happening between them right here and right now.

And Nico was torn between the need to run and the need to explore.

"You have amazingly soft skin." His voice sounded rough to his own ears and he cleared his throat. He wanted nothing more than to take her to his suite and take his time making long, slow, love to her.

Bronte realized she needed to take a step back.

The look in Nico's eyes for her was a heady mix of possession and predator. That sensual mouth was firm, tense even. The room spun, probably due to the fact she was holding her breath. She inhaled in an attempt to kick-start her brain.

Oh God, she loved the sensation of his demanding hands on her skin and the tingling at the base of her spine. She loved the way her cheek was pressed to his chest and the feel of the strong beat of his heart. The trouble was she was loving it all too much. The heat and scent of his body made her mouth water. The hot tugs in her belly and breasts were so new and so terribly seductive.

However, she was more than aware they were in the middle of a dance floor with her friends and acquaintances surrounding them.

Lifting her cheek from his chest, Bronte took a look around.

Sure enough, she spotted her brother's gimlet eye on them.

Alexander stood next to a Rosie who was watching them and grinning like a fool.

The music changed to a fast number and Bronte stepped back with a small smile of apology.

"I need a drink."

Hand in hand, Nico led her from the dance floor.

His eyes were narrow and thoughtful and she wished she knew what he was thinking. His hand kept hold of hers, then he drew her firmly to his side in a possessive gesture that had her brother eye him sharply and Rosie's eyebrows shoot into her hairline.

Nico signalled a waiter with a tray, who jumped to attention.

He took two glasses of champagne and handed her one.

Bronte accepted, smiled her thanks, excused herself and moved slowly around the room to mingle with the wedding party.

Her heart was going crazy in her chest.

She needed the time to pull herself together and had absolutely no idea what she said to people. Her entire focus, her consciousness, was on Nico, where he was and who he spoke to.

And all the while, every second, she was aware of his dark eyes tracking her every move.

She smiled, chatted and kissed the bride and groom.

The bride's mother was a little worse for wear and ordered her husband to dance with Bronte.

Peter Cavendish, an old friend of her late father, led her to the dance floor.

"You look lovely this evening, my dear." His gravelly voice sounded happy and relaxed now his speech was over. He told her he hadn't slept for weeks worrying about it. With a flourish that made her laugh, he twirled her around in an energetic waltz. "Your parents would be proud to see what you and Alexander have achieved, damned proud."

Bronte smiled mistily up into his rugged face.

And knew he was speaking nothing but the truth.

"They would have just loved this, wouldn't they?"

And just like that a heavy weight lifted from her shoulders.

Life moved on.

Ludlow Hall would never be the same, but Peter was right, her parents would have been proud.

"Absolutely," he replied.

With a quick peck on her cheek, he handed her to Alexander.

An Alexander who tightened his hold as he led her to the bar.

"What would you like?"

He ordered a mineral water for himself and turned to her.

His green eyes were filled with too much brotherly concern and she suppressed a sigh.

It looked as though they were going to have another fight.

"Make that two."

Eyeing him over the glass, Bronte braced herself for the lecture that was sure to come.

She watched her brother scan the room, his eyes narrowing when they settled on Nico, who was talking to Rosie.

He took a breath and turned, his eyes sharp as a blade met hers.

"What do you think you are doing with Nico?"

She knew that look and bristled.

"Dancing."

Alexander gave a grunt, sipped his drink and ran a hand over the back of his neck in a gesture she recognized. It was a gesture that told her he was very tired. She was about to ask him if everything was all right, when he spoke,

"That wasn't dancing." Alexander's green eyes stayed on hers. "You've no idea who you're dealing with. He'll eat you alive."

With a frown, Bronte met his gaze dead on.

"I thought he was your friend? The man who saved the day?"

Alexander pressed the bridge of his nose with his thumb and forefinger.

He appeared to be a man at the end of his tether and Bronte felt alarm slide up her spine. He looked exhausted. Burning eyes met hers and she was shocked at his expression.

"He is my friend. I owe him more than I could every repay. But Nico Ferranti is not good enough for my sister. You are so far above him..."

Baffled, Bronte simply stared at her brother.

He couldn't possibly be serious.

"I don't understand."

"Don't be fooled by the smooth charm and the polish. Underneath it, Nico is a born street fighter. He's totally ruthless. And he takes no prisoners. When he's finished with you, he'll walk away without a backward look. He'll break you, Bronte. And if he does that, he'll make an enemy of me."

Bronte couldn't believe she was hearing this.

"When did you become a snob?"

"Being a snob has nothing to do with it. I've seen him with women. He doesn't mean to hurt them, but he's not a man I want my sister involved with." When she kept her eyes on his, Alexander took a breath, it was clear to her he was struggling to find the right words. "He can't help it. He is what he is because he grew up too hard and he grew up too hungry. As a child Nico had a choice, to survive or die. He not only survived, he conquered."

That explained a lot.

Her voice was soft with sympathy for Nico the child.

"Surely that's something to be admired, something to be proud of?"

Alexander nodded.

"It is. But Nico Ferranti has no hard limits when it comes to sex. He has no soft spots. No tenderness or space in his heart for another." His eyes stayed on hers. "He's not for you."

Stunned, she shook her head.

"He's your friend. A friend you trusted your heritage to."

Not once did her brother's eyes leave hers as he nodded, accepting the truth of her words.

"I trust Nico Ferranti with my life. But not with my sister."

There were times and this was one of them, when Bronte detested her brother's overprotective attitude.

"So, you're warning me off a man you trust with your life? Honestly, Alexander, do you really think I would be stupid enough to fall for a man like him? I mean, let's be honest here shall we? You know perfectly well I'm not in the market for a long term relationship with anyone, am I? What on earth could I offer a man like Nico except for a few nights of hot sex?"

Her brother flinched, as his face went nuclear.

Maybe her words were too graphic for a brother she knew was no saint himself, but what was the point of lying about her personal goals in this instance?

"Christ, Bronte, I don't want to see you hurt."
Fair enough.
But Alexander wasn't thinking clearly, was he?

"What if I hurt him? Ever thought of that, or am I always to be the helpless victim in your mind?"

Pain, a deep sorrow, sparked in her brother's eyes.

And that sorrow burst the balloon of Bronte's anger.

She was so terribly tired of fighting with him over every little thing.

Now she rested her forehead on his shoulder and wrapped her arms around his waist to give him a hug.

"I'm sorry. I hate arguing with you like this. I know you're worried about me," she told him with a gentle sigh.

His response was to hug her back before his hand lifted to gently pull her hair.

And she knew she was forgiven.

"I'm leaving tomorrow. You can contact me through the office, Julie has my itinerary."

Bronte raised her head and smiled into eyes that forcibly reminded her of their late mother.

"Sounds exciting, Rome, Paris, Barcelona."

"It's work. Spot inspections of a couple of resorts."

The way he said it, made her frown.

"Trouble?"

"No trouble," Alexander said, gave her hair another tug. "I wish you would wait to meet your biological father until I can go with you."

His capitulation to wishes at last, made his face swim in front of her eyes.

"Are you sure you want to meet him?" she whispered.

"Not really. But I don't want you meeting a stranger on your own."

Bronte flicked a careful look at a Nico who was edging ever closer, and now chatting with the groom.

"It's all organized. And I'm not going to put him off until you return. I thought you were supportive of my decision to meet with him, to get to the truth of what happened all those years ago?"

Alexander's smile didn't reach his eyes which held a mix of raw emotions.

"I am." He assured her with a hug and then leaned in. His nose bumped hers. "I am, but surely I'm permitted to worry about my baby sister, a sister whom I love very much by the way."

It wasn't a sentiment Alexander Ludlow articulated very often.

Bronte knew how hard it had been for him, coping with the loss of their parents, of an inheritance that didn't exist, turning their home into a hotel in the teeth of her fierce opposition, never mind dealing with the fall out of her devastating news of her biological father, plus the messy end of her engagement.

He'd been amazing.

And she'd been too tied up in herself, in her needs, her feelings.

With a small cry she hugged him and they swayed together as she blinked back tears that came to her all too easily these days.

"I love you, too."

Alexander drew back, picked up his drink as his eyes searched the room.

"If you need me, I'm just a phone call away."

Bronte followed his gaze and found her own captured by Nico, watching them like a hawk.

Not once did Nico's eyes leave her as she circulated and half an hour later Bronte's nerves were shot to pieces.

"Ooooh, boy," Rosie whispered in her ear. "Let me know what happens if I don't see you later. I mean it. Give me a ring."

"How are you getting home?"

Rosie gave her a look that was filled to the brim with sheer mischief.

"Alexander's taking me."

"Good God, be careful with him, he's my only brother."

Rosie simply gave her a bland look.

"Don't you worry about him. He's big enough to look after himself. He barbecued my ear about your blind date with Anthony."

"You deserved it," Bronte told her.

"You should have told me Anthony hurt you, just wait until I see his sister."

"I handled it myself. He was nursing his thumb the last time I saw him."

"Ah, the Alexander technique. Apparently, Anthony's now walking with a limp."

"Brothers," Bronte said in disgust. "When is he going to learn I can fight my own battles?"

"Not him. It was Nico."

Bronte turned shocked eyes on her friend.

"Nico hurt Anthony?"

With big eyes, Rosie nodded. "And he didn't leave a mark. Alexander's very impressed."

Stunned, Bronte simply shook her head.

She turned and rammed straight into Nico who took her arm and led her back to the dance floor without a single word.

The look he had in his eyes for her had the butterflies in her stomach morphing into bats.

The band was playing another slow number and he slid her into his arms as if she'd always belonged there.

Her breath hitched again as he placed her hands around his neck.

They fit perfectly and moved together, swaying in time to the music.

When the band struck up a fast number, he spun her out and spun her back with a delighted smile as she laughed into his face.

Then her breath caught as she recognized the raw desire in his eyes.

Alexander's words swirled in her mind.

She was playing with fire and Bronte knew it.

But wasn't it about time she lost the good girl image?

"Nico ... I ..."

His finger stilled her mouth, those amazing eyes burned into hers as he rubbed his thumb over her bottom lip. An erotic, almost illicit little thrill shimmied up her spine.

"That is the first time you have said my name," he said, his voice deep with an emotion she didn't recognize.

When she raised an eyebrow, he rubbed her lip.

"Say it again." Heat flooded her cheeks and she stared up at him, confused. "Say it again. Please, Bronte," he murmured in her ear, his breath sending tingles of desire across her cheek.

"Nico."

Chapter Nine

Nico's gut tightened brutally as her voice, soft and low whispered his name.

Mio dio, it sounded wonderful.

Tension travelled up his spine, into his neck and it took him all of four seconds to work out why.

He wanted her too much, it was almost a need. The experience was unexpected and unwanted. Once he kissed her, he assured himself, these feelings would pass.

In a slow rhythm his fingertips stroked between her shoulder blades, down the smooth curve of her back and he permitted himself to enjoy the sensation of a skin as soft as silk. While his libido warned him to take it easy or it would surge even harder into life. He bent his head. With the scent of neroli and warm female surrounding him, he gave into temptation and nibbled the delicate flesh of her earlobe. Bronte shuddered in his arms with a little gasp, as his tongue licked and his lips kissed the erratic pulse under her ear.

"You are so beautiful, *cara*."

Low and husky, throbbing with desire, his voice sent arousal shimmering through Bronte's blood.

Her mind spun.

Oh yes, it had been too long since a man's cheek caressed hers.

She couldn't understand the language he murmured under his breath, but the sentiment and his physical desire for her was clear. His hard erection pressed into her soft belly. He was a big man and she shuddered. For the first time in a long time, she gave herself permission to relax, enjoy the moment, the sensations and the wonderful dreamlike state as he spun her round and round.

It took her a couple of heartbeats to realize he'd steered them to the side of the hall.

Nico opened a door behind a screen and whisked her into another room.

Her breath caught in her throat.

"What...?"

Stunned, she realized it was a private sitting room, a room which in the old days used to be her father's library.

Nico's dark eyes, watchful and intense, met hers.

It was one thing to flirt openly with him over dinner in a public place, quite another to be alone with him in a room that held so many happy memories.

The intimate moment on the dance floor had gone now, replaced with a wary caution as old as time itself. The caution of a single female faced with an aroused and predatory male.

She went very still as needles of tension of a different kind prickled her spine.

She'd assumed they'd be having dinner in the restaurant.

Then she raised her brows in silent question.

"I thought it would be more private for us to have dinner here," he said.

Did he indeed?

His accent seemed stronger, he appeared even bigger now she was alone with him and Bronte reminded herself that she had no idea who this man was or what he was thinking.

Or what she was doing here?

He seemed to understand her reluctance, because he dialled back the intensity in his eyes as he moved to take her hand in a comfortable friendly manner and brought it to his mouth.

His eyes held hers so intimately; she shivered as he kissed each finger. A sensation of the room spinning reminded her to breathe. A feeling of being pulled by an invisible force towards him almost overwhelmed her. Whatever this was, whether it was chemistry or a fatal attraction, her instincts told her to take great care.

To give herself space to kick-start her brain, Bronte drew

back and wandered about the room, amazed at the transformation from the old world order to the new.

She was only human.

And couldn't help the little pang of loss in her heart.

And then told herself to get over it.

"This is... very nice," she said.

All the time she was deliciously aware of dark eyes following her as she absorbed the changes this man had made to her home. The same imposing stone fireplace with a roaring fire in the hearth, along with the high, arched windows were all that was familiar. In the old days, this room would be heavy with the scent of her father's cigars and comfortable leather sofas the color of ripe blackberries.

Now heavy silk brocade curtains flowed onto the floor like a golden waterfall, held back by brass holders the size of a dinner plate. Three spacious sofas upholstered in a rich fabric the color of autumn leaves hugged a polished oak coffee table the size of a family car. And on the stone floor were dark rugs in matching muted tones.

Huge antique mirrors hung above serving tables which held clear glass vases overflowing with royal red arum lilies.

A dining table, lit with candles was set for two and sat in a small alcove. Intimate and romantic and all for her, she surmised. It was dressed with crystal glasses, white china plates and silver cutlery. It all looked quite lovely. She realized he'd organized a small buffet for them, too. Obviously, Nico was a man who didn't want to be disturbed tonight.

She turned to him as he stood perfectly still watching her.

Bronte sent him a nervous smile.

"This is fabulous." After another attempt at a smile she found herself wondering why he didn't say anything. "You must be pleased with the renovations."

Silence

He just kept looking at her with that dead on stare and the heat of it alone was scorching her skin.

Bronte looked at him for an endless moment.

A moth to the flame.

She couldn't breathe at the expression in those eyes.

Nico walked towards her.

And the jittery nerves in her stomach went crazy.

His eyes, filled with aroused desire, mesmerized her.

He reached out, stroked her burning cheek.

Fingertips, almost feather light, traced her chin, the pulse thundering below her ear, then down the front of her throat towards her breasts.

Her nipples sprung to attention so fast the sensation made her dizzy.

"Nico, what are you doing?" Her voice sounded too breathy.

"If you need to ask, I'm doing something wrong."

He held her hand, those eyes still watching her carefully. She couldn't read his expression. This whole thing was moving way too fast in one way and not fast enough in another. And not for the first time, she felt he could read her mind.

He brought her fingers to his mouth and nuzzled the tips.

"I am making you nervous, *cara*. But I can't seem to stop staring at you in that amazing dress. I need a drink, would you care to join me?"

No way.

She needed her wits about her.

Bronte shook her head and all the time he held her gently, his hands stroked her bare shoulders and down her arms.

Slowly, he brushed his hands back up her arms to tangle his hand in her hair, gently pulling her head back.

Nerves dried up her throat.

Why wouldn't her brain function?

"Nico, I don't think this is a good..."

Those eyes, dark with desire, studied the pulse thundering under her ear and he touched his fingertip to the spot.

"You think too much," he murmured, and lowered his head.

He was going to kiss her, thank God.

His mouth stopped a whisper from hers.

Those eyes asked a silent question as they stared into hers.

And she knew it was up to her to take the next irrevocable step.

Bronte swayed and her mouth found his.

Her heart was battering against her ribs, resounding in her ears, while his lips gently tasted her for the very first time. Slowly he took them both, sinking, into a deep drugging kiss. She had no idea it would be like this, could be like this. It was all there, the power and the strength. She opened her mouth and his tongue slipped in as he tasted her with thoroughness, so seductive, she almost wept.

Their bodies swaying together, his fingers explored her neck, as his other hand moved into her hair, gently tipping her head back to deepen the angle of the kiss. She'd heard of lights flashing before a person's eyes before, but had never experienced the phenomenon herself until now.

He tasted of pure sin and she loved it.

Bronte pressed her body against the hard length of his, tunnelling her fingers through his hair. And demanded more.

Nico caught her bottom lip between his teeth and she groaned into his mouth.

Through narrowed eyes he watched her emerald eyes mist and go dark.

A spear of hot and heedless lust shot straight to his shaft.

Hard and demanding now, his mouth plundered.

Even as she dropped away towards surrender, Bronte's fingers gripped his hair and held on fast. She heard him groan in his throat, but the sound was muted by the roar of her frantically beating heart. His body was so hard and so powerful. His mouth, so hot and so potent. Heat flooded and scorched her body from that one point of contact. His hands explored every inch of her naked back and she gave herself up to the sensations pulsing into her breasts and the slick trembling low in her belly. The need to feed and feed warred with the need to give and give.

Her fingertips constantly explored his silky black hair. God, he felt fabulous. Her breath mingled with his, rasping in her throat and those hands drove her out of her mind as they slid under the fabric of her dress, skimmed under her breasts, teasing and torturing, but never touching her aching nipples.

He was driving her crazy.

Bronte trembled on the brink of the abyss, ready to leap. A voice screamed in her head demanding to know what she was doing. She didn't even know this man.

Tearing her mouth from his, she gulped in a breath as her world lurched and tipped her out.

"No, Nico..."

Chest heaving, his heart jack-hammering, Nico laid his forehead on hers.

He'd never meant for it to go so far so fast.

He'd only intended to take a small taste, to enjoy the moment, but it had gone beyond good intentions into something quite, quite different. The silken heat of her mouth, the taste was so sweet; he could have feasted on it.

He closed his eyes shutting out the sight of her, but there was no way to close off his senses, the smell, the taste, or the softness of her silky skin.

She was inside him now. In his blood. In his very bones.

A kiss was not nearly enough he realized with dismay as his heart threatened to burst through his ribs. What was supposed to be a light, exploratory kiss designed to lower her defences had turned on him. He'd been ready to prepare her for a long and mutually fulfilling seduction where he set the pace and the tempo. He hadn't been ready for this clawing hunger which was more pain than pleasure between his legs.

The need to strip her, toss her onto the sofa and plunge into her, shocked, even terrified him.

Nico Ferranti *never* lost control.

Alarm uncoiled in his gut and finally entered his brain.

What the hell was he doing?

Then he lifted his head and looked into her eyes dark and smoky with desire. And he didn't care what he was doing. He kept his fingers on her face, stroking that soft, soft skin.

"You taste so sweet, even better than I imagined."

His voice sounded harsh and he cleared his throat to catch

his breath.

Those fabulous green eyes were huge, dazed with confused arousal and *Dio* help him, they almost brought him to his knees. She made him weak. The sensation was a unique experience and Nico found he didn't care for it.

He didn't care for it at all.

Perhaps it was time to re-group.

Perhaps it was time to think more carefully about the consequences of his actions with this woman.

He took a step back.

Since it had happened to her before, Bronte recognized the signs too well when a man was retreating from a woman. Her nails dug into the palms of her hands as she fought to control the deep ache of brutal arousal pulsing through her body. Dizzy with it, she tried not to be disappointed he'd pulled back.

After all, it was what she wanted, wasn't it?

Everything had been too intense.

Too much.

Too fast.

So why did she feel like bursting into tears?

"Nico? I..."

And she caught her breath as he caught her fingers and brought them to his lips.

She recognized that the shutters had come down over his eyes, they were cooler now.

"As I told you this afternoon, you are full of surprises. Do not look at me like that, so disappointed, so needy, *cara*, or I will take you right here, right now on the floor." He pressed his pelvis into her soft belly in a purely physical move that jerked her emotional antennae to high alert. "See what you do to me? Never doubt that I desire you. However, I have never, ever forced myself on a woman, Bronte. Do you understand me?"

He studied her thoroughly as her face burned then the heat drained away.

"Yes," she whispered, appalled by what she'd nearly let him do to her. And appalled that she did want him to take her right here and right now on the floor. "But, that doesn't mean that I'm going to let you... I mean, I don't have sex with men I don't know."

His dark eyes went wide in a way that told her she sounded pitiful.

"I would say we know each other very well."

"But, that's just a... a physical reaction."

"Damned right it is." Again he kissed her, this time hard and hot and impatient.

It made her head spin.

"I can't think straight."

"I must admit, Bronte, I am having great difficulty thinking straight myself." He drew back. Holding her hand as his thumb gently rubbed the sensitive skin of her palm winding her body even tighter. "So, what are we going to do about this? Wait until we are both half-crazy with lust?"

The Italian lilt in his voice was more pronounced, but it was the harsh tone that whipped over her heightened senses like a lash. Trying not to cringe at the hot edge of frustration in his eyes and voice, she lifted her chin.

"Why should I apologize for not leaping into bed with you? If I prefer to think about it before having sex with you, then you should respect my feelings."

"Trust me, I respect your feelings just fine." He rammed his hands in his trouser pockets and paced to the fire and back again. "Why do you not yell at me or throw something? We would have a good healthy fight and end up on the floor."

Was he serious?

"I never yell or throw things."

He gave a soft laugh and she breathed a sigh of relief he wasn't angry. But it did nothing for her raging hormones. Part of her wished she could get angry with him, be like Rosie and let it all hang out.

"Come," he said, and held out his hand. "I hope you are hungry."

Chapter Ten

Bronte took his hand.

She was hungry all right and it wasn't for food.

Her brain refused to compute everything that had happened between them tonight.

One minute she was ready to let him make love to her in every conceivable way. The next he was treating her like a friend.

She moved like an automaton as he led her to the table, sat her in a chair and poured her champagne.

He sat opposite and gazed, as if fascinated, into her eyes.

She had the distinct feeling he was putting on a show, an act.

And she didn't like it.

She didn't like it at all.

"Tell me about your life, your hopes and dreams, Bronte."

Was he serious?

Bronte simply stared at him.

Marshalling her thoughts from a brain still buzzing with the toxic mix of arousal and disappointment, she wondered how on earth she was going to handle this man. What on earth had she been thinking? She hadn't been thinking. That was the trouble. Her hormones and a complex, attractive man had got the better of her.

Those dark eyes studied her over the rim of his glass and Bronte felt like an insect pinned to a specimen board.

The selection of food, smoked salmon, tender loin of lamb and vegetables, looked wonderful and she was sure it must taste wonderful, too. In her mouth it tasted of sawdust. If only she was more experienced and a woman of the world. A woman who could handle a man like Nico. If only she was a little more street-wise instead of a provincial fool completely out of her depth and behaving like an unsophisticated moron.

"I am surprised you are not married," he said into the silence.

The question brought her head up.

Okay, he wanted to chat.

She could do chat.

No problem.

"I had a narrow escape."

Nico speared a pepper and drew back to study her face.

"What happened?"

"Things didn't work out."

She hoped he'd leave it at that.

No such luck.

"Why?"

Carefully, Bronte set down her knife and fork.

She didn't want to do this, go over old relationships, old heartaches, with this man.

Not now.

Not ever.

What business was it of his?

Tonight was supposed to be a quick roll in the hay, not a sharing of deep secrets.

Anger and frustration with him, with herself, curled in her stomach.

"He's moved on." Her eyes stayed on his. "These days I feel a certain amount of ambivalence about marriage. Anyway, what about you? Any family?"

She caught his surprise, the flash of pain and realized she'd touched a nerve.

It appeared Nico Ferranti could dish it but couldn't take it.

Too bad.

His gaze clouded.

"I have no family." The words were spoken as a challenge. "We are talking about you."

The look in his eye warned her to step back. And Bronte decided Nico couldn't have it all his own way. It simply wasn't healthy. Someone needed to take a stand against his incredible will.

She ploughed right on.

"Nope. You are talking about me. I'm talking about you. No

mother, father, siblings?"

He shot her a look of smouldering impatience mixed with something dark she couldn't identify.

"My mother died when I was ten. I never knew who my father was."

Immediately contrite, her hand moved across the table and found his. Easy sympathy for him flooded her heart. She knew exactly how it felt for a person not to know their biological father.

"Oh, Nico, I am so sorry. What happened?"

He pulled his hand from hers and picked up his glass, took a sip and stared at her with eyes that had gone so cold she shivered.

"I was a child. It is not something I care to discuss. As I said, we are talking about you."

She held his stare and their eyes clashed.

Okay, have it your way, she thought.

With a bravado she knew she didn't possess, she shrugged.

"What would you like to know?"

"Did you love him?"

Thrown by the blunt question, Bronte opened her mouth and then found herself being totally honest.

"I don't know. At the time I must have thought so or I wouldn't have said yes to his proposal. He's incredibly attractive and intelligent. Unfortunately he also has the fidelity of a tom-cat. He thought my family had money, which made him a fool and me an even bigger one for believing in him. I suppose it's better to find out before we tied the knot that we weren't suited rather than after."

She heaved in an unsteady breath and sampled a sliver of lamb.

"He *cheated* on you?"

His shocked tone made her smile and feel marginally better.

"Apparently, he got the girl who is now his wife pregnant. And I learned something very interesting about myself, too."

His eyes never left her face.

"Which was?"

"I don't forgive betrayal."

Nico ran his tongue over his top teeth, picked up his glass and sat back.

"What did you do?" A gleam entered his eye as a hot flush rose to her cheeks.

Licking her lips, she stared at her plate.

"Well, he asked for his ring back and the way he did it and the things he said... I..." She took another breath.

"What did you do, Bronte?"

Her eyes met his – she spoke very fast,

"I sold my two carat princess cut diamond set in white gold on eBay for ten pounds."

His shout of laughter gave her a jolt.

As did the speed of which he grabbed her hand and the soft kiss he pressed to her knuckles.

"Good girl."

She merely shrugged and nibbled delicately on another piece of lamb.

"He got his own back. He has a clever tongue and a sly charm. People think I started *Sweet Sensation* because I'm destitute and have no other skills to fall back on. They also believe I'm single and I don't date because he broke my heart and that I will never get over him."

"Hmm, so is that why you went out on a date last night? To prove that you are over him?"

Heat flared into her cheeks.

"No. Apparently Anthony's sister approached Rosie."

Nico took a sip of wine, watching her over the rim of his glass.

"Is Rosie the type of friend that would say you were, and I quote, gagging for it?"

With a shocked gasp, she stared at him.

Any guilt she might have felt that Nico had hurt Anthony drained away.

"Of course not. Is that what he said?"

He nodded.

"He is a man who cannot hold his liquor. You should have

no trouble from him." That piercing look was back in his eyes. "So tell me, why are you still single and do not date?"

He had her there.

Of course there was no way she could tell him the truth.

That she had too much emotional baggage to take into a relationship. That until she knew who she was and where she came from and made some sort of peace with it, how could she commit herself to a man?

Mind a complete blank, she said the first thing that came into her head,

"I suppose I'm looking not to get hurt. As I said, I will never marry."

He didn't even blink.

"I don't believe you."

"Excuse me?"

Nico merely shrugged at her icy tone.

"You are not a coward, you will love again. And you would make a lucky man a wonderful wife."

She ignored the weight pressing on her lungs at the wonderful wife comment and forced herself to keep her tone light.

"To be honest, I'm too busy to date. Work keeps me sane."

"You make wedding cakes and attend weddings. Yet you say you will never marry." He took another sip of his wine. "It makes no sense." He placed the glass on the table. She watched his fingers as they found hers.

Nico appeared to be genuinely interested.

But then her track record in reading men was not one to be proud of was it? Her fiancé's scathing remarks about her lack of sexual experience and the things he'd told her he needed from a 'real' woman still had the ability to make her feel physically ill.

She wouldn't fall for the charming routine, not again.

"You have smooth moves, Mr. Ferranti." Bronte removed her hand and clenched it in her lap to stop the trembling. "My love life and how I live my life is none of your business."

"So, why wedding cakes?" he persisted.

"It makes me happy. I don't suppose you would understand

that."

"You are not happy?"

Frustrated with him in more ways than one, Bronte took a breath and tried to explain.

"It's about capturing the moment. You know, when they hold hands and cut the cake and the look in his eyes for her. It's special."

He smiled in a way that brought her back up.

"Ah, you are a romantic. The trouble is these things never last."

Stung, she glared at him.

"There are no guarantees in life." She should know. "But I'm a part of the celebration of their love, the promises and the dreams."

He gave her a level look.

"And you do not want that for yourself?"

"I thought I had it for myself," she shot back.

Something bitter lodged in her throat.

Fury buzzed in her ears.

She threw her napkin on the table.

She'd had it all; the career, a close and happy family and a wonderful man who was safe, she thought. The road to their future had been all mapped out in front of them. Then the horror of losing her parents, the rejection from the man who said he loved her, the letter from her dead mother, the terrible discovery that...

The unexpected softness in his eyes as he watched her struggle to come to terms with her demons was an appalling temptation. Bronte almost wanted to tell him everything. This man was a complete stranger to her, so why did she feel the need to unburden herself to him of all people?

It must be the wine, she rationalized.

Trembling, she rose.

"I'm leaving."

He moved fast as she headed for the door, caught her and turned her into his arms.

"I did not mean to upset you, Bronte. Forgive me," he

muttered into her hair.

She closed her eyes.

No way was Bronte going to let him cut through her defences. He was an expert at seduction. She could sense it. And she he couldn't think clearly when he touched her.

Nico caught her face between his hands, dark eyes searched her face and his thumb rubbed her bottom lip.

Bronte almost groaned, had to clench her jaw to remain calm.

"I am sorry," he said.

Bronte read the truth and genuine regret in those grey eyes before she nodded.

He let her go.

"I'm going home," she repeated.

"Let us go dancing instead. What do you say?"

For the first time in her life, Bronte honestly felt that she was simply not on the same page as another human being. He'd kissed her as if she was the most wonderful woman in the world and then stepped back. She'd just unravelled in front of him. She'd barely been able to restrain herself from spilling out grief, sadness and fear. And now he wanted to go dancing? The man seriously gave her emotional whiplash.

She swayed on her feet while he watched her with a gentle intensity.

Why did he have to look so gorgeous?

Those eyes, they hypnotized her and made her forget everything but the need to be with him.

She let out a barely audible sigh and told herself she was a bloody fool.

"That would be nice."

Chapter Eleven

There was nothing worse than being confused.

Nico had been the perfect host, Bronte mused as he drove her home in the Bentley. Insisting on dancing every dance and holding her close, just not too close. As if he wanted to give her a bit of space to recover from her earlier turmoil.

Yet she still felt hurt.

And why shouldn't she?

Yes, she'd been the one to put a halt to their intimacy, but he hadn't put up much of a fight, had he? One minute he was all over her the next he held back. It wasn't every day she had an earth shattering kiss.

She slanted a look at him.

His hard jaw was firm, his attention fully focused on the road ahead. The Bentley slid into her driveway and he brought it to a stop outside her door and turned off the engine.

Fingers gripping the steering wheel, Nico didn't look at her.

The silence was tense.

Too tense.

Bronte decided to make an effort.

"Would you like a coffee?" And hoped to hell she didn't sound as pathetic and desperate as she felt.

He appeared not to have heard her, his attention riveted straight ahead.

Okay, it was better to find out that someone was moody ahead of time. She'd simply draw a line under this evening and put it down to experience. Her hand fumbled for the door handle as she struggled to keep her voice cool and unconcerned.

"Well, thank you for an interesting evening."

She turned to leave and his hand lay heavy on her shoulder.

"We need to talk."

His deep voice was stiffly polite.

Frowning, Bronte turned to stare at him.

His face was blank as he studied the steering wheel as if it held the answer to world peace.

She decided to nudge him along.

"I'm listening," she said.

He turned to look at her, his face serious.

"I do not know what to do about you."

Her brow creased as she watched him.

"You've lost me."

"I cannot upset Alexander. He is my friend. He will not approve if we have a relationship or an affair, and things are already tense between you."

Irritation with her brother and with Nico made her voice harsh.

"My brother does not run my life. Although he's doing his level best to interfere in every single thing. And *if* anything were to happen between us, Nico, we should be adult enough to deal with it." And she hoped to God she could take her own advice.

"I am not like you." Clenching his jaw, he stared into the night.

She blinked, trying to read his hard features.

"Ooooookay."

Then he turned to her and took a huge breath.

"Unlike you, I was not born with certain privileges. I have seen things that you can never imagine. I am not a man who needs or wants a wife, children or commitment. I am committed to myself and my business. That is it."

He took her hand and furious grey eyes glared into hers.

Her brows winged into her hairline.

"That's it?"

Studying her hand, he frowned, his finger stroking the sensitive soft skin of her palm. The move sent hot sizzles of awareness to every erogenous zone in her body.

"You must understand," he said in a hoarse voice. "I cannot give you what you need."

"And what makes you the expert on what I need?"

She removed her hand from his. And read doubt, confusion in his dark eyes. Well, that made two of them. What made him think she wanted anything more than a fling?

"Nico, I don't see you as husband or even boyfriend material. Frankly, you would be the last man I would choose as a life partner, even if I wanted one. And you don't have to do anything about me. I'll decide if and when I want to take a man, not just you, to my bed."

Silence.

She almost laughed out loud at his expression.

God, this conversation was so liberating, she should have put her cards on the table years ago and saved herself all the heartache. Why the indignant look of outrage? He seemed to have been rendered speechless in fact, so she ploughed on.

"I don't want complications, either. Believe me, my life is complicated enough." She shrugged in a way she hoped would show him she was a woman of the world and well used to dealing with this kind of situation.

Bronte gathered her courage in both hands. "I'm attracted to you. Call it an itch if you like." She patted his hand.

"An itch?" He stared at her hand in amazement.

And Bronte told herself she must have imagined the fury in his voice.

On a roll now, Bronte sat back to enjoy herself.

"Absolutely. And if you would like to scratch..."

The rest of the sentence was lost as his mouth punished hers.

This time there was no softness, no seduction.

Nico took, he demanded and she was with him all the way.

When he raised his head, he looked as if he wanted to strangle her.

"Get out of the car." The tone was rough and his accent stronger as he thrust open the door.

He stalked around to her side, hauled her out and marched her to the front door of The Dower House.

Stunned, upset and absolutely furious, Bronte twisted futilely in his strong grip.

He was angry because she agreed with him?

Typical!

One rule for the male and one rule for the female.

"Let go of me! You're so typical of the type of man who expects the little woman to be sitting panting by the phone waiting for him to call. Well, let me tell you I'm not one of those doormats you can wipe your feet on. You're being ridic..."

He held up a finger.

She received the warning in those dark eyes loud and clear and closed her mouth with a snap almost giving herself lock-jaw.

Just who the hell did he think he was?

Hot tears blurred her vision.

She fumbled her keys, dropping them in the porch.

With a harsh expletive, Nico picked them up and plunged the key into the lock.

Heart thundering in her ears Bronte felt torn between excitement and terror as he thrust her through the door.

Nico kicked it shut, threw the keys onto the hall table.

A single lamp lit his face.

Sheer temper glittered in his eyes.

Her wrap was torn from her shoulders.

Nico tugged off his jacket, tossing it on a chair and grabbed her.

Hot and demanding his mouth plundered, ravished hers.

God, it was terrifying and wonderful at the same time.

His body slammed hers against the door. Bronte couldn't breathe, couldn't think. Panic, desire and excitement whirled in her mind. His tongue forced its way into her mouth replicating the thrust of mating and she moaned as her mind was wiped clean.

Ruthlessly his knee spread her legs, his thigh pressing against her centre. Rough hands pulled down the straps of her dress as he burned a trail of hot, hard kisses down her throat. Nico groaned, exposing her breasts as she gasped in excited shock. Then that mouth suckled and his teeth tugged a too sensitive nipple, sending waves of liquid heat between her thighs. She trembled uncontrollably as he lifted her dress above her waist. Big strong hands cupped the cheeks of her bare bottom, kneading the soft flesh.

And Bronte froze.

"No!"

Her frantic cry reverberated around the hall like a gunshot.

Chest heaving, Nico immediately released her and stepped back.

Her face was deathly pale.

Eyes blinking, Bronte's slim fingers trembled on swollen lip.

Nico recognized shock when he saw it.

Self-disgust roiled in his stomach.

Cristo, what was he doing?

But she wanted him.

He could taste her arousal, her desire.

"I thought you were... I thought you wanted..." He couldn't breathe.

Hands not quite steady, he pulled up the bodice of her dress, smoothed down her skirt.

Able to move at last, Bronte slapped a hand on his chest.

Fury surged, thundering in her head and she could only stare into eyes that were darker than night.

"You thought what? That I'm easy, a slut?"

"No. I never thought such a thing."

"Liar." Her breath sobbed in her throat and it infuriated her. "I know I said I had an itch. But I didn't for a moment mean..." She heaved in an unsteady breath. "You had no right to kiss me, touch me like that."

Those eyes terrified her.

They were too dark now, too intense.

"We are attracted to each other. Look at you, your body desires mine," he said in a hoarse voice.

"That doesn't mean I... that I'm ready to..."

She folded her arms across throbbing nipples and realized with dismay that she was near to tears.

Nico took a steady breath and stepped into her.

"*Cara*, I am sorry." Voice soothing, his fingers stroked up and down her arms. "But why do you not wear panties? It was obvious this evening."

Mortification scorched her face.

Bronte closed her eyes.

"Oh, God... How did you ...?"

"The lights on the dance floor," he told her. The room spun and a roaring sounded filled her ears as Nico put a strong arm around her waist. "Come, sit down."

Nico led her into the sitting room and Bronte sank onto the sofa.

With a heartfelt groan she held her head in her hands.

How could this be happening?

No wonder Nico had been holding her so tight when they danced.

He'd been trying to save her dignity in front of all those people.

There must have been over two hundred people in the grand hall this evening.

Nausea seized her stomach as a wave of nervous exhaustion overwhelmed her.

Crouching in front of her with his eyes keen on her face Nico rubbed her cold hands.

"Try not to worry about it. Most people would not have noticed. You could only tell from the front."

Bronte rolled her eyes to heaven.

She glared at him, furious not only with him, but mostly with herself for being a fool.

"Oh well, that's all right then."

"But why?" He repeated the question.

She dropped her head into her hands and moaned loud and long.

"Because of panty line and Rosie said don't wear..." For the love of God too much information Bronte, too much information. She waved her hands in front of her. "Forget it. It's my own fault."

A cough, firmly suppressed, whipped her head up.

He found her funny?

His amusement drained from his eyes when he caught the stony look on her face.

"It was not as bad as you think," he said in a kind voice.

"Oh well, that's all right then." Pride and dignity rode to Bronte's rescue. "This whole fiasco between us was a bad idea. I apologize for giving you the wrong impression."

Those dark eyes held hers with an intensity that made her shiver.

What had she been thinking to get involved with this man?

No way did she have the skills required to deal with him.

She wasn't sexually experienced enough for him.

She didn't understand the nuances or the sophistication of the game.

And it was a game to him, she was sure of it.

Her eyes narrowed now as he sent her a slow, sexy smile.

"It has been a very long day, *cara mia*. You need rest."

Chapter Twelve

After a sleepless night, Bronte decided she wasn't going to let a mere man get under her skin.

Hair tied in a sloppy top knot and dressed in black yoga pants, vest and cashmere sweater, she padded into her kitchen in her socks the next morning. The missed call light on her answer machine beckoned. Pressing play she listened to three messages consisting of a long silence and the receiver being hung up.

Bronte frowned, a wrong number?

She shrugged because she had more important things to worry about.

Like how embarrassing had last night been?

Nico had morphed into Mr. Polite and *'Please do not worry.'*

Don't worry?

Easy for him to say.

The whole county now knew that Bronte Ludlow was shameless, never wore panties and was happy to prove it to hundreds of guests at a society wedding.

Here she was at eight o'clock on Sunday morning and wide awake thanks to a cold shower and a certain Italian who'd been the central figure in several hot and steamy dreams.

Since there was no point in worrying about something she couldn't change, Bronte did the only thing that relieved stress, she baked.

A stainless steel mixing bowl clanged onto the work surface and she got to work.

In no time the smell of cinnamon, apples and brown sugar filled the kitchen.

And she felt marginally better after a very strong coffee.

Sunday mornings were usually spent lounging around in her cosiest pyjamas catching up with the latest cake designs. Talking of cake designs, she pulled a large sketch pad out of a drawer and grabbed a pencil. Janine Brooke-Stockton was an old school friend who was getting married in three months. She'd changed her mind four times about the theme of her cake. Now Janine wanted a dramatic black and white theme for her wedding cake. It might not be Bronte's taste, but since the customer was always right, then a black and white theme was exactly what Janine would get. Fifteen minutes later the sketch was taking shape, but Bronte's weary mind refused to focus.

Flipping over to a new page, she drew her tormentor's face with quick, precise strokes. Absently, she spent time getting the firm and sensual mouth just right, highlighting the high cheekbones and working to get the super confident expression in those dark, dark eyes just right.

So what if her intuition told her something else was going on under that wonderful face.

So what if Nico Ferranti had a tortured dark angel look.

She had absolutely no intention of getting involved with him on an emotional level, so she should stop obsessing about a simple kiss.

Maybe she should call Rosie for some salient advice?

Maybe she should be less bloody selfish and let her best friend sleep late because Rosie was not a morning person.

Maybe Bronte Ludlow needed to get a grip and get a life?

Annoyed with herself and her fixation with a fabulous looking man, she drew horns sprouting from the top of his head, gave him a pitch fork and made his eyes diabolical.

The oven pinged and she rose to slide out her apple upside down cakes out of the oven onto a wire rack.

With lust curling in her belly, her eyes were drawn like a magnet back to her sketch.

Everything that had happened to her from the night before filled her mind.

When she'd danced with Nico it had been magical.

She loved how big he was.

She loved how he smelled, all spicy and clean and male.

She loved how he'd held her so tight, so close, as if he never wanted to let her go.

Had she ever been touched like that or kissed like that?

Never.

Now she wished she'd found the courage to let him just take her and be done with it.

But she realized that Nico wasn't a man who just took and walked away.

No matter what Alexander said about his friend.

Nico had taken a very big step back from her.

Okay, he'd been a pain at dinner when he wanted to know all about her life and yet kept schtum about his own.

At some point in his life, he'd been hurt.

She'd felt it as she'd recognized his pain.

Then scene in the hallway of her home had given her goose bumps.

Yes, he'd been rough with her and that was totally unacceptable behavior.

But... he'd pulled back immediately when she'd said no.

And a secret part of her had actually enjoyed it and what did that say about her?

It said she was a pathetic excuse for a female.

But God, his hands knew exactly where to go, what to do.

And now she'd been left hanging all night, all needy and achy.

And whose fault was that, she wanted to know.

Her own.

However, she wasn't letting him off the hook either.

He'd been blowing hot and cold with her since they'd met.

Son-of-a-bitch, she nearly snarled at the drawing.

He probably had a woman in every city.

Hadn't Alexander said that Nico was popular with the ladies?

No surprises there, since some of the women at the wedding had been virtually panting after him.

Pathetic.

She firmly pushed aside her own panting response last night to his undoubted sexual prowess with a grimace of something that felt like shame. And what would her brother think about his sister practically having sex up against her front door with his friend and business partner? She closed her eyes. Poor Alexander, he'd looked so stressed last night, and if he ever got wind of her behavior with Nico, he would be frantic. Hadn't she put him through enough?

Her tired brain moved relentlessly onto another issue.

Her brother had been her rock, along with Rosie, when her whole life had been turned upside down. And all because of a letter. How many times had she wished she'd never seen the damned thing, never mind read it?

She'd learned a salutary life lesson the hard way.

Secrets and lies and words unspoken bred mistrust, hurt feelings and broke hearts beyond pain.

Don't think about it... not today.

But her mind refused to let it go.

When she was overtired or stressed, her dreams were still haunted by the scene.

She'd been driving in her car, in a hurry, singing along to a song on the radio and had driven round a bend and into a scene straight from the bowels of Hell itself.

Straight into teams of Police, Ambulance and Fire crews desperately fighting to release the shattered remains of her parents from their car. She'd never forget, couldn't forget, the smell of petrol, the roar of power tools and men shouting.

And underpinning the whole... the smell of death.

The trauma of the loss of her parents had been nightmare enough, but then had come the discovery of a letter.

A letter written by the man she knew as her father.

She closed her eyes now, because she knew that letter by heart.

Bronte, my darling,

You have been a joy to us since the day you were born. Even now when we look at you, we can't believe we've been so lucky that we were given you as our daughter.

Every marriage has its tough times and ours has been no different. Twelve months before you were born, your mother and I separated for a time. Hindsight is a great thing and we now realize we were too young to handle the responsibilities of running Ludlow Hall and the estate.

Duty came to us too early after the death of your grandfather.

Both of us were to blame for what happened.

For a short time, your mother found solace and badly needed affection in the arms of another man. We came to our senses and realized we still desperately loved and cared for each other. But your mother was already pregnant with you. We want to make it clear that we never, ever thought of terminating the pregnancy. You have always been much wanted and very much loved.

If you are reading this it means we have left this earth too soon, before we found the courage to tell you the truth to your face.

Your biological father has no idea of your existence. That is a decision your mother and I have come to bitterly regret, but we made that decision when we were young and once done it could not be undone.

Your biological father is Carl Terlezki.

He is a wonderful man who cared very deeply for your mother at a vulnerable time in her life.

We hurt too many people all those years ago, Bronte. And now we have to hurt you, too.

We are so sorry, my darling.

What you do with this information is entirely up to you, Bronte, but we hope you contact Carl and show him this letter. Perhaps finding each other will bring joy to two people we have wronged.

Please find it in your hearts to forgive us for keeping you apart.

Your loving parents.

Bronte opened her eyes and found herself in the present and again found herself asking questions that could never be answered.

As a family, the Ludlows had been so close.

They'd shared so much.

Why hadn't her parents told her and Alexander the truth?

She had so many questions to ask and too many words were now left unsaid.

Then the problem with the will and the inheritance had arisen because she wasn't a Ludlow. Her parents had left her The Dower House. Alexander had been left Ludlow Hall, and all its debts. The Hall would need to be sold. And then she'd had to deal with her fiancé's decision that they were too young to settle down. He hadn't attended the funeral, saying it was a *'private, family matter.'* When in fact, Jonathan had been having an affair.

What kind of person did something like that to someone they were supposed to care about?

The room swam as tears gathered behind her eyes.

Her throat tightened.

Furious with herself for getting upset again over a man who'd done nothing but con her and her parents into believing he adored her, Jonathan was a man who didn't deserve a single tear shed.

She blinked her tears away.

Of course, she'd researched Carl Terlezki.

Google wasn't just Rosie's friend.

The man whose face now stared at her from her laptop screensaver was in his mid-sixties, slim, tanned and still handsome. He had a thick shock of white hair and apparently was a wealthy financier and a man who raised millions for good causes.

Although he appeared to have had relationships with women, it appeared her biological father had never married, nor had children.

At least none he acknowledged publicly.

She'd put his face on her screensaver just to torture herself with even more unanswered questions.

What if he didn't want to know her?

What if he thought she was after his money?

And what did she want from him?

In spite of her parent's lying to her, Bronte had to admit she'd had an idyllic childhood.

However, she still felt so very angry with them, the sense of betrayal a weeping sore in her heart.

So she'd sent Carl Terlezki a tentative letter, keeping it vague, telling him about the death of her parents and the discovery of a letter. Might she meet with him to discuss it? The reply had taken weeks since, he said, her letter had got caught up in other correspondence. Carl had asked her to phone him and forty-eight hours ago Bronte had done so. His deep voice on the phone had sounded sincere and very kind. She was due to meet him tomorrow morning at his office in the City. By his tone he sounded intrigued; he assumed she wanted him to donate funds to a worthy cause. He'd be delighted, he said, to meet the daughter of such a wonderful woman who had been such a good friend to him.

Bronte had no idea what she was going to say to Carl when she saw him face to face.

And of course, Alexander was less than happy about the situation.

Her brother didn't want to stir up a scandal, old news from the past that would certainly smear the family name.

Bronte could understand it, but for too many months she'd struggled with what was the *right* thing to do. Doing nothing was not an option. So she'd taken the decision to play it by ear. Hand Carl Terlezki her parent's letter and gauge his reaction to the news.

What was the worst thing that could happen?

He might turn away and want nothing to do with her.

Which was fair enough.

Who would blame him?

However, she was achieving nothing by sitting here brooding over what ifs.

Whatever would be, would be.

She'd just need to accept it.

No more tears, she told herself ruthlessly as she stared now at the drawing of Nico Ferranti.

She wanted him desperately, but was honest enough with herself to realize that if she took, she may lose something too. She'd lose a fundamental part of who she was.

Not only that, a man like Nico would never understand her.

Not really.

Not where it counted, like the love and loyalty of family, of tradition, of duty.

Bronte bit into another cake, topped up her coffee, still staring at the drawing.

Surely a fling or an affair would hurt no-one?

An affair sounded more sophisticated, less sleazy than a fling.

After all, her heart wasn't involved.

With a man like Nico, a man who knew the score, she could have a little fun.

He'd spelt it out clearly last night and so had she.

Therefore there was no risk to her heart or to his.

She could experience things other women took for granted without a second thought.

He wanted her and she wanted him.

They were single, unattached and free to do as they wished.

Feeling more settled Bronte rose and boogied her hips.

There was another way to relieve stress.

She plugged her iPod into her surround sound system, selected Rihanna and flicked it up to full volume.

Life, Bronte told herself, was too damned short not to have fun.

Chapter Thirteen

In the penthouse suite of Ludlow Hall, Nico lay on his back in his big bed, his heart bucking against his ribs.

Remnants of an erotic dream featuring Bronte in the starring role tortured his mind and his body. In a fluid movement, he jack-knifed off the bed, stalked across the room and slapped on the bathroom light, blinking at the man in the mirror. He took a shaky breath. He was so hard he could barely breathe. His pupils were dilated, full of arousal as well as a dazed bewilderment.

Perspiration beaded on his forehead and his skin felt clammy and damp.

This was ridiculous.

He was an experienced man of the world, not seventeen and unable to control himself.

Under a freezing shower, he fought to come to terms with the last forty-eight hours. If he believed in magic he would swear that Bronte Ludlow had bewitched him. His bones ached for her. She made him weak and that was simply not acceptable.

Never had a woman affected him like this.

Fury pulsed through his blood as he shivered under the onslaught of icy needles beating his physical response to the dream into submission.

With a towel slung around his hips, he stalked into the bedroom.

How the hell was he supposed to work, concentrate on running his business if he couldn't get a decent night's sleep? When was the last time he'd spent the night tossing and turning with dreams of wild sex with a gorgeous blonde?

Never.

He snapped on briefs. Digging out jeans from his closet, he hauled them on and tugged a cream sweater over dripping hair. She'd been sending him mixed signals since the first moment they'd met. He rammed his feet into Tod's loafers. He couldn't believe it when she was dancing with that young man and he realized she wore absolutely nothing under her dress.

Grabbing his car keys, Nico opened the door and strode down the hotel hallway to the stairs. He took the steps two at a time. Then he stopped dead when the memory of those huge emerald eyes full of spitting fury and aroused confusion tortured him again.

It made him feel physically ill each time he thought of the way he'd had her trembling against the door.

He'd been too rough with her.

And whose fault was that?

Itch?

He continued down the stairs.

He would give her an itch all right.

She was attracted to him was she? And he could give that itch a little scratch could he? And she would have men whenever she liked, would she?

What was she thinking talking about herself like that?

Which was an unfortunate thought he realized when lust burned in his shaft.

He stalked out to his car, closed the door with a thud and jabbed the key in the ignition.

Once they made love, he assured himself, this anomaly would pass and he would return to normal.

The Bentley screeched down the driveway of Ludlow Hall.

Little witch.

A few minutes later, Nico's car purred to a halt at the back entrance of The Dower house.

He checked the time.

Too early?

Too bad.

Stepping out of the car, the scent of warm apples, sugar and cinnamon poured across his senses.

Pure annoyance fired his blood pressure again.

So she made cakes while he suffered the agonies of hell.

The Dower House throbbed and boomed with the bass of a pop song.

Nico lifted his hand to knock the door and then shrugged.

She'd never hear him over the racket.

Ignoring the little voice that told him he was invading her privacy, he tried the handle and opened the door.

Strolling into the house, he cocked his head.

It appeared Bronte was singing.

Then he thought again.

Nope.

That noise could never be called singing, more like howling or screeching.

And he winced as she let out an endless shriek that didn't quite make a long top note.

Nico stepped into the kitchen and every particle of angry frustration drained away.

He couldn't help the big grin that split his face.

Blissfully oblivious she had an audience to her hips bumping and grinding to Rihanna's big hit, Bronte stripped off her top, swung it around her head and tossed it.

The sweater sailed high through the air to land at Nico's feet.

Without taking his eyes from her, he picked it up.

Absently, he rubbed the soft wool between his fingers. Absorbing the warmth from her body and inhaling her scent.

She wore black fitness pants slung low, low on her hips and a short skinny vest.

No bra and bare feet.

Still cheerfully unaware of his presence behind her, Bronte continued to sing her heart out as she shook her booty.

Blonde hair, piled in an incredibly sexy knot on top of head, accentuated a long and delicate neck. Her ears, small and perfect, hugged her scalp.

Nico had to laugh when he spotted a black sock over the kettle and another in the middle of the fruit bowl. Rihanna blasted through the speakers telling everyone to please don't stop the music.

Please don't, Nico begged, leaning his shoulder against the door frame to relax and enjoy the show. Guilt that he was witnessing something terribly private dug him hard in the ribs, but Nico ignored it.

He wouldn't have missed this for the world.

God knew she couldn't sing but the girl had moves.

Skipping to a fridge, her tight little bottom wiggled in perfect time to the beat and Nico bit down hard on a knuckle.

With a bottle of water as a microphone the fabulous Ms. Ludlow step-touched with a sexy swing of her hips, shook her booty and strutted her stuff.

Spinning round he saw her eyes were closed and that stunning face was flushed with exertion.

She opened her eyes and saw him.

And those fabulous eyes bugged right out of her head.

Jogging frantically on the spot, Bronte Ludlow screamed her lungs out.

Pure reflex had Nico catch the bottle of water that almost beaned him between the eyes.

"You *bastard!*"

The girl was on him like a wildcat. He was a big man who knew how to handle himself. Bronte was no match for him. The shock that she'd even think to attack him in the first place made him laugh out loud. A big mistake, he realized, when she growled in his ear. A growl that only made him laugh harder. A flying fist caught him on the chin as she clung like a limpet to his back. An arm locked around his neck in a tight strangle hold. Endless legs wound around his waist like a vice.

"*Cristo*, Bronte, stop."

Roaring with laughter, Nico couldn't catch his breath.

His eyes watered when Bronte did her level best to rip his hair out of his scalp.

When her teeth sank into his shoulder, he yelled,

"Okay, that is it!"

"How *dare* you come into my home without warning?" she yelled in his ear. "You almost gave me a heart attack."

She made a determined effort to twist his earlobe off and he'd had enough.

Nico landed back against a wall.

And he heard Bronte's breath whoosh from her lungs.

He spun, pinned her arms above her head and pressed his body against hers.

Her powerful knee thrust missed unmanning him by a whisker.

Panting now, her eyes spat green fire into his.

The feel of her struggling under him sent blood racing to his shaft.

And he knew he was in big trouble.

Her breath was panting into his mouth as she went utterly still and those green eyes grew wary now.

She trembled and not just from fury.

"Let me go," she panted. "I mean it."

Her voice was high as her breath heaved in short bursts and he couldn't take his eyes from her mouth. Her heart bucked against his and the scent of her shampoo and pure Bronte made his mouth water. A pink tongue licked her top lip and Nico knew he desperately wanted, needed, to taste, to take.

A soft whimper made him look into her eyes and what he saw there, arousal battling with alarm, made him stop.

He'd already taken a misstep with her last night and he wasn't going to take another with her today.

Chest heaving, Nico released her and stepped back, palms up in a gesture of peace.

God, she desperately needed to take a minute.

Her heart was threatening to implode in her chest and Bronte thought she *was* going to have a heart attack. For a second she'd thought he wasn't going to let her go, then when he had released her, she'd been disappointed.

What the hell was wrong with her?

Her emotions were all over the place.

And how much of that little dancing exhibition had he seen?

She spun and switched off the music.

The sudden silence in the room was deafening.

Their heavy breathing sounded too loud as she stared at him.

"What the *hell* is the matter with you? Have you never heard of knocking a damned door?"

Rubbing the side of his chin, Nico wiggled his jaw.

"I... um... realized you would not hear me above the noise of the music. You really should lock your door."

Since she was too busy looking at the dishevelled state of him, Bronte ignored the implied criticism.

"There's been an invention, perhaps you've heard of it? It's called a telephone. It's a very handy device. Before you visit someone, you give them a ring and see if it's convenient for them before you descend unannounced. You can leave messages and everything on it." Her eyes went into icy slits and she took a long, deep breath. "How much of that did you see?"

He rubbed the back of his neck, his scalp and winced.

"Um... I caught it from the part where you took off your sweater. Nice moves, shame about the voice."

He caught her eye and grinned.

Adrenalin still pumping through her system, Bronte's eyes narrowed on the knife block on the granite worktop.

She moved fast, but he moved faster to put himself between it and her and certain injury, if not death.

Now she bounced on her toes, like a fighter in the ring.

"You find this funny, big boy?" With a growl in her throat, she kept her knees loose as she balanced onto her toes and ran her tongue around her teeth. She'd had plenty of fights with her brother. And knew exactly how to inflict pain on a man. She'd give anything to wipe that stupid grin from his face.

"I find you absolutely fabulous," he said quite sincerely.

The tone of his voice and the look in his eye told her he meant every single word of it.

Okay.

Bronte's blood cooled rapidly as she took a deep, cleansing breath.

She took a long look at him and couldn't help it.

Her lips twitched as she saw that his hair wasn't all slick and sleek now.

Nope.

It stood on end, all tousled and tangled.

And was that a rip in the shoulder of his sweater?

His grey eyes were full of fun and barely suppressed laughter as dimples flashed in his cheeks.

An emotion Bronte didn't recognize caught in her chest.

Spinning to turn her back to him, she filled the kettle with water and plugged it in.

Pulling on a sock, she searched for the other one, found it in the fruit bowl and tugged it on, defiantly ignoring his rumbling laugh.

The urge to take another bite out of him, or to throw herself into his arms almost overwhelmed her.

She needed to recover her balance, put a little distance between them and get a grip.

"Coffee?" she asked now.

Her eyes slid to him as he settled himself in a chair at the kitchen table.

He grabbed a cake from the rack and bit into it.

"Please. Hmm, these are excellent. What are they?" He swiped another cake.

"Help yourself," she said. The sarcasm dripping from her tone went right over his dark head. "Apple turnovers. Miss breakfast?"

She placed a mug on the table with milk and sugar.

Those dark eyes sparkled into hers and he sent her a wicked smile.

For a moment she saw the little boy in the man and Bronte's heart simply melted.

"I did miss breakfast," he admitted.

"Was there something you wanted from me?"

"Oh yeah."

Bronte frowned and scooped ground coffee into a pot, filled it with hot water.

She was missing something here but couldn't work out what it was.

"Something important?" she asked now.

Glancing at him she saw those grey eyes were gentle on her now, the smile sweeter.

For some reason it worried her, although she couldn't exactly say why.

"I thought it was, but it can wait."

His attention was diverted by her drawing and notes of Janine's wedding cake.

When he turned over the page Bronte nearly fumbled the coffee pot.

Those dark brows drew together.

"Did you draw this?" It appeared he couldn't take his eyes from her drawing of himself.

Mortified, she poured coffee into his mug and slid into the chair across the table from him. "I'm afraid I did."

When deep grey eyes met hers she read humor mixed with appreciation and realized she'd been holding her breath. "Is this really how you see me?"

"Mmm hmm."

She sipped her coffee.

"May I keep it?"

Surprised, embarrassed and secretly thrilled Bronte shrugged. "Sure."

Nico tore the page from the pad and carefully rolled it up.

Feeling the chill now, Bronte rose, found her sweater and tugged it over her head.

"What are you doing here, Nico?"

Chapter Fourteen

Good question, he thought eyeing her over the rim of his cup.

What was he doing?

"I wanted to apologize again for last night." Those luminous eyes held his for an eternal moment. "And to make sure you were all right."

Bronte gave him a cheeky grin that he couldn't help but return.

"Apology accepted. As you can see, I'm fighting fit."

Little witch.

He desperately wanted to kiss her.

"Okay, I am not going to apologize for that."

"You should quit while you're ahead."

"Will you come to the Ball with me?"

"I'd like to, yes."

They smiled at each other companionably.

Sipping her coffee thoughtfully, Bronte frowned for a long drawn out moment then flicked him a wicked little look.

Nico realized he could sit there all day just watching the expressions cross her mobile face.

"Nico?"

"Hmm?"

"Are you any good at giving a woman a screaming orgasm?"

He inhaled coffee and choked.

Laughing, Bronte handed him kitchen roll, rose and energetically thumped his back.

"Sorry, sorry, I didn't mean to catch you unawares."

"What sort of question is that?" he croaked.

"Rosie reckons you must be a fully paid up member of the club."

She grinned at him with big wide eyes and Nico wondered just what the hell these women talked about.

"What club?" As soon as he asked, he wished he hadn't.

She simply shrugged, batted her eyes.

"The big "O" club."

"Never heard of it."

Terribly aroused and distracted by those fluttering eyelashes, he knew he sounded outraged. He was fast coming to the conclusion that Rosie Gordon was a bad influence on her friend. She appeared to be at the bottom, so to speak, of a lot of things.

"What's so funny?" he growled now, aware she was teasing him and that he loved it.

He wondered if she was prepared to face the inevitable consequences of her actions.

Still grinning, Bronte took the dishes to the sink and turned on the tap.

"Your face."

He moved fast.

Bronte felt the heat of his breath on her neck. Swishing liquid soap into warm water, she took her time cleaning the mugs.

When his arms slid loosely around her waist, she turned and looked up into those eyes, dark and filled with desire for her.

"What is the matter with my face?" That voice, deep and husky made her shiver.

It was a perfectly serious face now she realized and her stomach curled with a pleasant little kick of lust.

"You have a nice face." She patted his chin giving him a beard of bubbles.

His eyes stayed on hers as he drew back to study her.

"Do not start something you are not prepared to finish, Bronte," he said, arousal deepening his voice. He pressed his aching erection into her soft stomach. "I need to take you to bed."

Those dark grey eyes went too intense now, never leaving her suddenly hot face.

His mouth was so close, his breath mingled with hers as he slid his hands under her sweater to stroke gentle fingers over her too sensitive flesh.

Her body jerked and he smiled.

Magic fingertips glided over her skin, sending erotic shivers up her spine and a hot spear of arousal into her belly. His jaw clenched as she trembled and still he didn't kiss her. He wouldn't, she realized with sudden insight. Whatever happened next was her decision and hers alone.

Her hand reached up and her fingertips traced that stubborn jaw, over his cheek and up into his black, silky hair.

"Kiss me," she said and pulled that fabulous mouth to hers.

And there it was again, that punch of power.

Heat roared through her blood, almost making her frantic as he danced his tongue across her lips. His mouth cruised over hers, searching and tasting, but never taking.

He was being careful with her she realized and nipped his bottom lip to encourage him to give her more, much more.

Her breath panted into his mouth.

Nico was determined that this time he wouldn't make a mistake. This time she set the pace. But when she sucked his bottom lip into her mouth and her hands went on an erotic voyage of discovery under his sweater he was lost.

"Where is the bedroom?" he panted, running hot frantic kisses down that soft neck as he tugged off her top.

"Upstairs," she gasped, struggling to get his sweater off as he toed off his shoes.

"We will never make it," he moaned as she slid off his belt, shaking fingers unbuttoning his jeans.

He slid her fitness pants down her legs and she kicked them off.

Nico lifted her and she wrapped long legs around his waist.

Then she pressed her breasts against his chest and buried her hot face in his neck as she plastered her body against his.

She was shy?

"Sitting room, hurry, hurry," she implored him between open mouth kisses on his neck, his jaw, as her body pressed intimately against his.

His soft laugh brought her eyes to his as he carried her

through the house.

Setting her on her feet next to a large couch Nico cradled her face between his hands, rubbing his thumbs along her flushed cheekbones, her lips. Her emerald eyes were so dark with arousal and desire.

"I will take care of you. I will not hurt you," he promised as his eyes held hers.

She smiled and he nearly wept with relief when he saw trust there.

"For God's sake, Nico, make love with me."

She groaned as he laid her down, her arms reaching for him.

It appeared she wanted it fast and furious.

And he was with her all the way.

But something in the way she was trembling, something in her eyes, held him back.

Those big green eyes watched him as he settled himself on his knees between her spread legs. Her hands now clutched her small, but perfectly formed, breasts. Hiding them from his gaze. He bit his lip as it became crystal clear to him that Bronte was painfully shy of her body and bravely trying to hide that fact. He was a big man and could only imagine how he must look to her as she lay beneath him, looming over her, hard and ready to take everything she was prepared to give. He was used to making love with women who were supremely confident in their looks and their bodies, especially their surgically enhanced breasts. So it was a first for him to be attracted to a woman like Bronte Ludlow. A woman who was incredibly beautiful and yet insecure, unaware of her own allure, of her own attraction. Now he wondered what she would be like when she'd thrown off whatever body issues were holding her back. Which meant he would need to put his aching need of her on the back-burner, just for a little while. He caught her hands in his and placed them above her head, opening her body up to his gaze. Her breasts were small, but perfectly formed with nipples that even now were swelling and rigid under his gaze. Gorgeous. And that's when he caught a glimpse of embarrassment and a hint of fear in those wide green eyes. With each inhale and exhale, her lips trembled and he realized she was wound a little too tight. Something clicked in the vicinity of his heart and a tenderness he'd never have believed himself capable of entered.

"You must never be ashamed of your body, *cara*. You are beautiful, perfect to me, just the way you are."

She tried to smile, but the attempt was pitiful.

"I can't help it," she said now. "As a rule I don't do envy, but I'm so jealous of Rosie's boobs. In fact I've often thought of having..."

His finger gently pressed to her lips stopped the comment in its tracks.

He shook his head.

"Never think of it." He sat back on his heels and looked his fill at the woman he was going to make his in every conceivable way. Nico Ferranti wasn't a man who let his dick rule his head or his heart. He was too disciplined to accept or want instant gratification. At all times he was a man in total control of his emotions, of his physical needs. But he found it hard to maintain that control as he looked his fill at the woman who lay beneath him. There was one word being softly whispered again and again in his mind.

Mine.

His hand stroked her bent leg from knee to thigh again and again, until she began to relax and her trembling almost ceased. When she let out a long and contented sigh, he spoke, "You are a stunning woman. I love how your skin feels under my hand, soft as silk. And your bones and muscles are all long and lean." Then the palm of his hand stilled on her flat belly, felt the muscles quiver as his thumb rubbed the dip of her navel again and again. Had he ever had a woman so responsive to his touch like this? He couldn't remember. And now his throat went tight with an emotion he couldn't identify. "I can feel how your belly tightens when I touch you there. You are a gift to me, *cara mia*, a gift."

Now his hands smoothed and stroked her flushed skin as they reached up and over her ribcage, felt her heart thundering there. His hand slid up over her breasts and very gently, so gently, his hands cupped the small but perfect creamy globes and the pad of his thumbs rubbed and whispered tiny flicks over her hard little nipples. He saw the change in her. Her neck and cheeks heated as her eyes glazed, but it was the dampness between her legs that alerted him she was nearly ready to be taken. Now her breathing became fast again, this time with arousal rather than nerves or fear. He settled back on his heels as he lifted and brought those endless legs together and whipped the scrap of lace that were her panties up and off and tossed them to the floor. Then he spread those legs and looked his fill at the very heart of her. Her swollen and slick flesh reminded him of rose petals dipped in dew. And there was the hard little nub of her clitoris throbbing to the hectic beat of her heart. *Dio mio*, she was exquisite and so very ready for him. He inhaled the unique scent of his woman. And somehow he knew that if he was blindfold he'd be able to identify her by scent alone in a crowded room.

Again the thought whispered his mind.

Mine.

His heart seemed to open wide and the woman who lay beneath him, who was staring into his eyes so intensely, something, a message, was passed between them and Bronte Ludlow stepped right into Nico Ferranti's heart.

He didn't question it.

It felt right.

It felt real.

In that perfect moment, Nico made himself a firm promise.

That at all times he would put her needs before his own.

He would take care of her.

Protect her.

He placed the flat of his hand again on her belly, this time just above her pubic bone. And the other cupped her sex. All the time he kept his eyes on hers, and saw hers go wide.

"You need to understand something about me, Bronte. When I give you pleasure and watch you fall apart under my hands, your pleasure gives me the greatest pleasure, too. Therefore it is important to me that you hold nothing back. Do you understand me?"

Her response was a single nod of her head as her neck arched off the sofa.

He knew if he so much as whispered a little flick of his thumb over the throbbing bud at her centre, she'd fly apart. But he wanted much more than that for her and for himself. He wanted it all. He wanted Bronte screaming his name. After all, she'd asked him for a screaming orgasm. Who was he to deny her such a thing? It was his very great pleasure to bring her joy.

And now as his finger stroked her slick and hot flesh, never touching the hard little pleasure centre, he inserted his finger into her and immediately her body clutched him tight. He closed his eyes and his whole body shuddered because he knew now how she was going to feel around him when he made her his. But first thing's first. He inserted another finger, that made two now, and curled them in a *come here* gesture that stroked the spongy flesh of the spot that would make her scream when she came. And immediately he felt her womb go hard under his hand. She was panting now as her back arched, as her face flushed and her lips quivered with each trembling breath. Her hands were still held high above her head and Nico knew he'd never seen anything so beautiful in his life as Bronte coming apart under his hands. It was as if he'd known her his whole life. He knew exactly how to stroke to make her moan and how to make her body quiver. *Cristo*, he was so hard behind the fly of his jeans, he was ready to explode.

But now she was sobbing beneath him.

"Please, Nico. I can't...take..."

Without warning, he removed his fingers, both hands spread her wide and he dipped his head to taste her. The flat of his tongue licked her and he'd never tasted anything so wonderful in his life. She was sweet and tart and writhing beneath him. And when his tongue flicked her clitoris her whole body arched again as she screamed his name as she flew apart. But he wasn't finished. He licked and stroked her until she lay pliant on the sofa, as her legs and arms lay splayed, boneless, beneath him. Only then did he lift his head to smile with a satisfaction that seemed to fill his heart.

Oh yeah.

Bronte Ludlow had just had her first screaming orgasm.

The first of many.

He rose over her and watched her eyes go from dreamy to alert as her hand reached out to touch his face.

Nico bent to kiss her once, twice.

She was warm and willing and wet and ready for him.

So ready.

Nice and slow, Nico, he ordered himself.

Take it nice and slow.

His hand slid over the smooth skin of her hip, along her thigh and she trembled under him. Softly, softly his mouth brushed hers, tasting her, teasing a response as he nibbled a slow path along her bottom lip. Bronte sighed and opened her mouth, her tongue tangling in a silky, sensuous dance with his. And then her hands streaked through his hair to grip his scalp and pull him close for more.

A smile shaped his mouth as she moaned as he tore his lips from hers and moved lower to explore the soft skin under her ear and her body shivered, convulsed under his.

Her responses made the blood thunder through his veins.

Those soft panting breaths made him crazy for her.

When those nails ran down his back towards his ass he groaned into her mouth.

Her fingertips stroked and explored his back, his wide shoulders.

The man worked out and Bronte gave a little hum of pleasure in her throat as she reached down over hard abs and lower still. Her fingers searched under his jeans, feathering over a lean hip.

His hand stilled hers.

"Not yet, *cara*." His harsh voice, low and full of need, detonated a bomb of lust deep in her belly. And she arched her pelvis towards him as he removed a condom from the back pocket of his jeans.

Stripping down to his skin, Nico protected them both.

His fingers skimmed over her ribcage, down over her flat stomach and she gasped. Gentle fingertips stroked feather light slow circles around her navel and the hot liquid pull low in her belly was a heady mix of pleasure and pain. The scent of soap, his signature cologne and aroused male surrounded her. He rose above her, arms propped either side of her shoulders. A strong knee gently forced her legs apart. His eyes never left hers as his mouth twitched.

"You are ready for me." Voice low and accent thick with desire, his fingertips stroked the sensitive skin between her hip and pubic bone. Pleasure soared into Bronte's mind and she closed her eyes.

His index finger hovered over her centre.

"Open your legs. Wider."

A shuddering breath caught in her throat as his finger swept fluidly towards her buttocks and back up, almost reaching the tender little bud of tingling energy before sweeping away again. Two fingers slid into her and set a slow rhythmic pace. They dipped deep into her core then slicked around the bud again and again, faster and faster.

She couldn't cope with this, she just couldn't. Eyes wide, her head shook from side to side. Too fast, her heart beat was too fast, the breath in her throat caught. His eyes never left hers, not for a moment. Her mouth made the O shape and her hands, knuckles white, gripped his shoulders, every muscle in her body went taut, stretched tight like piano wire. Her back bowed as two fingers dipped hard into her, his thumb pressed the bud.

Her breath seized in her lungs.

"Come for me, Bronte. Let go."

A primal scream sounded in her throat. Every bone in her body almost snapped into tiny pieces as her mind fractured. A trembling, deep and dark built within her womb as the full body climax exploded.

The world went black for a split second.

Bronte screamed as her release gushed into his hand and her lungs burned before she took her first breath after orgasm.

The trembling wouldn't stop.

Panic flooded her system.

Nico held her shuddering body close.

He stroked the valleys and plains of her back, down her buttocks and up again, over and over.

She couldn't stop shaking.

"Hush, it is okay. Let me finish it."

"You're killing me." She sobbed into his neck.

His laugh vibrated through her as she clung to him as he settled into the cradle of her hips.

He fisted his shaft and pressed the head of his penis into her.

Bronte tensed as he pressed deeper.

Her body felt stretched too wide as it tried to accommodate him.

He was too big.

Her eyes flew to his as Nico held the position.

The concentrated tension in his expression as those corded neck muscles strained with effort simply amazed her. For the first time a man was waiting for her. Exquisitely slowly he entered her, inch by inch. She sighed into his mouth and let herself go as a voice in her head told her she would never, ever be the same again.

"Relax, *cara*."

Nico had never had a woman so responsive to him.

Her every tremble, every gasp brought him to his knees.

She was amazing.

When she tried to kiss him, he shook his head, desperate to concentrate purely on her pleasure. He suspected that this was her first experience of a penetrative orgasm. The fact that she trusted him enough to let go of her inhibitions made him feel so protective of her.

He needed to show her it could be so much better.

Bronte's endless legs gripped his back as her pelvis tipped to permit him to thrust deeper again and again. She felt so good. So tight and hot and wet. Her centre still pulsed. And he felt her next orgasm gather as she gave sharp high little panting breaths of pleasure that drove him out of his mind.

Take it slow and easy he muttered in Italian. But she pumped her hips faster. The muscles of her core gripping him ruthlessly as she raced towards completion.

Bronte screamed loud and long in his ear and then sank her teeth into his shoulder.

Hell, he had never felt anything like it. Her orgasm clenched like a fist around him, sucking him further into her centre. His sac ached, throbbed as it tightened relentlessly and he lost control. Fear clawed a path from his gut into his throat. But even it could not cope with the sensational build up. His skull almost fractured from pressure and he howled, gasping in release.

Nico lay on top of her, sucking air into burning lungs and still she milked him.

He laughed, happy and terrified at the same time.

Still connected, pulling her with him, he lay on his side, eyes closed.

He needed to give himself a minute.

When he opened his eyes, Bronte's serious emerald gaze studied him.

Her cheeks were flushed and she shivered in reaction.

"What just happened?"

Wisely, Nico controlled the grin and kept his face absolutely straight. And kept his voice gentle.

"We made love. You screamed... twice."

Stunned, Bronte simply stared at him.

Boy, oh boy, he had her there. And she had screamed twice. The man obviously kept a count of a woman's orgasms. She still had glorious aftershocks rippling through her system. A firm hand smoothed her skin from shoulder to hip as he nuzzled the delicate skin of her neck.

"You have a beautiful home. Shall we move this to the bedroom?"

Cold reality slapped Bronte hard.

How could she have forgotten what it was like afterwards?

She'd never had the wow, darling, you were amazing after sex talk. Jonathan's idea of pillow talk was to complain she was unresponsive and unimaginative.

Apparently all Nico wanted to talk about was the house.

Pushing him off her, Bronte leapt to her feet, hunting for her panties.

She couldn't look at him as she pulled on the scrap of white lace.

"Well thank you very much for the orgasms," she told him, her tone stiffly polite. "They were lovely."

Chapter Fifteen

From his swift intake of breath, Bronte knew she'd scored a hit.

"Why are you acting like this?"

She couldn't look at him. "Because I refuse to be used yet again by a man."

Especially by a man who knew exactly how to press a woman's buttons, literally and figuratively.

Nico hissed out a breath.

"Rewind, you have lost me."

The hard tone of anger in his voice made her wince.

She turned to him, folding her arms to protect her throbbing nipples.

"No matter how much sex we have, the house is still not for sale."

His eyes never left hers as heat soared into his cheeks then drained away leaving him white with fury.

Her stomach gave nervy little jerks.

Naked and totally comfortable with it, Nico stood proud and tall.

He hauled on his jeans and moved towards her.

God, he looked amazing.

Bronte forced herself to stand still and not step back.

His hands, hard now, gripped her shoulders.

Hot, angry eyes drilled into hers.

"You think I made love to you for the house?"

Why wouldn't her voice work?

"You seduced me. You're trying to soften me up."

By the appalled shock in those dark eyes, by the way his head jerked back, Bronte knew she'd made a terrible mistake. She closed her eyes against the anger in his and wished to hell she could take the stupid words back.

But it was too late for that.

Much too late.

He released her as if she'd burned him and shook his head.

"You are unbelievable. If you have any regrets about what we did, say so. Have the courage to tell the truth. But do not dare..." He took a breath, his voice a whip that lashed her from top to toe. "Do not dare to imply you were not a very willing participant."

Shitty, shit, shit.

He was absolutely furious.

And had every right to be.

How the hell was she going to get herself out of this in one piece?

"I am not denying anything. But it's obvious you are sexually experienced, very experienced from what I hear. You knew exactly what to do to me."

"And it is obvious that you are not experienced. And also very stupid."

Stung, Bronte followed him as he stalked through to the kitchen.

Nico picked up his sweater and yanked it over his head.

He threw hers and she caught it before it hit her in the face.

All her insecurities, all the little darts of poison that had been fired into her psyche for years by a man who'd tried to destroy her self-esteem rose like bile into her throat.

"I'm not stupid. I'm a realist. Why else would you hit on me? Why else would you want to have sex with me unless I have something you want? I'm hardly your type am I?"

He whirled around to face her, those eyes now the color of a stormy sea.

"How do you know my type? You know nothing about me. You have judged and found me wanting from the first moment we met. You appear to believe I am a man who seduces women for his own material benefit."

Her heart was going crazy in her chest, but she jerked up her chin.

"Can you deny that you still want my home?"

"No, I cannot deny it. But I would never *whore* myself to get it. You have just treated me like a damned stud," he roared at her.

Shaking with reaction, she realized she'd hurt him as well as made him very angry.

Oh God Bronte, what have you done?

She was trembling now, her voice a mere whisper, "I didn't mean you to take it in that way."

Not once did his dark eyes release hers.

"What *did* you mean? Do you know? Because one man treats you badly we are all damned? How fair is that?"

She had to close her eyes to his absolute rage.

"It's just that you've had hundreds of women. You have a certain reputation."

She opened her eyes and saw dark brows wing into his hairline.

"Where did you hear this nonsense?"

Bronte knew instinctively the worst thing to say would be that he'd been Googled.

She was losing the argument and rightly so.

What on earth had she been thinking having sex with this man?

She couldn't think straight.

"Look, let's draw a line under this. You like a certain type of woman and I know that I'm not it."

Her eyes slid to his and she saw with relief that Nico looked totally confused now and a lot less angry.

He dragged his hands through his hair in an expression of bewildered male frustration.

"I have never slept with a woman if I was in a relationship with another. I have never paid for sex. My needs are crystal clear and I never make promises I do not keep."

Fair enough.

But her mind kept coming back to the main issue.

"Why do you want me?"

Stunned dark eyes stared into hers and he was looking at her as if she was speaking in tongues.

He shook his head as if trying to clear it.

"*Mio Dio*, you have absolutely no idea. Have you?"

When she said nothing, he moved closer until his finger tilted her chin up and she had no choice but to look at him.

"What did your fiancé do to you?"

Deeply uncomfortable with the direction the conversation had taken, Bronte jerked her chin away.

"Why on earth bring Jonathan into this?"

Those eyes filled again with impatient annoyance and glared into hers.

"You brought him into this, straight after we made love."

She opened her mouth to hotly deny the accusation and then closed it.

He was right.

She had permitted Jonathan's words to affect her.

His vicious comments, filled with malice, poured out of her mouth before she could stop them.

"He said I was too frigid for him, because I wouldn't... um... do certain things to him. That I couldn't satisfy him and that's why he needed another woman."

Nico gripped her shoulders, gave her a shake.

"*Madre de Dio!* If you believed that then you are stupid."

"I was going to marry him, why wouldn't I believe him." Stung, she tried to push him away but he didn't budge. "You've just told me yourself that I'm not experienced enough for you."

She closed her eyes on his wide eyes.

God, she sounded absolutely pathetic.

He gave her another little shake and this time his forehead touched hers, his shoulders relaxing.

"I did not say any such thing. You *are* inexperienced. But that is not a bad thing. I love your responses to my touch, my kisses. Your breathy sighs and cries of pleasure increase my own."

Nico pulled her close and nuzzled the soft spot under her ear.

Feeling like a complete moron, Bronte wrapped her arms around his waist and leaned into him.

Her heart did a crazy little flip.

"I wasn't really thinking of him. I was thinking of me."

He framed her face with large hands and forced her to meet his dark eyes.

"You *were* thinking of him if you remembered his words and how he made you feel. Do you want me to tell you what it was like for me making love to you? It was magical, *cara,* and amazing." He brushed his lips, softly, gently, over hers and muttered into her mouth, "Trust me. You cried my name when you came."

Mortified that he said such things to her and with her lips still tingling from his, Bronte didn't believe a word of it. Men like Nico Ferranti didn't find women like her magical and amazing.

But God, she wished with all her heart that he did.

"It was probably a one off," she told him in a disbelieving voice. "I can't imagine that sort of thing happens every single time."

She bent to retrieve her yoga pants.

"I would not bother, *cara.* I will just take them off again."

Nico's voice was low and throaty, almost a growl.

Her head whipped up in time to see him move fast as he bent low and hauled her over his shoulder.

She yelped in alarm.

"Nico! Put me down."

A flat hand smacked her bottom hard enough to make her gasp.

"That is for doubting yourself and for doubting me. A one-off? I am Italian! I have never been so insulted in my life."

He strode through the house, heading for the stairs.

"Where are you...? Put me down..." she sputtered, split between laughter and dread as he marched up the stairs.

"I am continuing your education and from what happened earlier, you appear to be a very fast learner. Believe me, you will not be thinking of another man the next time I make love to you."

Torn between heady delight and sheer terror, she found her legs caught close to his body.

Nico ignored the fists drumming on his back. Which only added fuel to the fire of her temper.

Her insults deteriorated into expletives.

He found her bedroom and tossed her into the middle of her enormous bed.

In an attempt to escape, Bronte flipped over onto her stomach.

But Nico simply grabbed her ankles, pulling her back down the bed and straddled her legs.

His voice went soft and low.

"Your language is a disgrace. I would not have thought a well-bred young woman would know such words."

Panting, she lifted her head to see him remove two foil packages from the back of his jeans and place them on her bedside table.

"Get off me."

"No."

He whipped off his sweater and tossed it.

His eyes were dark and hot with mixture of arousal and irritation.

Those toned chest muscles flexed as he bent over her and she took a moment to enjoy the view of the plains and dips of his six-pack and that hard flat stomach. Fine silky hair ran from his chest to below his jeans in an inverted V. And she decided she loved the feeling of being weak and feminine. Her sweater followed his as a big hand squeezed her buttock cheek and a finger pinged the top of her panties. No matter how hard she tried to remain unaffected, an illicit thrill raced through her system to pool, hot and wet, between her thighs.

Bronte groaned.

"Nico." Her voice was almost a plea as he slipped a finger between her buttocks.

"I am going to take off my jeans. If you move one inch, I will spank you. How dare you bring another man between us and then doubt what we have shared. Trust me, *cara mia,* it will not happen again."

Bronte could not believe she was allowing a man to do this to her.

She was lying virtually naked on her tummy, too scared to move in case he did indeed spank her.

Her breath caught in her throat as he straddled her again.

However this time he knelt over her, a hand either side of her head as his erection pressed into the small of her back.

He couldn't be ready again, could he?

She turned to look at him, feeling horribly vulnerable and wonderfully aroused.

His mouth tasted hers as his hips rubbed his shaft against her buttocks.

His erection was hard and searching as it nudged the soft skin between her thighs.

Bronte arched her back.

His tongue, hot and silky slipped into her mouth and explored with a devastating thoroughness that left her gasping for air. He sucked her tongue into his mouth and she shuddered in wicked delight. He couldn't seem to get enough of her mouth.

Then he flipped her on her back and dragged her up to her knees in front of him.

His shaft jerking into her soft belly.

Nico moved onto his back, resting on the many pillows on her bed.

Unsure of what to do next, she knelt beside him.

His eyes, dark and brooding with arousal, met hers.

A gasp escaped from her throat as he unashamedly gripped his shaft and stroked from root to tip, pleasuring himself in front of her startled gaze.

Bronte couldn't drag her eyes from the blunt head of his swollen shaft.

Her tongue ran over her bottom lip and Nico moaned.

She clenched her thighs.

"Please, Nico. Let me touch you."

He simply lay there, relaxed, stroking himself in a way that made him grow harder and thicker.

Those eyes mesmerized her, she couldn't look away.

"Open a condom for me and come closer."

She did as he asked, mortified that she fumbled such a simple task.

And all the while Bronte's heart beat a rapid tattoo in her throat, until she held the tip of the condom between trembling fingers. Without words and never taking his eyes from hers, Nico took her hands placing his fingers over hers to slide the protection home.

His pupils dilated as he slid his hand between her legs.

Her womb clenched and Bronte moaned deep in her throat.

"You have no idea how beautiful you are, how swollen and heavy with need for me." His voice, deep and low, hypnotized her.

She gasped as he moved fast.

Flipping her on her back, he caught her wrists in one hand holding them above her head. His eyes, jet black with arousal took a long, lingering look at her body openly displayed for his pleasure. She trembled in reaction as he gently nudged her legs wider apart with a strong thigh.

Then he dipped his head and stared into her eyes with an intensity that made her shudder with something like fear and a brutal arousal.

"I am going to take my time and taste every part of you until you scream with ecstasy. I am going to bury myself deep within you until you come again. Are you ready?"

Yes!

But the sound that escaped her throat was a pathetic little whimper.

A whimper that appeared not to be enough for him.

"Do you want me to taste you?"

His lips nibbled a lazy path across her jaw, under her ear to the spot that made her purr her answer.

Bronte lifted her hips, wantonly wriggling under him, rubbing her too sensitive breasts across his strong chest. His lips smiled against her neck and he released her wrists, using both hands now to take what he wanted, to pleasure, to plunder and to explore her until she was nothing but a puddle of lust.

She took the opportunity to run her hands over his broad,

strong shoulders as her heart thundered in her ears. His mouth savoured a pebbled nipple, teased the sensitive flesh with the tip of his tongue, then suckled hard in a way that made her gasp and grip his head, pulling him closer. He paid its twin the same attentions making her cry out as the liquid pull deep in her belly responded to his touch. With care he skimmed his fingertips over her ribcage, closely followed by his hot mouth. His tongue lingered over her flat tummy, paying particular attention to her belly button. This time there was nothing soft about his exploration and she almost shot off the bed.

Nico had never, ever had a woman so responsive to him, she shuddered and trembled under him and it aroused him unbearably.

Again he told himself to take great care with her, to give her mindless pleasure. Again he caressed her soft breasts. They fit perfectly into the palm of his hands. God, her skin smelled fabulous, a mix of both of them. And each part of her, the underside of her breast, her belly, her hip had its own unique taste.

She groaned and her eyes closed as his fingertips smoothed the too sensitive skin along her hip bone and travelled lower to the tender spot between her thigh and her mound. Her hands travelled across his shoulders and then her nails dug into his flesh as he cupped her just the way she liked it. She jerked as he changed tempo, rose up and crushed his mouth to hers in a passionate, bruising, breathless kiss.

She gasped and cried out as he plundered down her flesh devouring her with his hungry mouth, his teeth nipping with gentle little bites, desperate now to taste and take.

Gripping her hips, he growled, pulling her hot, slick core to his mouth and feasted.

"Oh, God!"

His mouth suckled, his tongue licked and speared into her.

Ruthlessly he used his tongue as a weapon of pleasure bringing her to a fast, raging orgasm that had her bucking under him. He held her legs wide and open. She wanted to drown in him, sink into him as he forced her up again until she gripped the sheets in sweaty, trembling hands. She screamed her lungs out with another orgasm so deep, so prolonged, that reality shattered and the world went dark.

Nico devoured, lapped and drank the evidence of her release.

And he wasn't finished. With one sharp inhale, he entered her. The ache in his loins was beyond anything he'd ever experienced, the burning of his bones eased as he slid in and out. She was so tight, so wet, so hot he couldn't speak, didn't need to. He shoved up her thigh and thrust into her faster, harder. And discovered with a feeling of pure joy that she was with him all the way, her throaty cries synchronized with her hips as they rose to meet his, thrust for thrust. Then he felt her body gather again as her breath hitched, every muscle from her toes to her fingertips went rigid.

"Let go, let go," he commanded breathlessly. Her body jerked and she rocked his world as she came apart in his arms.

From a distance, Nico heard himself roar as he held her tight and emptied his seed within her.

Then a deep sob escaped from his throat as he collapsed, gasping for air on top of her.

He rolled to his side, turning Bronte and taking her with him.

He closed his eyes.

His heart thundered inside his ribs, against her back, as he settled her in the spoon position and her body miraculously still rippled around his. Mini aftershocks followed one after the other. He seriously didn't know whether he was ecstatic or devastated. He'd thought it couldn't get any better than the first time they'd made love and he'd been so wrong.

Nico clenched his jaw as again her internal muscles milked every drop of life giving liquid from him. He shuddered and buried his face in the fragile nape of her neck. If they kept this up, they would be dead within a week.

She was slick with healthy sweat and he was in just as bad a state.

He was not a snuggler, never had been, but he wanted to stay like this, joined to this woman, forever. Reality dug him hard in the ribs telling him he would pay a high price for this day, but he ignored it, simply enjoying the moment, muttering endearments in Italian and pressing soft kisses to the sensitive skin, baby soft, below her ear.

And all the while, he was stroking her hip, her thigh as he held her close.

At last she calmed, relaxed, her body still reluctant to release his.

She was a miracle.

Nico didn't question his too intense feelings.

They were what they were and that was the beginning and the end of it.

He knew for certain that Bronte was destined to play a crucial part in his future.

Although how the mighty had fallen in less than forty-hours was a complete and utter mystery to him.

They must have slept.

When Nico awoke he was no longer inside her.

A little cry and a sob brought him back to himself.

Bronte whimpered, curled up in a foetal position near the edge of the bed. Her shuddering sobs fractured more of the steel door that protected his heart. *Dio Mio*, had he hurt her? He couldn't bear the sound of her distress. Desperately, he pulled her, sobbing, into his arms. It took him a heartbeat and then another to realize she was in the grip of a vicious nightmare.

She muttered words he couldn't grasp.

Appalled, he watched rapid eye movement under eyelids so fragile they reminded him of tissue paper. Tiny beads of sweat prickled across her brow and top lip. With infinite care, he pressed his lips to her brow and stroked her gently bringing her back to him.

"Bronte, wake up." And he thanked Christ when her eyelids fluttered and her breathing calmed. "Wake up, you are dreaming."

Chapter Sixteen

Dazed, Bronte jerked awake and stared up at a marvellous face she was coming to know as well as her own.

Nico, good God, she was in his arms and he was murmuring words in soft, rapid Italian.

Heat scorched her cheeks and other intensely intimate parts of her as reality dumped her firmly in the present.

Still groggy, she refused to let her mind linger on the instant when she'd found her parent's bodies lying under blankets at the side of the road.

She would not permit a nightmare triggered by anxiety to destroy this wonderful moment.

Stretching like a cat, she ached gloriously in parts of her she never even knew existed.

Nico's mouth brushed over hers.

"I am going to run you a bath, *cara*. Lie still until I come for you."

He rose and strode naked in all his glory into her bathroom.

Indulging herself, Bronte admired his tight buttocks and long, lean, muscular legs.

The thud of ancient water pipes heralded hot water gushing into the antique clawed bath.

Nico hummed in a deep baritone.

Still sleepy, she listened to the sound of swishing bubbles, then the water ceased and he strode to her side of the bed.

He lifted her as if she weighed nothing, kissed her forehead and carried her into the bathroom.

Bronte nuzzled his collar bone, determined to enjoy a minute that was quite unique in her experience.

With care, he stood her in the bath.

A move that brought her eyes level with his.

He cupped her face between his hands and studied her with

an intensity that made her shiver.

How did he do that?

"Are you okay?" She nodded but he didn't appear convinced. "Do you have nightmares often?"

Bronte cleared her throat as his grey eyes scanned her features.

"I haven't had it for months."

He frowned.

"Is it always the same?"

Her pulse fluttered.

"Yes." She shivered.

"Lie down in the water. You are chilled, *cara*. I will use the shower."

Warm water, scented with jasmine, eased out aching muscles.

Bronte didn't want to think of her ex-fiancé at such a time, feeling it was unfair to Nico.

But she had to admit that in the years of intimacy she'd shared with Jonathan, she'd never experienced anything like the sex she'd shared with Nico. The man was an amazingly generous lover and how lucky was she? Not that she was keeping count, much, but she'd come three times.

Wow.

She sank into the water and relived the experience.

She'd never known it was even possible.

And weren't men supposed to need time to recover?

Someone obviously hadn't told Nico Ferranti.

Drowsily, she kept an eye on him through the opaque glass of her walk-in shower. He was quick, efficient and exited with a white towel slung low on his hips. He towel dried his hair, and then ran his fingers through it. The easy intimacy, the sheer domesticity of the moment, caught her throat.

She caught herself wishing *if only* and told herself to behave and live in the moment.

Those dark eyes now cruised possessively over her face and her body.

Saliva dried in her mouth.

Her breasts, bobbing among creamy bubbles, tightened and

her nipples hardened into rosy bullets.

Nico's sharp eyes missed nothing.

He gave her that slow, sexy smile, revealing those adorable dimples and Bronte knew she was toast.

He crouched beside the bath.

His fingertip stroked her breast rubbing a nipple.

She couldn't help it, she pulled back.

He frowned.

Those eyes, sharp as a blade, stared into hers.

"You have beautiful breasts."

With the horrible nightmare still jerking her chain and Jonathan's voice telling her she was built like a boy, Bronte gave a tiny shrug.

"They're only breasts. I'm not defined by them."

Those slashing brows flew into his hairline.

"Of course you are not defined by them." He frowned. "I hope you are not thinking about implants?"

"I've, um, thought about it."

Her teeth bit her bottom lip and she couldn't look him in the eye.

"You are not happy with your breasts?"

"I don't think about them," she lied.

He grinned.

But his eyes remained sharp on hers.

"I have no complaints about any part of you, *cara*. Would you like me to wash you? I am very thorough." That accent, intimate and terribly erotic, had her catch her breath.

She eyed him.

"I just bet you are. No thank you, I can manage."

Nico grinned and captured her mouth, exploring it thoroughly with his.

Gentle but passionate, it was a kiss full of promise of good things to come.

His forehead touched hers.

"Do not fall asleep in the bath, you still look drowsy. I will make coffee."

Mr. Bossy was back and Bronte found she didn't give a

damn.

"That would be nice." She sank into the water until bubbles reached her chin.

He rose, the hunger in his gaze evident.

Nico growled in his throat as he left.

And she couldn't help but smile.

Bronte replayed the amazing events of the day in her mind and knew Sundays would never be quite the same again.

Part of her couldn't quite believe that what she'd experienced was real. If this was an affair or a quick fling, then Nico appeared to be taking it very seriously indeed. But perhaps that was how men of the world behaved when they were with a woman? She supposed a playboy was called a playboy for a reason. It wasn't as if she had experience of these things.

There was absolutely no point, she told herself, in trying to analyse what was happening between them. He'd told her he found her amazing and she believed him. She'd satisfied him and that gave her a wonderful feeling for the first time in her life of immense feminine power. Bronte Ludlow had made Nico Ferranti tremble. He'd called her name in the throes of physical passion. And how wonderful was that?

"Bronte! Do not fall asleep," Nico yelled from the bottom of the stair.

Oooh, bossy much.

"I'm coming!"

She leapt out of the bath.

Wrapped in a towel, she tiptoed into her bedroom and stopped dead.

Pillows were strewn across the polished floor of dark oak. Her usually pristine Egyptian cotton sheets and duvet looked as if they'd been through a hurricane. Evidence of energetic sex lay everywhere.

With a shrug, she ignored her perfectionist tendencies.

Ignored that siren call to bring order back to her bedroom

and her life.

She dug out black skinny jeans and matching polo neck from her closet.

After tying up her hair, she pulled on cosy socks and padded down to the kitchen.

He'd been a very busy boy.

The kitchen table was set for two. In the middle of the table, a heavy white platter was piled high with wholemeal sandwiches filled with what appeared to be slivers of lean ham and cheese.

Nico turned with a smile for her that would melt the polar ice cap and Bronte simply stared.

Her breath caught in her throat at the look in his eye for her.

Dressed in jeans and his sweater, she noticed he hadn't bothered with shoes. With the tousled hair, the five o'clock shadow on that strong jaw and the glint in his eye, the man was gorgeous. And he was looking at her as if she was his sun in the morning and his moon at night.

She managed to reach a chair before her legs gave way.

He genuinely cared for her?

Seriously?

A shaft of alarm, a portent of disaster slid into her heart.

Desperately, she told herself she was imagining it.

Hadn't Nico laid all of his cards on the table?

Hadn't he told her in words of one syllable that he didn't want commitment?

And hadn't Alexander had made it crystal clear that Nico had no place in his heart for a woman?

Those were the facts.

Hot on the heels of those facts, came feelings.

Feelings she couldn't deny.

But he'd been so gentle with her after her nightmare.

Then he'd run a bath for her.

By warning her not to fall asleep he'd shown her that he cared for her.

Now he was feeding her, too.

Dismay squeezed her lungs as she studied the food

meticulously prepared, for her.

When he placed a bowl of fresh strawberries on the table and poured her a cup of coffee Bronte could barely breathe.

He must not care for her.

She had nothing, no future, to give him.

He was a man who moved fast in all things she realized now.

However, the timing could not be worse.

This was not the time for her to become heavily involved with any man, never mind a man like Nico Ferranti.

"*Cara?*"

She blinked as he crouched in front of her and Bronte forced herself to smile into his eyes. As ever, he smelled divine. If she bottled it, she'd make an absolute killing.

Gentle fingertips stroked her cheek.

Telling herself she was overthinking things and overreacting as per usual, Bronte took a deep breath and picked up a sandwich.

"You've been busy. Thank you."

"It is my pleasure. I enjoy looking after you."

He did?

Oh God.

Her mind desperately searched for a neutral subject when the phone rang.

Saved by the bell, she thought as she rose and moved across the room to pick up the receiver.

"Hello? Bronte speaking."

There was a long silence before the person hung up.

She replaced the receiver.

Nico moved to stand next to her.

"Wrong number?"

With a frown she shrugged at him.

"I don't know, they didn't speak."

The missed call light was flashing. It must have come in when they were in bed. Pressing play, she cocked her head listening to the long silence with a spooky feeling in her gut that someone was there and almost certain she could hear faint breathing.

Then they hung up.

"Do you receive many crank calls?"

With a slow shake of her head Bronte remembered the messages earlier.

"Strangely enough I had three that hung up early this morning. I turn the volume off on the extension in the bedroom on weekends."

Nico frowned now.

"If you continue to have problems call the telephone company."

"I will, but it could be one of those automatically generated sales calls."

Putting the calls out of her mind, she turned and spotted her sketchpad on the table.

"So, what are you going to do with my drawing?"

His eyes searched her face and she pumped up her smile as she returned to her seat.

He sat next to her.

"I will frame it."

Sipping her coffee, Bronte choked.

"Good grief, why?"

At ease Nico leaned back in the chair stretching out long legs.

"Because it will remind me to keep my ego in check."

"You've lost your mind."

"It is how you see me, no? You see me as the devil."

He took her hand in a relaxed friendly fashion but his eyes were too watchful.

Bronte ordered herself to be very careful.

"I believe I was a little bit pissed off with you at the time."

Nico barked out a laugh.

"Not a terribly ladylike expression, *cara*."

"Well, there are times when I'm not a lady."

His fingertips stroked the back of her hand.

It appeared that Nico was a terribly touchy feely sort of man. Not that she was complaining.

"You cannot change who and what you are," he said.

Perfectly true, she admitted.

She picked up her cup and eyed him over the rim.

"So, you're going to run Ludlow Hall for a month?"

He nodded as he shovelled in a sandwich, wiping his fingers on a white linen napkin he'd unearthed from God knew where.

"I am, yes. We will be working together."

Her brows rose.

"We will? I usually have *Sweet Sensation* meetings with Julie."

He shook his head. "*Si,* but from now on you will be meeting twice a week with me."

"Very well, if you don't trust me."

Her chin tilted and he tapped it with a gentle finger.

"So quick to take offense. Pull in your horns. Has it not occurred to you I might want your company?"

He did?

She told herself to keep calm.

Her vivid imagination was working overtime as usual.

What could happen in a few short weeks?

"If that's what you want. But I'm certain you will be bored to death with icing designs, fillings and flavors, color schemes and flowers. Not to mention hysterical brides."

Nico merely shrugged. "You are incredibly creative. It will be a joy to watch you."

It would?

She had to ask, "Then what?"

He gave her a long, slow smile.

"Then Alexander takes over running Ludlow Hall again, and things return to normal."

Well, she'd asked and she'd received an answer.

The right answer.

And Bronte wondered why she didn't feel relief.

One minute she was worried he might actually care for her and the next she was worried he might not.

She didn't want him to care and she didn't want him to leave.

Maybe she needed to visit a psychologist after all, because she was certainly losing her frigging mind.

"Nico?"

"Bronte?"

"What is it you do? I know you own hotels and have other interests. But you don't appear the type of man to get your hands dirty. Even if you do make too much money."

He shook his head.

"I look forward to the day I understand why you have a complete disdain of people making money."

Nico took a sip of coffee before he answered,.

"I acquire things. I suppose the best way to explain it is that I invest in people and match them with opportunities. Years ago I discovered I had a talent for recognizing people and technology in their embryonic state. I invested and the rewards were great, fortunately for me. The hotels belonged to my late grandfather. I kept the flagship and sold off the rest. Then I met Alexander, we became partners, and invested in the cream at the very top of the business. Together, we run the Ferranti Hotels and Spas." He shrugged. "That is it."

If he had a wealthy grandfather then what, Bronte wondered, had he been doing on the streets?

None of it made sense and none of it was any of her business she reminded herself.

"Bronte?"

Her attention snapped back to Nico who was watching her with a quizzical look in his eyes.

"Hmm?"

"Tell me about your nightmare."

Not a chance.

She shook her head.

"It's nothing, honestly."

Nico leaned forward.

His hand reached for and found hers.

"Sometimes, *cara mia*, it is good to talk about such things."

She opened her mouth to tell him she was fine and then he rubbed slow circles on the back of her hand with his thumb.

"I drove right into the middle of the emergency services when they were removing the remains of my parents from their car..."

With an expletive, Nico grabbed her and Bronte found herself on his lap as strong arms held her close. He murmured soft words in Italian into her hair and Bronte snuggled right in as her eyes stung and her voice went too husky. "I don't think I'll ever get over it."

Big hands held her face as he stared into her eyes and she read shock along with a steady support.

"I am so sorry, *cara*." Those dark eyes stayed on hers. "Can I stay tonight?"

Logic yelled 'no way' and her heart cried 'yes.'

Bronte did what came naturally.

"I would like that."

Nico's brilliant smile would have cracked glass.

He moved in for a long, lingering kiss that had her pulse skipping and her tummy tugging with arousal.

The tip of his nose touched hers.

"Do you have wine?"

She smiled, inhaling the now familiar scent of him.

"I do indeed, red or white?"

He rubbed his nose against hers.

"Red. I am Italian."

Chapter Seventeen

The buzz of her alarm had Bronte reaching out in the dark, groping for her Smartphone as she switched on a low lamplight.

"Ooof," she gasped, struggling to free herself from under the heavy weight of Nico's arm.

"*Dio*. What time is it?" His deep voice growled in her ear making her quiver in response even as he ran a hand over her hip and down her thigh.

Squinting bleary eyed at her phone, she groaned.

"Five-thirty."

"Go back to sleep. It is the middle of the night."

She rubbed her body against his, skin to warm skin and stretched like a cat, arching her back.

"It might be for you. But some of us start early. I like to get a jump on the day."

Nico simply rolled on top of her, burying his face against her neck.

She smelled so good, all warm and sweet and tempting.

"Good idea."

The only thing he was going to jump this morning was her. Slim arms circled his neck. Her body pressed tightly against his, soft and pliant as she willingly opened and offered herself to him. He took a long, slow taste of her soft, moist mouth. His tongue was stroking hers as he shifted to fit his body into the perfect cradle of her hips. With a sigh he slid into her, one slow inch at a time. She was so hot and so wet and so tight. Fevered pleasure had him shudder. Then he caught her hips and pulled her to him to surge deeper as far as he could go. And he was home. He'd never felt anything like the way her body gripped his, joining them in a way that felt so right.

He ached for her, for them and for what they had found together.

But it terrified him, too.

Bronte had a gentle soul and he wasn't an easy man to live with.

He didn't do love.

He didn't do commitment.

Did he?

He tried to take a deep calming breath as his heart thundered in his ears and Bronte's high gasps of boundless pleasure fed his desire, his hunger, for her. The wild side of him, the dark and hard side of him wanted to pound into her. But despite his starving need, he forced himself to kiss her with exquisite care, almost with reverence. He took her slowly up and over the edge and they fell together.

As if he'd waited his whole life for this one moment, everything inside him shifted, settled and calmed.

He was home.

Bronte gave him kiss for kiss.

She adored the feeling of his thick body buried deep within her.

"Nico, I've never, ever felt anything like this in my life, never."

He nuzzled his favourite spot under her ear as his body shuddered again.

"I think we have found something very special, *cara mio*."

Through half-closed eyes, she watched him as his tongue took long slow licks of her nipple. His mouth closed around the hard bud. His tongue tip flicking, dancing and then he was sucking the nipple until she cried out. Still inside her, his low growl vibrated through her body as he used the flat of his tongue to take big long licks like a big, lazy cat over her throbbing nipple and her womb clenched tight.

Unbelievably he hardened again, grinding his hips in a circular movement against hers.

Then his mouth was hot, hard and demanding.

He took her by surprise and she gasped meeting his hard thrusting tongue and sucked it into her mouth as he groaned as if in agony.

Fire blazed over his skin and his control snapped.

Nico couldn't breathe as he pounded into her and God help him she was with him every single step of the way. The walls of her body surrounding his pulsed hot and wet and so tight. He was losing it. He knew it and couldn't help it. Her high cries, almost sobs, only added fuel to his already roaring fire.

The smell of her, the feel of her and the sound of her had him piston harder. Her fingernails dug into his shoulders as her body arched as she screamed his name. Then her body clamped down hard on his, milking, dragging hot life-giving fluid out of him as she pulsed around him.

Utterly spent, Bronte dropped her arms and legs on the bed as he flopped on top of her.

Her heart and his were thundering as one.

"Nico." Her voice was high and breathy.

Immediately he rose on his elbow.

Shame burned Nico's cheeks as he ran an unsteady hand over her skin. What was he doing rutting her like an animal? Where had the legendary Ferranti control and finesse gone?

"Did I hurt you?"

Bronte stared up into his face.

His hard features were so masculine and too serious.

She gave him big eyes.

"Is that how all Italian men make love? Because if it is, I must find an Italian for Rosie."

She caught the flash of relief before he buried his head in her neck.

"I can never get enough of you, Bronte." He raised his head and stared deep into her eyes. "Are you sure you are all right?"

She gazed at his mouth before running gentle fingers through his hair.

All right?

Was he serious?

Her body felt truly alive and was vibrating like a tuning fork.

She'd made Nico tremble with desire, for her.

How totally unbelievable was that?

Her eyes sparkled into his.

"Now that's what I call a jump start to the day."

Things had moved fast, Bronte realized as she dressed carefully for her appointment in the City. But then Nico was that kind of man. The most important thing was not to kid herself. Her heart and his were safe and sound. Remarks, little things, may ring a bell or two of alarm. But she told herself she'd imagined the glimpse of vulnerability when he'd held her tight in bed this morning. It was so typical of her to worry over nothing these days. A habit that she fully intended to break.

Bronte parked her mini in the car park of the Gherkin building in the middle of the financial district of the City of London.

She wore a black business suit by Armani, teamed with four inch heels in ivory patent with a black patent toe by Chanel. She carried a matching clutch bag. Simple diamond studs glittered in her ears. And she wore a single diamond on a chain at her throat.

What was a woman supposed to wear when she met her father for the first time?

Jerky nerves caught in her throat as she was taken through various offices and gatekeepers who eyed her with polite interest.

Carl Terlezki's office was a low-key lesson in exquisite good taste.

Long couches in soft suede the color of bitter chocolate hugged a long narrow glass coffee table. A glass wall framed the city. His PA, Tamara, was an immaculate, middle-aged women dressed in black with a helmet of blonde hair. Her blue eyes scanned Bronte from head to toe, not in an aggressive way but she was obviously intrigued.

"Mr. Terlezki is on a call. I'll take you in as soon as he's finished. Can I get you a coffee?" Her tone was friendly but polite.

A coffee was the last thing she needed and Bronte had an attack of anxiety as she wondered now what the hell she was doing? And desperately wished Alexander was with her because she felt physically ill with stress and nerves. She was going to change a complete stranger's life forever. Perhaps coming here like this was a terrible mistake?

She stood to leave.

A door opened.

A gravelly voice spoke,

"Tamara, when Bronte arrives show her…"

He entered the room and she went utterly still.

He was taller than she'd expected and leaner.

And terribly good-looking with his clear tanned skin, sharp intelligent eyes and thick grey hair.

Their eyes met and the way he caught his breath stopped her heart.

Carl Terlezki walked forward.

His eyes were the color of the sea, the blue hazed by dark grey.

And his hand reached for hers.

"My God, you are the living image of your mother."

Emotions long held in check threatened to spill over and Bronte waged a bitter war of attrition to remain calm.

"How do you do?" she whispered.

He grasped her hand like a man handed a lifeline, emotions whirled in his eyes and she realized he was as thrown as she was.

Neither of them noticed his PA leave the room or heard her quietly close the door.

He blinked.

"I am so sorry for your loss." He cleared his throat and looked around the room as if seeing it for the first time. "I'm sorry. My PA seems to have disappeared. Would you like a coffee or tea?"

He appeared to have forgotten, he still held her hand.

Bronte felt him tremble, saw the distress in his eyes and realized this was a man who had loved deeply and suffered for it.

Strangely enough, seeing his distress gave her the strength to carry on until the bitter end.

With a breath she squared her shoulders and looked him straight in the eye.

"I don't know how to tell you this and I've worried about it for months, Mr Terlezki. But you are my father."

Carl Terlezki read the letter again and again.

He stared at the fabulous creature who sat before him. Her nerves and stress were self-evident. He couldn't believe it. Cynthia Ludlow was dead. Intellectually, he knew it was true and he'd grieved for her and for what might have been when he'd heard of the accident. But this, this brought it home to him in a way that shook him to his very core. Emotions whirled now in his mind. Anger, regret, hurt and outrage that the woman he loved never told him he was a father.

They'd kept his daughter from him for over twenty-six years.

His hand, he saw with dismay, shook as he returned the letter to Bronte.

"Can I take a copy of it?"

What a stupid question to ask of his only child.

But he had absolutely no idea what to say to her.

Bronte stood.

The poor man looked as if he'd been hit by a train. And she knew precisely how he felt. He needed time to come to terms with the shock and betrayal. Well, she knew what that felt like, too.

"I understand the shock of this news. Believe me I've had no idea what to do or how to react in this situation."

He rose and shook his head, his eyes swimming with emotion.

"No, don't go, Bronte. Please stay."

Carl took her hand and led her to a leather couch the color of clear honey.

"Did you have a happy childhood?"

She squeezed his hand, amazed that his first thought was for her.

"Absolutely I did. They... my parents... loved my brother and me very much."

"Alexander, yes, he was a handful as I remember. How is he?"

Shocked, she could only stare at him.

"You knew my brother?"

He smiled in a way that broke her heart.

"Ah, yes. He was an energetic six year old who loved the steam engines at the British Engineering Museum. They kept him occupied for hours."

She looked at him feeling totally helpless and spoke from the heart.

"He's taken the truth very hard. He feels hurt and angry and betrayed. What are we going to do? How do we deal with this?"

Her father took a breath, squared his shoulders and patted her hand.

"How about we take it one step at a time? We get to know one another?" He gave her a heartbreakingly brave smile. "You can ask me anything and I promise to tell you the truth. And you must tell me everything about your life."

She blinked frantically as his face swam before her.

"I don't know if I can ever forgive them for this."

He didn't attempt not to understand her.

"One thing I've learned in life is that sometimes love is not easy, or fair, or right. People are only human. And human beings are not perfect, Bronte. They make mistakes, especially when they try to protect the ones they love."

He held out his hand to her, his eyes brimming with emotion.

"Shall we make today the start of a new beginning?"

Nico leaned back in Alexander's chair in Alexander's office at Ludlow Hall and stared unseeing into the log fire that shed a warm glow over the room.

The meeting with senior staff had gone well and the assistant manager was a smart cookie, which, he acknowledged, made his life a hell of a lot easier. He checked his cell phone again and found no message from Bronte.

He knew she'd gone into the City for an appointment.

Probably something to do with a wedding he supposed.

What did he want from her?

His libido spiked and he shook his head.

Apart from amazing sex, she was a hell of a package. Bronte Ludlow was so much more than just a fabulous body or a heart-stopping face framed by a silver waterfall of hair. He adored her style. She was beautiful, loving, funny and sexy as hell. He really *got* her in a way that he'd never done with any other woman.

So what did she want from him?

He frowned now, remembering her words that she'd never marry.

The little witch had told him he wasn't husband or even boyfriend material.

He smiled now thinking that that had been his line, was it not?

And he had no idea how he was going to take back the stupid words he had spoken.

A couple of quick knocks on the door brought him back to earth.

"Come in."

Rosie Gordon popped her dark head around the door to give him a cheeky grin.

He had to smile.

"Hey. Are you busy?" she wanted to know as she entered the room.

"Not at the moment," he told her and eyed the box she held with interest. "What can I do for you?"

She plonked the box on his desk and herself in a leather bucket chair.

"You can give me a coffee and I'll let you have a taste of one of Bronte's new mini triple chocolate muffins with a toffee cheesecake centre."

He found himself grinning, picked up the phone and placed the order for coffee.

"Has Bronte returned from her meeting?"

Rosie blinked, a wary look entering her eye and he wondered what it meant.

She nodded. "She's on her way home."

A knock at the door and Julie, Alexander's PA, entered with a tray of coffee and a hello for Rosie. After she'd left and Nico had poured, he bit into a tiny muffin and a little bit of heaven melted on his tongue.

"How does she come up with these ideas?"

"It's part of her creative make-up."

"Sì. It certainly is."

Rosie watched him over the rim of her cup with a speculative gleam in her brown eyes and he wondered what was coming.

"Are your intentions towards my best friend honorable?"

He gave her a smile that didn't quite reach his eyes.

She didn't flinch as she held his stare with a little nudge of her chin.

Nico decided he liked Rosemary Gordon very much indeed.

"My relationship with Bronte is between her and me."

"Okay," she said in a cheery voice. Then her brown eyes went hard. "But if you hurt her you'll answer to me."

He nodded.

"You are a very good friend, Rosie. And since you are such a good friend, tell me everything about her ex-fiancé."

Rosie wrinkled her cute little nose in distaste.

"Jonathan? He's a poor excuse for a human being."

"Grazie, Rosie, but that tells me nothing." He could see she was debating with herself. "I know he hurt her. And from what I can gather and have observed, I believe he was cruel to her."

What he had no intention of telling Rosie, was that it had been Jonathan who told Anthony that Bronte secretly liked him. And Bronte herself had told him how her ex had spread rumors about her in their close-knit community. Along with the phone calls she was receiving, Nico firmly believed that someone was out to make mischief for her. But he couldn't do anything without facts.

Rosie took a breath and met his eye.

"If he was a woman I'd call Jonathan an evil bitch of the worst kind. He's charming and a liar with an eye constantly on the main chance. When she sold his ring on eBay, Bronte became his sworn enemy and that's something I don't believe she realizes. He was a controlling bully and did everything he could do to destroy her self-esteem, not that she had much of one to begin with. The way I see Bronte and the way I know you see Bronte is not how she sees herself.

"You're going to need to be careful, Nico, she's vulnerable."

He frowned, picking his way gingerly through an emotional mine-field.

"*Si*, she is still missing her parents. She is still grieving. To find them like that, *Madonna mia!*"

"It's not just that..." Rosie bit her lip and shook her head.

Loyalty was a trait Nico respected, but not at the moment.

"I only want to help, Rosie."

"What's going on in Bronte's life at the moment is her business, Nico. It's not mine and it's not yours."

He had to admire her loyalty, even if it did leave him with very little to go on.

Another thought entered his head.

"Have you had a number of calls received at The Dower House where they hung-up?"

By the look on her face he could see she had.

"Yes, there were two on the answering machine and a couple picked up by the girls. We assumed they were wrong numbers." Her eyes met his and she frowned. "Has Bronte been receiving crank calls?"

He nodded.

"Any other... unpleasantness?"

She snapped her fingers and pointed to him.

"Yes. On our website we had a visit from a particularly nasty troll who made sexist remarks about Bronte and called her a bitch. I've moderated the comments." Anxiety entered her dark eyes. "What's going on, Nico?"

He had no idea.

But he was going to find out.

Chapter Eighteen

Bronte drove home in her Mini Cooper, almost on automatic pilot.

Her new father, as she saw Carl, had shown great courage and a generosity of spirit she could only admire. Of course, she had no idea what was really going on inside his head. But they'd agreed to get to know one another and agreed to take it slowly. She'd accepted his invitation to have lunch with him in a couple of days and he'd told her he would always be there for her.

Before she realized it, she was in Ludlow chapel on the grounds of the Hall with her hand on the door of the family crypt. In the early days of bereavement she'd found no comfort, no solace here. But these days spending time with the dead brought her a type of peace.

Eyes burning, she sank into a carved oak pew remembering the day she'd read the letter Alexander had discovered in their father's safe.

Fate, she decided now, was an absolute bastard.

She didn't apologize for swearing in her head in a holy place because she was too bloody angry. Fate had taken her family, her home and her ability to have children. Endometriosis meant her chances were slim to none of being a mother.

There was no point in sitting here bemoaning that life was not fair.

Look how unfair it had been to her father?

Loss crushed her.

It squeezed her lungs as she fought for control.

Emotions, long buried, floated to the surface of her psyche.

Bereavement, she knew now, had an edge of ambivalence about it. Along with guilt, bitter regret and anger for words unspoken there were unhealed sorrows that needed to be expressed. And unfinished mourning completed. She'd been through denial and the truly desperate bargaining with God but Bronte couldn't seem to find acceptance.

Now she wondered if she ever would.

Grief left her too vulnerable these days, abandoning her in a wasteland of sadness.

With a shaky breath, she rose and pressed a hand to her parent's memorial stone.

"Mama, I wish you'd told me."

There, right there, was the wound. A running sore that coursed through her soul along with anger. She was bitterly angry with her dead mother. And guilt kept that anger gleeful company preventing true healing.

And she had no idea what to do about it.

Alexander continued to find the reality that she was his half-sister rather than a full blooded sibling too hard to bear. He'd lost his parents. He'd lost his home and now he felt threatened by her biological father. And after talking with her father, she realized that Alexander was acting out because he was terrified he was going to lose her, too.

Which was ridiculous.

No matter what Alexander did, Bronte could never stop loving him.

Everyone had their tipping point she supposed.

Their family had always stood together no matter what, but that had been an illusion Bronte reflected, heartsick.

No matter how hard she argued that knowledge was power, her brother did not want to dig up the past.

His choice.

But Alexander was suffering.

And she couldn't do a damn thing about it.

Bronte stood and rummaged in her jacket pocket for her car keys.

Going over old ground was a lesson in utter futility.

She should count her blessings.

And learn to deal with the positives in her life instead of the negatives.

Not only did she have her brother in her life, she had a friend who was like a sister to her, a heady new lover and a business to run. Plus, she had a new-found father in her life.

If she secretly dreamed of Utopia, where she had a wonderful husband and a couple of children running around The Dower House, well she just had to get over herself and damn well get on with it.

Striding out to her mini, Bronte ran through her schedule for the day. Rosie was due back at *Sweet Sensation* after lunchtime. She had a consultation with a bride who wanted a cake with a Brazilian carnival theme. Nothing much surprised them these days, but they'd managed to persuade the bride that feathers, firework sparklers and wedding cake were a volatile combination. Fortunately, the client wasn't a bridezilla and had agreed to multi-colored edible beads, miles of ribbon and an eye popping topper of a Swarovski crystal crown. Since the woman loved sparkly things, Rosie had come up with a diamond and silver theme to tone down the beads and ribbon, or to get rid of them all together.

As far as Bronte was concerned the role of *Sweet Sensation* was to give the bride a cake to remember... for all the right reasons.

Her black mini sped down the road from Ludlow Hall, roared through the driveway of The Dower House and whipped round to the rear of the property. She forced a smile and waved at a trainee pastry chef busy in the back of one of the vans.

For a moment she stared unseeing into her gardens, knuckles white as she gripped the steering wheel. *Sweet Sensation* was her baby.

She'd given herself to it twenty-four-seven.

Now it was a thriving, busy business.

Awards and accolades had rained upon her wedding cake designs

The diary was full for twelve months ahead.

Here was her future.

So why the hell did it feel so empty?

At the end of a productive afternoon, Bronte took time to try and clear her mind.

She checked her diary for the following week and cast an eye over the wall mounted white board itemizing the months' events.

Three chest freezers, each one the size of a family car, were filling up nicely with carefully labelled containers of butter cream icings in twenty different s. Along with emergency fruit cakes, muffin batters and sponges of all shapes and sizes. The trainee pastry chefs were coming along well, too.

Rosie had called to say she would drop in to Ludlow Hall to pick-up a supply of the chef's new menus.

Potential couples were offered complimentary dinner and room for a night to test drive the hotel. And business was brisk, she was delighted to see by the appointments scattered through the diary.

The weather forecast had issued a country-wide alert, and predicted a punch from the Arctic meeting a kick in the teeth from Siberia. A double whammy for the British Isles and minus 20 degrees. The weather warning had gone out with neighbors being asked to keep an eye on the sick and elderly.

Dusk fell at three-thirty, along with the temperature, and Bronte padded through to the sitting room with her laptop to check out other top wedding cake designers. Competitor analysis was an ongoing exercise and one she took very seriously with diligence and determination. Tomorrow, she promised herself as she sank into the couch in front of a roaring fire, she'd check out her suppliers' new price lists. They were tricky buggers who occasionally slipped in a price increase. One of the smaller companies was lagging behind their delivery dates, which was totally unacceptable. *Sweet Sensation* paid their invoices on time, so she expected the same courtesy on quality and delivery dates. One more strike and the supplier was out.

An hour later, a vehicle approaching the house crunched on the gravel drive, its headlights illuminating the rear of the house.

Expecting Rosie, Bronte wandered into the kitchen to switch on the kettle.

RECKLESS NIGHTS IN ROME

The door opened behind her.

"I bet it's cold enough to freeze..."

She turned.

Rosie, she realized with a gasp of alarm, had been crying.

Before she could ask what on earth was the matter, Nico, in his signature designer suit and black cashmere coat stalked in firing instructions in Italian into his Smartphone.

His face was fierce.

Rosie, too pale, stared at her.

Ice clutched Bronte's heart.

"What's happened?"

Nico finished his call.

He removed his coat and wrapped it around Rosie.

Then he pushed Rosie into a chair and turned to face Bronte.

The look on his face had her pulse in her throat roar in her ears.

Nico placed his hands on her shoulders.

She braced herself as his eyes stayed on hers.

"Alexander has been in a car accident in Rome."

She shook her head.

Her heart jolted one, twice, to hammer in her ears.

"No, no."

Those dark eyes never left hers for a second.

"He is alive, Bronte."

Nico wrapped his arms around her and held her tight.

His phone rang.

He snatched it with one hand and kept a hold of her with the other.

Rosie stared straight ahead, tears flowing unchecked down her pale cheeks.

"Grazie, grazie."

He pressed Bronte into a chair and crouched in front of her.

Those dark grey eyes fixed on hers and she held on to him as her whole world fell apart.

Fate couldn't be cruel enough to do this to her again.

Could it?

"He is unconscious but stable in the emergency room of San

Pietro Fatebenefratelli Hospital in Rome. My jet is fuelling and will be ready to leave as soon as we get to the airport."

She blinked.

Her brain simply would not compute.

"What happened?"

He shook his head and took a breath.

"He was stationary at a junction and a car hit his car. That is all I know."

"He's alive? You're certain?" Rosie's voice was hardly a whisper.

Nico turned and looked Rosie dead in the eye.

"*Si*. He is alive."

Rosie pulled it together and stood to stare down at Bronte.

"Right, Bronte, we need to get you packed."

"But, I can't leave you here alone."

She was aware of Nico's fingers massaging the tension in her neck.

All business now, Rosie handed Nico his coat and turned to Bronte with a hint of the old fire in her huge brown eyes.

"Of course you can. I'll stay here to look after the place and terrorize the trainees. As per usual, we're ahead of schedule. You're at the other end of a phone, a laptop." She gave Bronte a nudge. "You're going to Rome not Pluto."

"Pack light," Nico instructed. "We can pick up anything we need there."

His phone rang.

Bronte, eyes glued to his face, watched him frown.

Fear gleefully caught her throat as Rosie gripped her hand.

Nico ended his call and his dark eyes were filled with an anxiety that made her want to howl.

"They are taking him for a CAT scan."

Sheer stubbornness willed back tears that threatened to flow.

If she started crying, she'd never stop.

"Okay, okay, right. I'll pack."

Chapter Nineteen

In the Ferranti company jet, Nico tapped on his laptop.

A satellite phone lay on the table between him and Bronte.

The latest update from the hospital was that Alexander may have a detached retina. No word on whether or not he was conscious. Anxiety attempted to bloom in Nico's chest and he stamped it down hard. There was no point in worrying until they had something to worry about.

He flicked a look at Bronte.

Not a word had she spoken since they'd left the house. Not one tear had she shed. In the car, through customs, she'd walked like a zombie. Now, she was quiet and biddable as she sat in a vast leather chair.

Too quiet, Nico decided.

Wherever she'd retreated to inside herself, it couldn't be good for her.

Dressed in black slim jeans and a sweater of grey cashmere, she sat with long legs tucked under her. Her hair was tied back in a silver braid. Her beautiful face looked too pale, too vulnerable and too devastated. A glossy magazine sat on her lap. An untouched notebook and pen lay on the table.

She hadn't turned a page of the magazine, but simply stared straight ahead.

He imagined the day's events must have brought back dark and painful memories of her parents' car accident.

He almost missed the shudder. A lightning vibration of her body that alerted him to the fact she was clinging to her emotions by a thread.

Rising, he signalled the steward and requested a blanket.

With great care he removed the magazine from Bronte's nerveless fingers.

Wrapping her in the blanket, he lifted her in his arms and

knew he'd done the right thing when she turned her face into his chest with an earth shattering sob. The steward moved before them to the rear of the plane and opened the door to a bedroom suite. He folded down the bedspread, asked if they wanted anything else and then closed the door.

Nico laid her on the double bed and Bronte turned on her side to curl into a tight ball. He unzipped flat boots of polished black leather and eased them gently off her feet. His jacket, tie and shoes followed before he lay down beside her and took her in his arms.

Bronte, he realized moments later, cried with as much fervour as she made love, with passion, energy and with her every part of her heart.

The storm raged and his heart ached for her, and for the ruination of his Armani shirt.

"I can't bear it. I can't bear to lose him like this," she sobbed into his chest.

With deep shaky breaths, she rolled onto her back and sniffed, blinking up at the ceiling of the plane.

Nico took the opportunity granted by the lull to grab a couple of face towels from the en-suite bathroom. Lying on his side next to her he propped up on an elbow and wiped saturated cheeks.

"Alexander is very much alive, *cara*. Hang onto that until we see him."

Drenched emerald eyes, huge with distress, met his.

"Nico, he thinks I'm angry with him because he won't listen to me." She swallowed audibly. A fat tear rolled into her hairline. "But I'm not angry with him. None of it was his fault."

Since he had no idea what she was talking about, he simply nodded.

"Good, he will be pleased to hear it."

He watched, helpless, as she fixed her eyes again on the ceiling.

Her bottom lip trembled and she bit down hard on it as her eyes flooded.

"I'm so scared."

He frowned, rubbing the abused lip with his thumb.

"*Cara mia*, we will not panic until we need to panic. Let us take it one step at a time."

Blinking rapidly, Bronte turned to him as if seeing him for the first time, her eyes now bright and focused.

"You are absolutely right." She sat and swiped her cheeks. Her attempt at a smile broke his heart. "God, I must look a mess. I can't keep falling apart like this."

He cupped her face between his hands and forced her to look at him.

"You look beautiful. The love you have for your brother is beautiful, too."

And Nico reminded himself fiercely that this was neither the time nor the place for his libido to spark.

So he contented himself with a burning kiss on that soft vulnerable mouth.

Bronte couldn't remember landing at Leonardo Da Vinci airport, or being rushed through customs, or the drive through Rome's hectic traffic to the hospital.

She simply focused on putting one foot in front of the other and held her breath as a smiling nurse opened the door to Alexander's room.

The woman was smiling.

That was a good sign.

Right?

They entered the room and the bleep, bleep of a heart monitor rang too loud inside her skull.

Her eyes clung to the still form lying in the bed.

A sob caught in her throat.

Alexander's face, his poor face, was swollen, battered and bloody.

Nico's strong arm around her waist steadied her.

Her brother's left arm was in a sling.

The other had fluids dripping into a vein.

Heart in her mouth, Bronte placed a hand tentatively on his leg.

"Alexander?"

Alexander's good eye opened.

He struggled to focus.

"Hey, baby face. Those tears better not be for me."

Relief hit her too hard and Bronte threw herself into Nico's arms and did cry like a baby.

Nico didn't appear to mind too much as he stroked her hair, and studied the condition of his friend.

"You look a mess, my friend."

Alexander narrowed his eye at the intimate body language of his best friend and his sister.

"Airbags, two of them."

Bronte plucked tissues out of a box on Alexander's bedside table. She heroically blew her nose. Her head pounding in reaction to the sudden release of adrenaline.

"You look bloody awful," she said in a wobbly voice.

Alexander winced as he attempted a smile through his split lip.

"You don't look so hot yourself. Wound yourself up good and proper, didn't you? Typical."

Stung and purely for form, because her brother would expect no less, Bronte glared at him.

"We didn't know if you were dead or alive."

Nico smiled at the steel in her voice and ran a gentle hand down her hair.

"I will leave you both to it and speak to the doctor."

Outside Alexander's room, Nico leaned back on the wall, pinching the bridge of his nose.

He heaved a great big sigh of relief.

Close families, they loved, they fought, but always they stood together.

His hand rose to touch the envelope in his pocket.

Then there was the other type of family, dangerous, destructive and cruel.

A hard ball of bitterness burned hot and bright in his throat.

The day of reckoning for *his* so-called family was fast

approaching.

But first he had to deal with more important matters.

He would ensure Alexander had everything he needed.

And then he would look after Bronte.

Nico moved to the nurse's station to request a meeting with Alexander's *medico*.

"For God's sake, you're not bloody sleeping on the floor," Alexander told his sister in a tone dripping with disgust as Nico entered the room.

The nurse checking Alexander's blood pressure spoke to Nico in Italian.

"She said," Nico translated in a silky voice. "The patient must remain calm. He is not calm."

Bronte huffed out a breath and caught Nico's bland look.

"Okay, okay, I'll go. But I'll be back first thing in the morning." Then she frowned, her expression full of sympathy for her brother. "I can't find a spot that's not bruised on your face to kiss you."

"How about my ass," Alexander muttered under his breath.

Bronte's emerald eyes glittered as they narrowed dangerously and Nico whipped an arm around her waist.

"I will telephone in the morning," he told Alexander.

"Yeah, right. Nico?" Alexander's good eye blinked and he gave his friend a crooked grin. "Thank you for bringing her."

Leaning back against the wall of the hospital elevator, Bronte muttered something about the ingratitude of her brother and a boot up the ass.

Out of the corner of his eye, Nico watched her sulky face and sulky mouth.

Little devil.

She still looked pale, but her fighting spirit had returned with a vengeance, he noted, as his lips twitched.

"You can hardly blame him, *cara*. You buzzed around him like a hornet." He tapped her chin as it came up. "Do not even think of taking it out on me. Unlike Alexander, I am able to give as good as I get."

Bronte kept quiet remembering exactly how he gave as good as he got.

A black chauffeur Bentley purred to the kerb as they exited the hospital building.

Nico opened the door and she slid inside.

"Where are we going?" she asked.

With interest, she watched the bright lights of Rome whiz past.

"To my apartment."

Surprised, she looked at him. "Not a hotel?"

"No, I have a place in the City."

The car whisked them through the colorful metropolis of the City that never slept. At night Rome always reminded her of a fantasy. A beautiful, vibrant and magnificent City with its ancient buildings lit up, as were the wide expanse of beautiful parks. People were always in a great hurry in Rome. They walked fast, talked fast and drove like lunatics. And that thought brought her back to what had happened to Alexander. Her brother had had a lucky escape. He would need plenty of rest and recuperation.

Bronte shivered.

It was as cold here in Rome as it was in England.

Although why she'd expected it to be warmer, she had no idea.

The sense of her life spiralling out of control, the sense that fate again may test her by taking another loved one, had drained away now leaving her numb and strangely disoriented.

None of the events of the past two days seemed real now.

Tension rolled from her shoulders, up the back of her neck, to tighten around her forehead, finally to rest behind her eyes.

A wave of old memories, memories of her last visit to Rome with her parents washed over Bronte now. She remembered vividly the way her parents had walked hand in hand, strolling through the streets of Rome, as her father had pointed out immense statues. They'd enjoyed people watching in a cafe in

Via Cola di Rienzo. Her mother raising an eyebrow, while giving her daughter a secret little smile, as an attractive man passed by. They'd done the usual tours; The Coliseum, The Trevi Fountain, The Spanish Steps and the Piazza Della Republica.

An intense feeling of great loss, a deep and abiding sadness she'd buried deep in her psyche crept into her lungs. Bronte's eyes stung and her throat closed. She found she couldn't swallow. Oh God, she missed them. She missed the life they'd had together so damned much.

Now she wondered what on earth would her parents think of her brazen behavior with a man like Nico? She couldn't begin to imagine what her mother would think of her asking a man she'd known for less than thirty-six hours to give her a screaming orgasm.

Where the hell had her self-respect gone?

Where the hell had the *real* Bronte Ludlow gone?

What the hell was she doing going to his apartment?

Was she crazy?

A hotel would be better.

Safer.

In a hotel, she would have her own space to think, to feel real again.

And all the time Bronte's tortured mind took her on a rollercoaster ride, she was aware of Nico's dark eyes on her, watching her.

The atmosphere in the car had changed too, it had become tense, edgy even.

The car cruised to a stop in the Prati district outside a smart apartment building.

Nico wrapped an arm around her waist, guiding her inside.

An elevator whisked them up to the top floor.

The penthouse.

Why was she not surprised?

It was so typical of Nico Ferranti.

A man who liked the good things in life.

The best things in life.

A man who took what he wanted.

A man who had made love to her so beautifully, that she knew instinctively that he'd spoiled her for anyone else.

He unlocked double doors into a palatial open plan expanse with glazed walls surrounded by wide balconies.

Bronte bit down on her bottom lip, taking in the space and the spare minimalist decor.

The exclusively masculine feel of the place was intimidating.

Testosterone seemed to leak out of every black leather sofa, chair and lamp.

She didn't like it.

The space could do with flowers and plants she decided.

Something to humanize the room.

Maybe silk cushions on the leather sofas and chairs to break it up.

"What would you like to do first?" Nico asked standing very still, just watching her.

Dark eyes stayed on hers and that weird wave of vulnerability washed over her again.

She was alone with Nico Ferranti, in Rome.

It didn't feel real.

The day's events had taken their toll on her, she realized now, especially after spending the night in Nico's arms. Meeting her biological father for the first time had drained her. Then the opening of old wounds as she'd visited the family crypt. Add in her brother's accident. And the rush to Rome, along with the heady relief Alexander was going to be okay.

Everything, she realized now, was all too much.

She felt punch drunk and terribly disoriented.

What she needed was something to anchor her to the earth instead of her emotional centre bouncing around like a damn ping pong ball.

At the moment, Nico seemed more foreign to her, too, in this environment.

His strong features appeared too harsh.

Too powerful.

Unaware that his guest was heading for a complete breakdown, Nico's eyes narrowed as he continued to watch her.

"Would you like to take a bath? Food?" he asked now.

Silence.

Hysteria built inexorably from Bronte's solar plexus.

Dear God, she was going to lose it, right here, in front of him.

She blinked rapidly determined not to break down.

The man would think she was certifiable.

What was she doing?

She was so terribly tired and he looked as if he could swallow her in one big bite.

God, he probably expect her to give him another night of hot sizzling passion.

And she just didn't have it in her.

"Bronte?" Nico pushed her gently onto a sofa, grabbed a stool and sat in front of her. "What is it, *cara mia*? Speak to me."

He didn't touch her and for that she was eternally grateful.

Shaking her head Bronte looked into his face and it was as if she was seeing him clearly for the very first time.

Her vision clicked into focus.

Who was this man?

What the hell was she doing?

She leapt up like a jack-in-the-box, her fingers twisting the leather strap of her bag.

"I'm terribly sorry, Nico. I can't do this."

He rose, too, took her hand.

She snatched it back.

"Please don't touch me."

His brows winged into his hairline, but he took a careful step back.

"Okay, I think you need a stiff drink. I do, too. Just relax here a moment."

Nico moved into the open plan kitchen, helped himself to large brandy and went to pour her one, too. Then he changed his mind and poured her a glass of white wine, all the time keeping a close eye on her.

He placed the wine on a small table.

Bronte sank to the couch and picked up the glass.

She looked at him.

He wasn't angry.

But she wondered how he was going to take it when she told him she didn't want to have an affair with him or anything else for that matter.

Making himself comfortable in a chair, his eyes narrow and thoughtful, Nico took a sip and waited through a very long silence.

"I don't know who I am anymore," Bronte confessed, and wondered if he had the telephone number of a very good psychiatrist, because God knew she needed one.

"Why do you feel like that?"

"It's my behavior. Especially recently, it's just not me, Nico. I can't be someone I'm not."

"Do you want to know how I see you?"

Face flushed, Bronte shook her head, staring unseeing into the liquid in her wine glass.

"I can just imagine how you see me."

"I see a strong, beautiful woman who works hard and never gives up. She's funny and warm and loving. Her family and friends love her very much."

Bronte simply shook her head.

He knew nothing about her.

"I thought I could do this but now I can't. I'm sorry."

"What is 'this'?"

She stood and paced as her mind whirled off in ten different directions.

"Being here with you. I should be in a hotel near the hospital to be close to my brother. I don't usually jump into bed with men I hardly know."

"*Si*, I should hope not, *cara*."

By his tone, she could tell he wasn't taking her seriously.

Now she pressed her fingertips into tired eyes.

"For the first time in my life, I decided to be selfish and act on my feelings with you. I was attracted. No strings. No expectations. No promises. You were perfect."

His eyes quizzical, Nico sent her a slow smile.

"I do not know whether to be flattered or offended."

Bronte rubbed the tension easing slowly from her neck and sent him a sad look.

"If I stay here with you it will be under false pretences. I should be at a hotel."

"I do not understand."

She owed it to him, after everything he'd done for her, to be nothing less than honest.

"Well, we're having a hot affair. And I'm sure you'll want constant monkey sex. I'm not the type of person you think I am."

She jumped as he roared with laughter and shook his head.

Nico rose, took her in his arms and pressed a soft kiss on her forehead.

"Oh, Bronte, monkey sex? What on earth is that?"

Smiling into his chest she inhaled the scent that was pure Nico and sighed.

"Something Rosie said."

His big body shaking with laughter, Nico lifted her chin and kissed her with a soft delicate brush of the lips.

"But we are not having an affair, *cara mia*. Neither of us is married."

"What are we having?" she wanted to know.

With a gentle hand he stroked her hair.

"We are in the early stages of a relationship. Let us make a promise to each other. We must only have the truth between us. Agreed?"

His eyes held hers.

And Bronte read a mix of understanding and humor.

"Agreed."

"If you do not want to sleep with me and have *monkey sex* then you tell me. Agreed?"

She let out a breath feeling incredibly foolish.

"Agreed."

"If you want me to do something, then you tell me. Agreed?"

Nerves, Bronte realized with relief, she'd only had an attack of nerves.

"Agreed."

Pulling her close, Nico nuzzled her hair.

"What happened to you in the car? You changed."

"Memories," Bronte told him.

"Sad memories?"

"Yes and no. I came to Rome with my parents years ago. We had an amazing time."

Lifting her chin, his thumb stroked her bottom lip and the little pull in her tummy reminded her of his fatal attraction as her eyes clung to his.

"You need to learn to speak your thoughts rather than keeping them locked inside your head," he said, as he kissed her.

Their agreement for the truth between them had Bronte opening her heart.

"I wondered what they would think of me if they could see me now."

Those dark eyes studied her face.

"And what conclusion did you come to, *cara*?"

Her throat tightened and her eyes stung.

"They would be ashamed, disappointed in me."

Nico shook his head vehemently.

His eyes never left hers for a moment.

"Never, I do not believe that for a moment. Look at what you are doing with your life, working hard and running the business. It is a great success. I heard plenty of people on Saturday night say how proud your parents would be of you and Alexander." His mouth nuzzled hers. He raised his head, eyes gentle. "You are still grieving for all that you have lost, *cara*. And you have had an emotional day. Rome has brought back happy memories that have made you sad. That is all."

A heavy weight lifted from her heart.

She felt free for the first time in a long time.

Her parents *had* loved her... unconditionally.

She remembered that now.

They wouldn't dream of judging her.

So, who was she to judge them?

"Nico?"

"*Si*, Bronte?"

"I'm starving."

He took her to a family run trattoria.

They ate pasta and drank red wine.

Wine which brought a light flush to Bronte's cheeks.

And Nico discovered she had a passion for ice cream, particularly white chocolate.

On the return to his apartment, he realized she loathed the interior decor with the same passion she had for ice cream.

Well, the decor was easily fixed.

A few calls and it would be in hand.

After Bronte had made emotionally charged calls to Rosie and a person called Carol cancelling a lunch date, he'd urged her to take a warm bath... alone. And then he'd left her deeply asleep in his bed. By the end of this evening, the girl was near collapse. Her face appeared too pale with dark circles of sheer exhaustion under her eyes. Rising every morning at the ungodly hour of six am (or even earlier) was taking its toll on her.

But he had a plan to fix that.

Dressed in a thick duck-down quilted vest, jeans and heavy boots, Nico narrowed his eyes as he lit a long slim cigar and sank into a recliner on the covered balcony of his penthouse. He exhaled and smoke rose in the frosty air. He studied the sky. It would snow tomorrow. He could smell it. Blowing smoky circles, Nico carefully analyzed the ache in the region of his heart, and the butterflies in his gut, with a mixture of deep regret and excitement.

There was a risk he was heading for a fall.

Without him being aware of it, Bronte had slipped into his heart.

And the time had come for him to face facts.

He cared about her.

Perhaps he cared about her too much?

Shrugging his shoulders, he smiled, and considered the

changes in his heart and in his head.

When the hell had he ever cared whether a woman liked his decor?

Never.

When had he ever cared enough to comfort a woman?

Never.

But then, he'd never made love with a woman as unaffected and wonderfully naïve as Bronte. Was that it? When he thought of the hard, polished, world weary women he usually indulged in, he shuddered. He found it difficult to remember a face and that made him cringe.

Now he wondered if he was going through a mid-life crisis?

Was that what this was all about?

Thirty-four was surely too young for such a thing.

Or was it?

In the car he'd watched her lightning change of mood.

And now he wondered what was behind it and what it meant.

For a moment he thought he may need to take her to a hotel, to let her go and be alone with her thoughts.

He could understand her feelings of grief and her deep sense of loss.

She had been incredibly close to her parents.

It was understandable.

And Alexander's accident had brought it all back.

Nico remembered his own mother and her unconditional love for him. Her death had broken him. He could admit it to that fact now. But he had been a child of ten, a skinny street urchin, dirt poor and starving.

Bronte, on the other hand, had been blessed with two loving parents and a loving brother.

He inhaled smoke as his mind proceeded into another issue.

The letter he received from a lawyer requesting him to meet with his father and his half-brother in Rome in two days preyed on his mind. And wasn't it interesting, how they'd crawled out of the woodwork once he was wealthy and successful.

Apparently the old man was seriously ill.

Tough.

Nico hoped he burned in hell.

The man had left his mother to die, sick and alone and never acknowledged his younger son, Nico.

According to his late grandfather, his father had seduced his mother. A married man with a young son, he'd dabbled on the fringes of organized crime.

In the letter Nico had received, the lawyer said they didn't want anything except to meet him. His brother wanted to introduce Nico to his family. He had a wife and two kids apparently.

Nico smiled to himself.

Fat chance.

He would not permit his sordid past to touch the life he had worked hard to build.

And no way would it touch the embryo of what he may build with Bronte.

No way.

Their relationship was too new, too vulnerable.

Cristo, they came from two different backgrounds.

He was a tough, streetwise sewer rat and Bronte was the cool English lady with an impressive heritage. For the first time in his life, Nico could see a future stretch in front of him with her at the centre of it all. It scared him how much he wanted it. He craved the routine and a home with Bronte at The Dower House. And one day, perhaps, they'd be blessed with a blonde-haired little girl and a dark-haired little demon with big green eyes like his mother.

Nico shivered with the strength of the sudden premonition.

He had to laugh at himself and the ridiculous situation he now found himself in.

Dio, he was being fanciful.

How could this *thing* have happened to him in just a few days? Bronte was perfect for him, he admitted now. He'd known it as soon as he had first set eyes on her. But his intuition told him something was wrong with her. Something was tormenting her. It was there in her eyes when she didn't think he was looking. He'd noticed it from the very beginning. There were times when she was mentally absent from him. Something dark lurked at the back of her eyes, keeping her in the past, instead of being in the present moment. He wondered what it meant.

Frowning, anxiety now curled at the base of his spine.

Nico hoped to God she wasn't in love or still had strong feelings for her ex-fiancé.

The man must be a fool to have had her and let her go.

But he shook his head, inhaled and blew out a stream of smoke, staring into the night sky.

There was no point in worrying over something he could not change.

Bronte was still grieving and that made her vulnerable, although she hadn't been terribly vulnerable yesterday morning when she had nearly scalped him.

He laughed out loud.

She was spectacular when she lost her temper, a wildcat.

Life with Bronte Ludlow promised to be very interesting.

Nico would put good money on it that he would never have a boring moment and how amazing would that be?

However, it was true that she was a little repressed sexually.

And he laid the blame for that firmly at the door of her ex-fiancé.

Now Nico studied the tip of his cigar with narrowed eyes.

He was almost certain the bastard had made comments about her breasts.

She had a hang up about them.

Well, he would fix that, too.

Although he fervently hoped she was not planning implants.

He hated those.

Bronte did not have an ounce of vanity in her.

Unbelievable really, since she was the most beautiful woman he'd ever seen.

What had the bastard done to her?

And monkey sex?

What on earth was that?

Chapter Twenty

"I'm not sure about this, Nico."

Bronte twisted and turned in front of a mirror, studying the back of a shocking pink strapless sheath. Her feet were bare. And she tugged at the bust and hem of the garment.

The dress was too wide at the top and too short.

"I like it," Nico said in a silky drawl. "I like the color. It suits you."

Bronte shot Nico a dark look.

She hated clothes shopping with a passion.

Hated it.

How the hell had he managed to talk her into this.

And who asked for his opinion anyway?

"You would," she said, and didn't bother not to sound bitter.

No matter how hard she'd argued until she was blue in the face that she could afford to buy her own clothes. Nico had steamrolled over all her objections and brought her to a place she just *knew* was ridiculously expensive.

And it seriously annoyed her that Nico refused to believe she absolutely detested shopping for clothes. Add in shopping with a man, and shopping for clothes was a whole new experience. Two hours into the new experience and Bronte decided it was not fun. She should have been at the hospital with her injured brother, but Alexander had made it clear he would see them this afternoon. His visitors would be allowed half an hour because he was having tests. A precaution only and he hoped to be discharged from hospital tomorrow.

Nico had organized rest and recuperation for Alexander at his villa on Lake Como.

After a heated telephone discussion between a relentless Nico and Alexander, her brother had *reluctantly* agreed to a four week stay.

When Bronte had mentioned going home tomorrow, Nico wouldn't hear of it.

He had a meeting in Rome on Thursday, he said, so they should stay until Friday.

Since Rosie, sounding happy and ruling *Sweet Sensation* with a rod of iron, was all for Bronte taking a well-deserved break.

Bronte had found herself outgunned and outmanoeuvred.

Dressed in casual Armani, Nico now lounged in a fancy chair looking gorgeous.

He made her do a little twirl in each dress.

A twirl that pressed Bronte's hot button every single time.

The bastard was thoroughly enjoying himself.

Madame Carlotta, the smart, middle-aged woman who owned the shop, was French.

And she forcibly reminded Bronte of a bird of prey.

Clucking her tongue now, Madame sent Nico a reproving look.

"Bronte is not comfortable in this design, Nico. It would sit in the back of her wardrobe. What is the point?"

Madame held up another strapless little number, which probably cost four figures, and led a protesting and fed-up Bronte into the changing room.

She was sick and tired of being poked and prodded, measured and sighed over as if she was some sort of damned freak.

Her temper bubbled and brewed.

She'd endured two hours of sheer hell without a break, without even a sip of water.

How much longer was it going to take to find a dress that met with Nico's approval?

She didn't notice Madame's secret smile as she zipped her into a boned sheath of blue silk, the color of a summer sky, that fitted her like a glove and showcased her legs.

Who the hell cared about her legs?

Bronte stalked out, stood in front of Nico and struck a pose with attitude.

Who in their right mind would want to be a model she asked

herself.

And if he made one smart remark, just one, she would deck him.

Nico sat up straight, made a twirl sign with his finger that made her growl deep in her throat.

Bronte turned in a slow circle certain the top of her head was about to explode.

"We'll take it," he said.

Thank you, God.

Madame clapped her hands.

"Excellent choice. And it does not require altering."

Green eyes blazing Bronte whirled on them.

"It doesn't need altering. How amazing is that?"

She unzipped and stepped out of the dress.

Naked except for white lacy panties, Bronte picked it up and tossed it into Nico's smiling face before she marched into the changing room and slammed the door.

Madame removed the garment from a laughing Nico and took it to a table.

Clucking her tongue, she folded the dress in tissue and shook her head.

"She hates shopping, Nico. Never did I think I would live to see the day you would bring me such a woman."

Delighted, Nico grinned at her.

"I never thought I would live to see the day either."

Madame patted his cheek.

With an expert flick she plucked the black credit card out of his hand.

"She is very beautiful. Excellent bones. She can wear anything. It will be a pleasure to dress her. The items will be delivered later today."

Face flushed, eyes spitting fire, Bronte stalked out of the changing room dressed in black from head to toe in jeans, knee high flat suede boots and polo neck sweater.

She'd tied her hair in a high pony tail.

Nico held out her black quilted jacket.

She thrust her arms into it and gave him a look that would

have melted titanium.

And he thought she looked absolutely spectacular.

Only manners that had been drummed into Bronte from childhood held her back from storming out of the door.

She held out her hand.

"Thank you for all your help and assistance," she said not meaning a word of it.

Madame cleared her throat, eyes sparkling as she shook hands.

"I hope to have the pleasure of seeing you very soon."

Nico held open the door and Bronte breezed past him.

"Hell will freeze first," she muttered.

Taking a deep breath, Bronte inhaled the wonderfully cool air of freedom.

She spotted an empty table at a cafe across the square and made a beeline straight for it.

Ignoring the interested looks of the local populace, she plonked herself in a chair.

Picking up a menu, she waved it at a good-looking waiter who sprang to attention and flicked an interested glance at Nico as he sat next to her.

"I'll have a large hot chocolate, heavy on the marshmallows," Bronte told the waiter with big a smile that made him blink. "A smoked cheese and ham baguette. A glass of Frascati, make it a large one. Oh, and a bottle of still water, thank you."

Rummaging in her big bag, she brought out a packet of ibuprofen.

The waiter raised a brow at Nico who told him, "I will have the same, *grazie*."

The water and wine arrived.

Bronte popped a couple of pills into her mouth, took a sip of water, closed her eyes and sat back.

After a while, she blew out a long breath, opened her eyes and met those dark slightly perplexed eyes.

"Something tells me you do not enjoy shopping for clothes," Nico mused.

Har har, har har.

"Funny, very funny."

His eyes widened and those lips twitched as she took a sip of hot chocolate with a little moan of pleasure.

"You never cease to surprise me, *cara mia*."

"Think of me as a plant for a moment." Bronte almost laughed out loud at his bewildered expression. "Would you feed and water a plant or would you leave it to die without sustenance?"

A heartbeat later and she saw the light switch on.

"Ahh, I should have realized. You needed a drink? Why did you not say so?"

She looked at him through narrowed eyes as Nico put up his hands in a gesture of peace.

Bronte continued, "I had no idea I would be spending two hours in that place being poked and prodded as if I was some sort of oddity. If that woman muttered or tutted one more time I was ready to... What?"

She took a breath as Nico stared at her in stupefied amazement.

"Why do you believe you are not beautiful?"

A flush of mortification washed over her cheeks.

She wriggled in her seat.

What was he talking about?

She was okay looking.

Her school days had been hell with her pale hair and coloring.

The jeers about her too skinny legs and pancake flat chest still had the power to hurt.

"I don't think about how I look." Liar, her conscience dug her hard in the ribs. Yes, but that was the breast thing, not her appearance as such.

Nico sipped his wine, eyeing her over the glass.

She was actually unaware of her own impact on others.

"I want you to look at all the men in the cafe."

She stared at him, shrugged and dug out her glasses from her handbag.

He had a light bulb moment.

"You are short-sighted?"

Bronte tossed him a belligerent look.

"A little. I need them when I'm driving or when I'm working."

"How do people look to you without them?"

"From a distance? Blurry. Why do you want me to look at men?"

"Just do it."

So she did.

Every single one gave her a little nod, a couple even winked.

Her brow creased.

"What's the matter with them?"

A laugh burst from his chest and she smiled back at him as he roared with laughter.

Nico took her fingers to his lips and stared into her eyes.

"Never change. I adore you, Bronte."

He read the wary confusion in her eyes and cursed his tongue.

Too soon, Nico, too soon.

Their food arrived and he smiled his thanks.

Relaxed, he sat back.

Fascinated, he watched her wolf down her food.

Most women he knew made a lettuce leaf last for an hour.

"Why do you always wear black?" he wondered now.

She shrugged.

"It's easy. I can't be bothered to work out what to wear every day. When I'm working I wear my chef whites. In summer, jeans and T-shirts."

"Don't you find black boring?"

She went utterly still.

Ooops.

Bronte put down her sandwich with great care and met his gaze dead on.

"Nope. Why? Do *you* find black boring?"

Her raised brows dared him to reply in the affirmative.

Nico attempted to climb out of the big hole he had just dug for himself.

"Not at all. It suits you with your coloring. Very dramatic." He shrugged. "I am thinking about the ball."

Her eyes grew huge.

"What was that dress we bought this morning?"

"That was a dress for this evening."

"What's happening this evening?"

"We are going dancing."

Her jaw dropped as sheer delight entered her eyes.

She leaned over and gripped his neck, pulling him close.

The green of her eyes appeared more vivid up close in daylight, with tiny flecks of amber in them. Her nose had a sprinkling of freckles he had not noticed before. The scent of her surrounded him and that fabulous mouth smiled.

"You're taking me dancing?"

And she leaned in and gave him a long and very lazy kiss.

Nico gripped her ponytail and kissed her back, only his was hotter and harder.

His heart turned over as he tasted her soft, silky mouth. And he wondered if she realized that it was the first time she'd made the first move with him. It meant so much to him Nico surprised himself with the well of emotion it opened up in his chest.

With a very wicked look in her green eyes, Bronte ran a finger down his cheek.

A little thrill ran up his spine.

She was flirting with him and he loved it.

"After we visit Alexander I'm going to need shoes."

He gaped at her.

"But... I thought you hated shopping."

She pressed a gentle kiss on his surprised mouth.

"My darling," she drawled. "That was for clothes."

She sent him a pitying look as he tried to recover from the shock of being called *darling* in that low sexy purr that had electrified his groin.

He'd been called darling before, lots of times, but it had never affected him like this.

"*Shoes* are an entirely different thing." Eyes a dreamy emerald, Bronte gave a couple of shoulder rolls and a little wiggle of her fingers. "I'm in Italy, the shoe capital of the world. Bring. It. On."

Unthinking, she reached out and stroked the back of his hand with feather light fingers sending a jolt straight to his hard shaft as she continued,

"You're the expert on Rome. Where do we go first to put a big fat dent in my credit card?" He opened his mouth to protest and she placed her finger on his lips as her eyes met his. "Oh no, Mr. Hotshot. You can buy me one dress... but the shoes are all mine."

She looked utterly determined and Nico found he didn't want to argue.

"If you are happy, I am happy." He glanced at his watch. They had an hour before they could visit Alexander. "I have sent flowers and fruit to the hospital, but I was thinking we should pick up a few magazines for the patient."

They arrived to find Alexander looking brighter and more like himself.

Chestnut hair damp from a shower, he sat against a waterfall of snowy pillows dressed in navy soft cotton jogging bottoms and T-shirt. His right arm was in a sling. With relief, Bronte noticed the swelling had gone down over his eye, which already boasted a rainbow of colors spreading over his cheekbone.

Sitting gingerly on the edge of the bed, she squeezed his calf and rubbed his leg.

"These pj's are a *big* improvement on that girly hospital gown. How's the shoulder?" she asked.

"Sore. But it'll be fine." Alexander winced as he made himself more comfortable and nodded to the flowers, glossy magazines and overfilled basket of fruit. "Thanks for these."

Bronte gave him big eyes and tucked her tongue firmly in her cheek.

"Who helped you with the shower? The blonde or the brunette?" she asked, referring to the attractive young nurses lurking at the door.

Alexander flicked a long suffering look at Nico.

A Nico who only shook his head as if to say, *'Don't look at me. I have no control over your sister.'*

Which was the absolute truth.

"Neither," Alexander said now. "His name was Jorge. I believe he's from Scandinavia."

Bronte bit down hard on her bottom lip as he sent her a dark look.

"It's not funny. How would you like a member of the same sex making sure your bits were squeaky clean?"

Bronte's shoulders shook as she cried with laughter and wiped her eyes.

"God, wait 'til I tell Rosie."

Genuine alarm entered her brother's eyes and he stabbed a finger at her.

"Don't even think about it. What have I ever done to you? Rosie Gordon will dine out on this for months." Alexander turned panicked eyes to Nico. "You've got to help me here. I'll never hear the end of it."

Nico moved in, his fingers squeezing Bronte's neck as he whispered in her ear.

"*Cara*, be nice."

Her brother still looked too pale.

Although he was putting on a very brave face, Bronte could see he was in pain.

So she decided to cut him a break.

"Okay, I won't tell her. But only if you agree to four weeks recuperation at Nico's house at Lake Como."

Alexander glowered at her, narrowing his eyes.

"I've already said I would, haven't I?"

Yeah, but she knew her brother.

What he said and what he did were two entirely different things.

"Swear."

She spat on the palm of her hand and stuck it under her brother's nose.

Nico squeezed her neck again and she felt his body shake with laughter.

"I don't believe this," Alexander told her, with a snarl. "What are you, twelve?"

"It's up to you. If you don't swear, I'll phone Rosie right here, right now."

With a look that could melt solid steel, he spat on his palm and gripped hers.

"You'd better stick to the bargain."

"Think yourself lucky, big boy." She flashed him a huge smile. "It could have been a blood oath."

Alexander groaned as a nurse entered with a blood pressure machine and a tray that contained sharps.

As his sister, Bronte knew it was her sworn duty to ensure her brother took his medicine like a good boy.

"Man up. It'll only be a little scratch."

Nico's grip on her neck tightened in warning.

"The helicopter will pick you up in a couple of hours," he said to Alexander. "Everything is ready for you at the house, including a nurse."

Defeated, Alexander gave them a look that reminded her of an abandoned puppy.

"Yeah, yeah, yeah, but it had better not be Jorge."

Nico bit his lip.

"I believe her name is Lydia."

Perking up at the news, Alexander brows winged into his hairline.

"Really? Blonde, brunette, red-head?"

"Ah, I believe she might have been a brunette... when she was younger."

"Aww, come on, Nico." Alexander winced as the nurse took his blood pressure. "Well, at least I'll have my laptop and can get some work done."

Alarmed, Bronte sent Nico a look.

But Nico was busy flicking fluff from his sleeve and didn't

meet her eye.

"It breaks my heart to tell you," he said to Alexander, "that your laptop was damaged in the accident. However, I have a comprehensive library of books, DVDs and music. And a full complement of staff to see to your every need. All you have to do is to get well."

"For Christ's sake," Alexander said in disgust.

A couple of doctors arrived and it was Nico and Bronte's cue to leave.

Nico spoke to the medics in Italian and appeared perfectly happy with what their report.

He pressed Alexander's good shoulder.

"I'll phone you later. If you need anything, just ask."

Bronte kissed his cheek.

"Take good care of yourself."

Her brother looked hard at Nico for a long moment, and then met her eyes.

"You, too."

It was not often that Nico Ferranti found himself out of his depth.

But he had never ever seen a woman buy shoes the way Bronte did.

It was a sensory experience for her. Totally focused, she studied the high heel in her hand from every angle. Her fingers stroked and smoothed the butter soft leather. Then she smelled them, which made him grin at the assistant who appeared to share her devotion.

Trying them on was a whole new experience in itself.

She bought four pairs.

One pair for the evening and the others because she 'just couldn't resist.'

"Why are you looking at these?" he wondered. "This is the men's department."

Like a lover, she stroked a pair of boots and sent him a sly smile, which was more powerful than a punch to the gut.

"This might come as a surprise to you, Nico, but you are a

man. Try them on."

Her arms wound around his waist as the assistant went off to find his size.

She gazed up into his face with wide eyes.

"Big feet? Hmm, you know what they say about a man who has big feet?"

Laughing into her naughty face, his breath caught in his throat.

But before he could kiss her senseless, the assistant returned with his boots.

He tried them on then did as he was told by Bronte and walked up and down.

"Do you love them?" She wanted to know.

"They are comfortable."

"No, do you love them?"

The look in her eye reminded him of a zealot priest.

He nodded.

"Absolutely, I love them."

Thrilled to bits, and without a blink at the bill, she handed over her credit card to the assistant.

Swinging her purchases with one hand, she tucked her arm in his as they strolled down the Via Borgognona.

"I feel another coffee coming on," she sang.

Steering them to an empty table, Bronte piled their boxes onto an empty chair.

"You should not spend so much of your own money," Nico blurted it out before he thought about how she might take it.

But although her eyes flashed, she just gave him a cool little smile and crooked a finger.

He leaned closer.

"I work hard. The business is in the black. I can afford a few of pairs of shoes, Nico. Say thank you."

"I apologize. I did not mean to offend you. *Grazie*, for thinking of me."

Her annoyed expression was replaced by one of genuine bewilderment.

"Has a woman never bought you a gift?" she demanded with

a glint of temper in her eye.

The thought had never occurred to him.

Those emerald eyes widened in amazement as she shook her head.

She poured sugar into her cappuccino, stirred it and then slapped down the spoon.

"All I can say is that you are mixing in the wrong company, Mr. Ferranti." She took a sip of her cappuccino, held his gaze. "And it's a damned disgrace."

He looked stunned.

Bronte eyed him over the rim of her cup.

What sort of women did he usually mix with?

Okay, that was an incredibly stupid question, Bronte. Don't even go there.

Frowning, the more she mulled it over, the thought occurred to her that Nico appeared to live an incredibly isolated existence.

She was distracted from that thought when a smartly dressed couple with a small child, a boy of around three years old with glossy curls and happy chocolate eyes, sat at the next table. The father said something to Nico and he laughed as they entered a conversation in Italian she couldn't follow.

Left to her own devices, Bronte's gaze wandered over the rest of the customers in the café.

Busy place.

And Italian men were incredibly attractive, she'd give them that.

Then she spotted a big man sitting in a quiet corner staring intently at Nico.

She pulled her glasses out of her bag and took a better look.

Weird, he looked like an older, harder version of Nico.

Maybe he came from the same part of the country?

By his expensive clothes, she surmised he was a businessman.

The man caught her eye.

She shivered at the chill in eyes scarily like Nico's.

His mouth thinned as he jerked a nod at her.

Bronte kept an eye on him as he paid the bill and left.

Yes, he was tall and broad, too.

He even held himself like Nico as he walked.

Laughter from the other table brought Bronte's attention back to the couple with the adorable little boy.

"What are they saying?" She smiled at them thinking she should mention the man to Nico.

"They asked when we are going to start a family."

Her heart took a stumble in her chest.

To distract herself, she gave Nico a teasing look.

"There speaks the man who never wants a family or commitments. I hope you told them we're not married."

Dark eyes, perfectly serious now, held hers.

"A man might change his mind if he found the right woman."

A fist to the gut would have hurt less.

But the implication was clear that Nico was referring to her.

Dear God, he cannot be serious.

Giving what she hoped was an unconcerned smile, Bronte sipped her coffee.

However, she couldn't help but shiver with the sudden chill in her belly.

As ever when it came to her, Nico didn't miss a trick.

"Come, *cara*, you are getting cold."

They said goodbye to the family and Bronte ordered herself to pull it together.

It was ridiculous that an innocent remark should have the power to destroy her peace of mind.

But her heart felt as frozen as the icy wind that whipped through the streets.

Fat flakes of snow whirled around them and they picked up the pace.

Chapter Twenty One

Her cheeks stung with cold as Nico opened the doors to the apartment.

He placed their shopping bags on the floor and Bronte gasped.

Gone were the masculine furnishings.

And had there been a glass fire set in the wall before?

There must have been but she hadn't noticed it.

Stunned, she wandered through low linen sofas in a stone color with huge cushions in toning jewel shades. Her fingers smoothed ivory cashmere throws. Her gaze slid over glass coffee tables laden with huge Venetian glass bowls in corals and reds. Everything was pulled together with rugs in vivid matching shades. A soft warm glow came from various lamps placed strategically around the room. The atmosphere was welcoming and cosy. Gorgeous fresh flowers with vibrant, exotic blooms in hot colors were everywhere, on the dining table, serving tables, even in the kitchen.

She pressed trembling fingers to her lips as she turned slowly to face Nico.

He'd shrugged off his coat and was leaning against the doorframe watching her with a big grin.

"You like it?"

Was he kidding her?

"What's not to like? It looks fabulous."

Confused, she walked towards him.

"But why? Why would you do such a thing?"

"I do not spend much time in this apartment. I saw it through your eyes last night. It needed a change. My main residence in Italy is on Lake Como, although I never spend much time there."

Bronte nodded, she knew he travelled a great deal and

noticed he called it a residence, not a home. Arms wide, she spun in a circle to take in the change.

"How on earth did you manage to do this in one day?"

Nico stepped into her and pulled her into his arms.

His hands slipped under her sweater and feather light fingers stroked her skin, sending wave after wave of shimmering desire through her.

"*Cara*, I told you. I identify talent and let them do the work. This is an example of an incredibly efficient company whose business is to stage expensive properties for sale. They are involved in the interior design of my hotels. I gave them a ring last night. I did not, as you say, get my hands dirty."

"Wow, if this is an example of how you do business I'm impressed."

A wicked gleam came into his eye as his forehead rested on hers.

"How impressed?"

She ran her hands under his sweater, exploring the muscles and tendons of his chest as he backed her into the bedroom. Then she pulled his head down for a scorching kiss. Sucking his bottom lip into her mouth her fingers found his belt. She flipped open the button on his trousers, eased down the zip as her hand slid inside his jockeys and found him rock hard.

Her breath came in quick pants as he lifted her in his arms.

"Very, very impressed," she told him with a little purr, and gave herself up to the magic of the moment.

Something had changed.

The feel of his hands on her, the way he touched her, kissed her, was quite different.

His lips had changed, too. Those kisses scorched a path down and through her entire body.

This time when he entered her it was with exquisitely slow hip thrusts.

His eyes held hers with an intensity she found mesmerizing.

His fingers linked tightly with hers.

"Stay with me, Bronte. Look at me. See what you do to me."

Her breath sobbed in her throat as his eyes darkened, his breathing harsh as he tried to control her orgasm. As she fell apart, he caught her scream with his mouth and then followed her into the abyss.

His fingers stroked her naked back as her shudders calmed.

Safe and warm in his arms, legs tangled, Bronte dozed and simply enjoyed the moment.

A firm smack to her bare bottom brought her wide awake.

"Hey, what was that for?"

Nico scooped her up, striding into the shower.

He set the water for warm rather than hot and dumped her under it.

Roaring with laughter at her shriek, he pinned her to the wall and kissed her senseless until her system sizzled again with need.

He raised his head, water beading on thick black lashes.

"Dancing, remember?"

She gave a little mew of pretend discontent and batted her eyes at him.

"Oh, I don't know. Hot sex in the shower or dancing?" She bit down on her bottom lip and gave him big eyes. "Decisions, decisions."

He pumped soap into his hand from a dispenser and rubbed it over her breasts, rinsed until the water ran clear, then reached down between her legs.

Her eyes rolled back in her head.

The man had magic fingers.

"*Cara mia.* I can do both. I am Italian."

Her laugh was smothered by his mouth tasting hers.

Bronte put the finishing touches to her make-up.

She shook back her hair, shimmied into the sky blue dress and zipped it up.

The neutral Jimmy Choos looked fabulous.

She knew the five inch heels would kill later.

But no pain no gain.

Then she picked up a matching clutch bag she'd snuck past the ever vigilant Nico.

A quick spritz of Baby G and she was ready.

"Wow."

She turned.

Nico leaned against the bedroom door looking wonderful in a sharp dark suit with a matching shirt unbuttoned at the neck.

His eyes, dark and brooding, studied her from head to toe as if he'd never seen her before.

A little shiver of apprehension scurried up her spine.

"What's the matter?"

He moved into her, pressed a hot kiss to her cheek, and sniffed her neck.

"I'm going to have to fight them off tonight."

The driver of the Bentley held the door open and Nico handed her into the back of the car.

The lights of Rome streamed past as Nico pulled her close and tucked her under his shoulder. Holding her hand he did his habitual rubbing of her knuckles. Excited nerves fluttered madly in Bronte's stomach. Along with a growing sense of unreality, a horrible spaced-out feeling, that she was beginning to realize was the result of too much stress. She really needed to get a handle on her emotions or she would end up on the therapist's couch.

The car purred to a stop outside a nightclub which had a queue as far as the eye could see.

Eyes wide, Bronte turned to Nico.

"How long will we need to wait?"

"Not long," he whispered, his voice low and husky.

A wave of paparazzi surged toward the car calling out in Italian as their cameras flashed. She blinked as Nico pulled her closer as a team of black-suited security men linked arms to push them back.

With a huge smile for Nico, a doorman ran down the steps to open the car door.

Then they were whisked past the crowd and press, and into an area cordoned off from the rest of the club. The VIP lounge.

She gave him a fulminating look, squeezed his hand.

"You own this, don't you?"

His lips twitched.

She wondered if there was anything he didn't have an interest in.

"I have a partner," he murmured in her ear.

Bronte slanted him a look.

Tall and powerful, eyes narrowed, Nico surveyed the room missing nothing.

In this environment he was in his element.

And it gave her a pang that she was totally out of hers.

Nico Ferranti, Bronte realized with a chill, was the ruling King of this particular jungle.

A glass of champagne in her hand, he led her to a corner furnished with contemporary sofas. They sipped companionably as she watched, fascinated, by the beautiful people. She recognized some of them from glossy magazines.

He was toying with her hair as she turned to him.

"Was that who I think it is?" Her gaze followed major European Royalty.

"Mmm hmm," he whispered, nuzzling her ear, sending a little shiver over her skin.

A dark-eyed, dark-haired beauty, in a black dress that looked as if it had been sprayed on, sashayed up to Nico. She bent and pressed amazing breasts into him and tried to give him a hot kiss on the mouth.

In a move Bronte could only admire, he managed to avoid the kiss and the breasts. Nico flicked a cool look to another man, security she supposed by his earpiece, who stood against the wall. He moved to the woman's side, held her arm, and whispered something in her ear.

As she was led away, the woman's smouldering eyes held a mix of hot lust and despair.

And Bronte found herself feeling very sorry for her.

Is that what she would be like when this fantasy ended?

She'd better remember to keep her dignity intact.

The cool closed expression on Nico's dark face only

hardened the chill deep in her belly, reinforcing the feeling that she was way out of her depth with this man.

She'd better remember why she was here.

For the first time in her life, she was indulging in a hot affair with a hot man, having fun and living life to the full for once.

Nothing more and nothing less.

But something in the woman's eyes tugged at Bronte.

"Who was she?"

Nico turned and his look held a burning impatience, along with a warning.

"No one."

Stung by his attitude as much as by the tone, Bronte lifted her chin.

"Whoever she is, she is a human being and deserves to be treated as one."

Why was she making a big deal of this?

How would she handle it if he froze her out her like that, with utter contempt and disrespect?

The problem, Bronte knew, was that she couldn't handle it.

She noticed the way his jaw tightened.

"She's someone I once knew," he told her with reluctance.

For some reason, that just was not good enough.

"Did you have a relationship with her?"

He sighed in frustration, pulling her into his arms.

"I would not call it a relationship. It was a long time ago."

So he'd just used the woman for sex?

How charming.

But then, a little voice whispered, isn't he using you for the same thing?

"Shall I take a wild guess and say it didn't end well?"

His eyes met hers.

"It ended badly, my fault. She wanted something I could not give her."

"She loves you."

He shook his head, looking her dead in the eye.

"No, she loves what I can give her. If I was penniless, she

would not look at me."

He slanted her a cool look as he pulled her to her feet.

Taking her hand, he towed her through the crowd to the dance floor.

But before she could respond, Bronte yelped as strong hands gripped her waist and spun her round.

Out of the corner of her eye, she saw Nico move to intervene.

"Bronte Ludlow, what the hell are you doing here?"

With a delighted laugh, Bronte threw herself into the arms of a tall, tanned man with movie star good looks.

"Oliver."

Lord Oliver Bartholomew's blue, blue eyes sparkled into hers.

He held her at arms' length, looked her up and down and let loose a long wolf-whistle.

"I won't ask how you are, I can see for myself. Where have you been all my life?"

He pulled her to him and dropped her backwards with a passionate kiss.

Then he swung her up as she mussed his sun-kissed hair and patted his cheek.

Still smiling, she grabbed Oliver's hand and turned to Nico who stood absolutely still and gave them a bland stare.

Her pulse jerked at the possessive look in his eye and she heard Oliver chuckle in her ear.

The trouble with Oliver was he was almost like Alexander, a protective older brother and perfectly capable of putting Nico through his paces.

Now Oliver frowned at Nico's sullen face, and she dug him hard in the ribs.

Her message was clear.

Behave.

Wisely, Oliver controlled the grin and kept his face straight as he squeezed her hand in response.

She did the introductions and the men shook hands.

All the time eyeing each other like two alpha wolves sniffing the air.

"Where's Lucy?" Bronte asked, in a futile attempt to break the tense atmosphere.

With one eye on Nico, Oliver merely pressed hot little kisses to the inside of her wrist.

Bronte nearly groaned out loud as Nico narrowed his eyes into slits.

This was ridiculous.

"I'm divorcing her and marrying you."

"Try it, pal," a woman drawled. "And you'll never father children."

With high mutual screams, Bronte and Lucy Bartholomew jumped around like lunatics.

The men grinned at one another and Nico pressed a finger to his ear.

"What are you doing here?" Lucy demanded.

Bronte decided that married life certainly suited her old school friend. She wore a mini dress in ivory lace that contrasted beautifully with her skin. With legs up to her armpits, cropped black shiny hair and dusky complexion, she looked fabulous. A supermodel, Lucy had been scouted at the age of sixteen and never looked back.

"I'm staying with Nico for a few days. Alexander had a car accident... he's going to be absolutely fine," she added quickly as Lucy gasped. "Nico flew me over yesterday."

Lucy cast her expert eye over Nico Ferranti as Oliver introduced his wife.

She turned to Bronte with raised brows and wide eyes.

"Hubba bubba, he's gorgeous. How did you meet him?"

Bronte filled her in.

Lucy caught her in a bone crushing hug.

"How are you holding up?" she whispered in her ear.

"I'm doing really well."

Her friend studied her with serious eyes for a moment.

"You look happy and that makes me happy." Then she gave her a naughty smile. "He's certainly an upgrade from dear old

Jonathan."

"He certainly is."

Bronte turned and found Nico watching her carefully.

She caught his eye and he sent her a slow, sexy smile.

"Now that looks like a hungry man and I don't mean for food," Lucy drawled into her ear.

Oliver gave Bronte a quick kiss on the cheek, and slipped an arm around his wife.

"Darling, if we don't get a move on, we'll be late."

Lucy pecked Bronte's cheek, waving at Nico as she was dragged off.

"Speak soon, honey, I'll break my diet and pay you a visit."

"Nice people." Leading her onto the dance floor, Nico slid his arms around her, swaying to the beat of the music. "For a moment I thought I had competition."

Bronte batted her eyelashes and he sent her a delighted grin.

"Oliver was the first boy to see me naked." She laughed at Nico's pained expression. "I was eighteen months old and he was eight."

"They look good together."

"They've known each other all their lives. They were meant to be."

"Ahh, Bronte the romantic. Come, let us dance."

She had to hand it to him, the man had moves.

Not only that, he could sing, too.

He hummed in her ear to a sexy slow number, twirled her until her head spun to fast music. And rocked and rolled the night away.

Yes, Nico would be the possessive type, she mused, as she shared hot, searing kisses in the back of the car on their way home.

And Bronte decided she didn't give a damn.

Tired, but still nicely buzzed, Bronte sat on the edge of the bed in Nico's apartment.

Taking off her shoes, she caught a glimpse of her reflection in a floor to ceiling mirror propped against the wall.

What had happened to Bronte Ludlow, pastry chef and owner of *Sweet Sensation*?

The sleepy-eyed Bronte in the mirror, looked like a woman who was wildly in love with the man of her dreams.

No, not in love she corrected herself, in lust.

Her heart was safe.

With a white towel slung low on lean hips, Nico entered from the bathroom and pulled her to her feet.

Now he stood behind her, firm fingers smoothed and pressed the flesh across her shoulders. She watched them both in the mirror. They looked good together. They looked right.

Tipping her head back, she enjoyed the moment.

He slid down her zipper, lifting her as the dress pooled at her feet then drew her back against him.

Eyes dark with longing met hers in the mirror.

And the connection was scorching hot and instant.

Her eyes widened in surprise as he placed her hands around his neck then stroked her breasts, his thumbs circling rosy nipples.

She was riveted by the frantic pulse in her neck.

Was that woman with the wild, dazed eyes really her?

Embarrassment flooded her cheeks as she lowered her lashes.

Nico tipped up her chin, his eyes more intense as they met hers in the mirror.

"Watch, see what happens to you when I give you pleasure," he said, without taking his eyes off her face. A gasp escaped from her throat as he ripped off her panties. Hot lips found the spot below her ear that made her purr like a cat. "Hold on to me."

Nico pressed hot kisses along her jaw and she tipped her head back to give him better access. And she utterly surrendered every part of herself to this man. His hands now roved wherever they wanted. It was as if he commanded her quivering flesh. Everywhere he touched her, more than burned. It scorched her skin.

How could she permit him to do this to her?

Fascinated, she could hardly breathe as she watched his hands reach lower, fingers tantalising and teasing her navel.

The woman in the mirror trembled, licked her lips as she rocked her pelvis back and forth in wanton invitation. Under the towel, his rock hard erection jerked into the small of her back.

"Open your legs," he moaned in her ear.

Eyes huge, she complied.

His fingertips stroked around the throbbing bud between her legs. Heat licked under her skin as the orgasm built. It felt good, too good, to have him touch her there. Gentle fingers stroked those sensitive lips, swollen and slick. The evidence of her arousal wept upon his fingers as a dark pleasure shuddered through her.

He took her hand, licked two of her fingers and placed them between her legs.

"Oh! No... I..." Then without a word, his fingers covered hers as they pleasured her.

The woman in the mirror moaned as her legs gave way and together they sank to the floor.

"Watch, see how beautiful you look." Sitting her between his legs, his fingers guided hers into secret places.

"I can't..."

Still his eyes stayed on hers.

"I love looking at you when you come. Let me show you."

His fingers, slick and wet, swirled teasingly around the spot.

That little nub now stood proud and ready.

Oh God, she was burning up, her breath panting now.

Bronte reared up and her cry of release pierced straight into his shaft.

The tenuous control Nico exerted over his raging libido snapped.

He lifted her, tossing her onto the bed. Emerald eyes, wide with aroused surprise, flew to his. He read excitement mixed with nerves and it only made the fire in his groin burn even hotter.

This was no slow seduction that gripped him now, this was a

ravenous hunger.

He was starving.

And he fell upon her.

He loved the smell of her skin.

The taste of her mouth, that flat stomach.

He simply could not get enough of her.

Frantic now, his teeth tugged her nipple, as his hands ruthlessly explored.

Her little cries of pleasure drove him crazy.

The searing lust in his loins sent him over the edge as she bucked under him.

He flipped her onto her hands and knees, lifting her hips ruthlessly and entered her with one hard thrust, then rode her fast and hard.

She screamed and he held still, breath gasping for control as she fisted around him, the after-shocks drained his life-giving fluid and he followed her into oblivion.

Bronte's legs clung around his waist.

Exhausted, she dropped her head on his shoulder as he carried her into the bathroom.

Drowsy, she lay relaxed between his legs, up to her neck in bubbles in a stone bath in the shape of an egg.

He simply held her, his cheek against her hair as he muttered words in Italian.

She could stay like this forever she mused as her mind drifted.

"Come, *cara mia*, you are almost asleep."

Wrapped in a huge white bath towel, he carried her into the bedroom.

Taking great care, he dried her and then tucked her into their bed.

And Bronte felt her eyes sting.

Had anyone ever cared for her like this?

She couldn't remember.

Wouldn't it be wonderful to always be cared for like this?

Naked, she slid under the duvet and into his arms.

Her last thought before she sank into a dreamless sleep was that life just didn't get any better than this.

And she ruthlessly ignored the little voice in her head.

A voice that warned her that good things never lasted and to make the most of it.

Chapter Twenty Two

"I have a meeting."

Bronte looked up from her breakfast.

Today Nico wore a power suit and looked more like the man who owned Ludlow Hall than the man who'd burned up the dance floor last night.

"I have plenty to do. Nico, don't look like that. I don't mind."

She rose, gave him a hug and pressed a kiss on his smooth cheek.

He caught her in a rib crushing embrace, pressing his mouth to her throat.

"Take this." He handed her a Smartphone. "I noticed you using one at home. If you need me, my personal number is at the top of the list. I need a favor?" He gave her an over bright smile that had her narrow her eyes.

"Yes?"

"Pop into Madame's and try on three evening gowns she has selected for the ball. The driver will take you anywhere you want to go."

The pleading look in his dark eyes melted her heart.

"Only three?" At his nod, she gave in. "Okay, but I don't need the driver."

"This is the one."

Madame clapped her hands as Bronte turned in front of her. The designer label made her deeply uneasy. It probably cost a small fortune. But she had to admit, the dress was a dream. Chiffon Elie Saab in ivory and gold silk. Strapless and fitted across the bust, it fell in a glittering waterfall from her hips.

It could have been made for her.

"I'll take it."

"Would you like to try on...?"

Bronte interrupted her with a firm little smile.

"No... thank you."

Madame patted her hand.

"I'll have it boxed and delivered to Nico's apartment." She slanted Bronte a look. "You make him happy. Take care of his heart; he does not give it easily."

"Excuse me?" Stiffly polite, Bronte stared at her.

The woman blushed and took a breath.

"I apologize if I have offended you. Nico is very dear to me." She moved to the window and stared out into the street. "See those boys?"

Bronte moved to her side and saw a couple of very dirty little boys, around nine years old, playing with an ancient football. "He was one of those a long time ago." She turned back to Bronte and smiled. "Nico Ferranti has done well for himself, no?"

He had indeed.

Yet another piece of the puzzle that was Nico, Bronte mused, taking a seat at the same café they'd visited the day before.

Raising her face to the winter sun, she relaxed and soaked up the buzz of Italian voices, the scent of coffee. Just enjoying the moment and the spell Rome had cast over her.

A shadow fell across and she opened her eyes.

The man who had been watching Nico in the cafe yesterday stood before her now.

He wore a grey suit under a camel coat that hugged his wide shoulders.

Imposing, was her first thought.

Her second was he looked just like Nico, but older – late thirties?

He had the same aquiline features, perhaps sharper, with none of Nico's easy humor in his eyes.

Eyes that appeared almost black.

"*Scuse signorina*. You are English?"

The Italian accent was stronger, the voice deeper.

Those dark eyes pinned her to the chair as she nodded.

"May I join you?"

Before she could respond, he settled himself into the chair next to her.

Alarm battled with rabid curiosity as her mind raced.

What on earth could he do to her in a busy café in broad daylight?

Something of her thoughts must have shown in her face.

His mouth kicked.

"I will not harm you, Miss Ludlow. I wish to speak with you about Nico."

She blinked in surprise.

"I have no intention of discussing him with you or anyone else."

His mouth twisted in what could have been a smile.

He placed a business card on the table.

Gabriel Ferranti, CEO of Ferranti Construction.

Bronte placed her palms on the table ready to leave.

Then something in his eyes had her pause.

What was it they said about curiosity?

"Who are you?"

Gabriel stirred sugar into an espresso as the waiter served her another cappuccino.

He watched her carefully.

"I am his brother."

Her eyes flew to his face.

"I'm sorry, but Nico has no family."

The expressions in his face were fleeting, but she caught the shock, replaced by pain, replaced by bitterness and a cold anger.

Perhaps she could have been a little more diplomatic?

Gabriel nodded and placed the tiny cup very carefully on the saucer.

But before he could open his mouth a voice came from behind her.

"*Bastardo*! How dare you speak to her?"

Bronte's head whipped up.

Alarm gripped her heart, her lungs.

Not only at the freezing tone of Nico's voice but at the

suppressed violence that accompanied it.

Nico's dark eyes lasered into the man who sat beside her at the table.

Gabriel stood now, his eyes just as furious as his brother's.

And they were brothers.

There could be no doubt about it.

Bronte's breath caught in her throat.

My God, they could have been twins.

"Are you unhurt?" Nico's furious eyes held hers and she read a dark agony before he hooded his lids.

"I'm fine," she said and desperately tried to catch his eye.

Gabriel's snort of derision brought Nico's head up.

"How dare you approach her," Nico thundered. His voice shook with anger and for a moment Bronte thought he was going to strike out.

She gripped his hand.

"I would have no need to approach her if you had the good manners, and shown a modicum of decent behavior, to respond to our letters and answered our telephone calls."

Nico's voice trembled with suppressed violence. "You *dare* to talk to me about manners and decent behavior? I have nothing to say to you."

Gabriel leaned in closer and spoke in Italian, his voice viciously angry.

Whatever he said, they were nose to nose now and Nico responded through his teeth in Italian.

It brought a hot and angry flush to Gabriel's face.

The whole cafe had gone deathly quiet and Bronte realized every single person was listening.

She stood, trying to squeeze Nico's hand.

He was holding hers so tight he'd almost cut off the blood supply to her fingers.

Desperate, she used a tone her mother had perfected when dealing with her and Alexander when they were at each other's throats.

"Gentlemen! This is not the place to have this conversation. You're drawing too much attention to yourselves."

Gabriel nodded his head and his eyes met hers.

The expression in those dark eyes was so like Nico's it brought a hot lump to her throat.

Bronte recognized desperation when she saw it.

"I apologize for upsetting you, Signorina Ludlow."

With a final remark in Italian to his brother, Gabriel gave her a stiff bow and left.

For a moment Bronte felt lightheaded until she realized she'd been holding her breath.

"What...?"

Nico turned to her, his lips white.

Those eyes were black as coal and lasered into hers.

"Not here. What the *hell* were you thinking?"

Confused, Bronte blinked.

The tone of his voice, hard and cold, had jittery nerves dancing horribly in her stomach.

Her feet fought to keep pace with her racing heart as he strode through the streets, his grip on her arm felt like a vice.

Hang on a minute.

How was any of this her fault?

He was the one who told her he had no family.

And apparently, he'd lied.

He had a brother and God knew what else.

"Nico, slow down."

Her voice sounded high and panicky and it seriously ticked her off.

He ignored her and if anything his pace increased.

He pushed her into the elevator ahead of him.

And she'd be damned if she was going to let him get away with manhandling her like this.

Chest heaving, Bronte rubbed her arm and spun around to face him.

"You lied to me."

He looked as if she'd slapped him.

A bleak sadness whirled in his stormy grey eyes.

He refused to speak to her.

The very air sparked and crackled with a tension that was running too high.

She hated confrontations like this.

They always ended in tears.

Usually hers.

This is the stuff of nightmares, she thought, as he marched her through the door to his apartment.

She jumped like a rabbit under the gun as the door slammed behind them.

Bronte braced herself.

Nico threw his jacket and coat on the floor, loosened his tie and unbuttoned the neck of his shirt.

Genuine distress flooded into his eyes when he looked at her.

And Bronte pressed her fingernails into the palms of her hands.

"You do not know him. So, explain to me. Why were you speaking to him?"

"I..."

Bronte closed her mouth when she realized she had no good answer to his question.

At least, no good answer that would satisfy the fury in his voice.

She realized that to tell him she'd spoken to his brother because he looked and sounded so much like Nico himself made her look and sound utterly ridiculous.

How could she tell him that she'd wanted to understand what made Nico tick?

It was as plain to her as the nose on her face that something had happened to him as a child.

That much was clear to her.

How could she tell him she needed to understand the events from his past that had made him the man he was today?

To help her come to terms with the feelings she had for him, feelings that terrified her.

Face composed, voice level, she studied his face and answered his question with a question of her own.

"Why did you lie to me?"

His eyes were darker than night and she shivered as the shutters came down.

His face was cold and hard.

There was no sign of the Nico Ferranti she knew.

No sign of the man with whom she'd fallen irrevocably in love with.

"My personal life is none of your business," he told her in a tone that was like a whip over her frayed nerves.

Bronte nodded.

The clipped response was just what she'd expected.

He was treating her exactly like he'd treated the woman in the club last night.

Nausea rolled up into her throat and she moved on legs that weren't quite steady to the bedroom.

He followed her, pulled her round to face him.

"My father is dying."

Her eyes clung to his.

His father?

Okay, so he had a brother and a very sick father.

That explained the undercurrent of sadness within Gabriel.

"I am sorry, Nico."

"Apparently, he wishes to see me."

"You've never met him?"

"No."

Pity for him rose into her throat but Bronte knew better than to show it. He would never forgive her. Instead she sank to the edge of the bed. And she saw something else. Saw it quite clearly. Nico Ferranti did not forgive. She'd seen that last night with the woman at the nightclub. Nico saw things in black and white with no grey areas. The man had defined lines about how he ran his life.

And Bronte knew she'd stepped over a line with Nico today by talking to his brother.

He sat on the edge of the bed now with his head in his hands.

"He is your father and you have a brother? A family?"

He lifted his head and shot her a look of smouldering impatience.

"*Why* did you speak to him? My family has nothing to do with you."

It had everything to do with her, she thought.

She loved him.

As she sat right next to him, she could admit it now.

He was so alone in his life.

Nico rose and stalked into the sitting room.

He poured himself a cognac and swallowed it in one.

Bronte stood at the bedroom door, uncertain and unsure as she watched him.

And it took all the courage she had to gather herself and say the words he needed to hear.

"You should make a real effort to build a bridge between you and your family, Nico. I know what it's like to have a parent die with words unsaid. Words unspoken breed anger, they breed fear and they breed mistrust."

Nico turned to her and looked as if he wanted to strangle her.

"What are you talking about?"

She felt a glimmer of hope.

At least he was listening to her.

"I'm talking about my mother. There were things... she should have told me. Desperately important things that I had a right to know."

She jumped as his brandy glass shattered against the wall.

"You have no right to interfere in my life," he roared.

Chin high, eyes flashing, Bronte stood her ground.

"You will live to regret it every day of your life if you do not listen to what your father and your brother have to say. What happened to *'We must always have the truth between us.'*?"

Eyes weary now, he stared at her and shook his head.

"You know nothing about me. You do not understand."

"Then tell me. Make me understand."

With a heavy heart, she witnessed him struggle with inner turmoil and felt so helpless.

There was nothing she could do for Nico if he refused to trust her.

She turned away.

"I lost my mother when I was ten." He sank into a sofa and laid his head back. Eyes wide, he stared hard at the ceiling. "When she became pregnant with me, my grandfather threw her out, disowned her. Her lover was a married man with a young son. She died in poverty, sick and alone. After she died, my grandfather had an attack of conscience and took me in. He reminded me of the circumstances surrounding my birth every single day."

She cleared the lump in her throat, her heart breaking for the sad little boy she saw in the man.

A man who had never fully healed, she realized and sat opposite him.

He took a deep breath and continued.

"My grandfather was a vicious and unforgiving bastard. But at least he gave me an education. He told me everything I need to know about my biological father. My father left my mother and me to starve on the streets. I will have nothing to do with him or his son."

Bronte blinked.

Her mind racing, surely he could see that his grandfather was just as responsible for what happened to Nico and his poor mother?

"Your grandfather?"

"He died twelve years ago and I built up my business from his legacy." He turned tormented eyes to her. "I will have the rest of my life tainted by my father, Bronte. He is dead to me."

Okay.

She could understand his feelings.

Even if she didn't agree with them.

But there was a fatal flaw in his thinking.

She wondered why he couldn't see it.

"Why would you listen to the views of a bitter and angry man who turned his back on his daughter and her baby?"

She moved to sit beside him, took his hand and rubbed the back of his knuckles.

He stared at the ceiling, jaw clenched as she continued.

"Yes, your father might be a monster and your brother even

worse, but unless you hear the facts for yourself, how will you ever know the truth?"

He pulled his hand from hers and stood.

She recognized the expression.

It was the same one on his face when he'd dealt with the woman in the nightclub.

Uncompromising.

Unforgiving.

Cold.

Hard.

Nerves dried her mouth.

"I do not wish to discuss it further."

"I'm being your friend, Nico," she whispered.

The expression in his eyes chilled her to the bone.

"You have listened to my enemy and taken his side. Is that how you treat a friend?"

"I have not taken sides, Nico," she whispered.

She had not taken any side.

But her conscience told her that she had hurt him.

"Yes, Bronte, you have and you know it." The look on his face made her eyes sting. "I made a choice years ago on the path I wish to take through life. You have no right to interfere with that decision."

Her heart broke in her chest, she could actually feel it.

The blinders she'd been wearing were torn from her eyes.

Alexander was right.

Nico had no heart, no forgiveness.

He was never the man she thought he was.

Even worse, he would never become the man she knew he could be.

What a terrible waste.

And even though her heart was breaking, she still couldn't give up.

Not without a fight.

"I'm the best friend you will ever have, Nico. Words unspoken break hearts. You should remember that."

He gave her a cold, level look.

And she knew she'd lost him.
"You should pack," he said. "We are leaving."

Chapter Twenty Three

"I spoke to our boy. He's loving Lake Como and a little bird tells me you, Missy, were doing the rumba in Rome with a hawt Italian."

Rosie danced into the kitchen of *Sweet Sensation* on Friday morning and stopped dead.

Every surface shone like a mirror.

She and her team had left it in pristine condition yesterday.

However, this morning stainless steel glittered and glass gleamed like polished diamonds.

"Can I take it you had a call from Lucy?" Bronte muttered, rubbing the stainless steel gas hob, too keenly focused on the job in hand to look at Rosie.

She needed to keep busy.

She needed to stop her mind reliving over and over again the roller-coaster of the last week.

How could she climb so high and fall so far in such a short time?

The journey home had been a living hell.

Nico hadn't looked at her or spoken a single word.

Every time she closed her eyes he was there.

She hadn't slept a wink last night.

Her eyes swam and a hot fist gripped her throat.

Oh God, she had so much to do.

The whole thing, their affair, the way they'd broken up, was nothing short of a waking nightmare.

She put her back into polishing with a concentration and energy that made her best friend narrow her eyes and purse her lips.

Rosie watched with interest as Bronte scoured the hob as if she'd found the source of the Ebola virus.

"Er... can I just say the kitchen was spotless when I left it last night."

Frantic now, breath panting, Bronte polished the hob with a dry cloth.

"I know it was."

"Need a hug?"

Rosie put her arms around her.

Exhausted, Bronte placed her aching head on Rosie's shoulder.

"I'm not crying."

Rosie rubbed her back.

"Did he hurt you?"

With a sigh, Bronte slumped into a chair and pressed her fingertips into burning eyes.

"No, I hurt him."

Rosie stared, wagged a finger.

"Not possible. You don't have a nasty bone in your body."

Which was a typical Rosie thing to say.

She wasn't Miss Sweetness and Light all the time, Bronte knew herself too well.

She had her temper just like the next person.

"I hurt him by trying to help him."

"Well, that's all right then. Whatever you did, you did it with the best of intentions. He's a big boy. He'll get over it."

"I don't think so."

"Okay. What did you do?"

For the first time in her life, Bronte knew she couldn't share a secret with her best friend.

Because it wasn't her secret to share.

She may have crossed one line with Nico, but she certainly wasn't going to cross another.

She rubbed Rosie's hand.

"He doesn't trust me with the truth."

Rosie scanned her face, then gave her a small smile.

"You care for him?"

Bronte nodded then rested her brow on folded arms.

"I more than care for him." She raised her head. "I'm in love with him."

This, she realized, was the last thing she needed.

Nico was furious with her.

Last night when they'd arrived home, he'd cut her dead.

And Bronte admitted now (wasn't it just great to be wise after the event) that it simply wasn't in her make-up to have intimacy with a man without a deep emotional connection.

What on earth had made her believe she could do it?

What the hell had she been thinking?

She stood, paced with jerky steps to the window and back again.

Rosie watched her with big eyes.

"What am I going to do?" she demanded, eyes too bright.

Her best friend ran her tongue along the edge of her teeth.

"What I'm about to say, I say with love. Have you told him about your mother's letter? Have you told him about your father, how you've found him? Have you told him about your own personal situation?" Rosie raised a brow. "By the surprised look on your face, I'll take that as a no."

Stunned, Bronte stared at her friend.

She'd been so full of hurt, righteous indignation and she'd taken the high ground about Nico not opening his heart to her, to trust her. But she didn't walk the talk, did she? And she'd thought him judgemental?

"I'm a hypocrite."

Rosie made a face.

"I wouldn't go that far."

Keeping a weather eye on Bronte, she got up, opened a cupboard and took out two mugs.

"You've had a lot of big life events on your plate lately. And you have a few more to deal with at the moment." She poured coffee from a pot and handed the mug to her. "What was going to be a quick tumble in Rome has turned into something quite different. But you cannot expect Nico to trust you if you don't trust him."

Bronte took her coffee to the French doors and stared unseeing into her garden.

She leaned her throbbing head against the window with a distinct feeling of déjà vu.

"It's too late for that. He told me he'll never marry or have children, but what if he changes his mind? The chances of me having a family are virtually zero. And if there's anyone who desperately needs family, it's Nico."

Jonathan had rejected her when she'd needed support.

And he'd been quite happy to tell her why.

Perhaps he'd realized that she'd never really loved him the way he needed to be loved?

Perhaps he'd realized that Bronte had held a part of herself back from him?

The physical attraction between her and her fiancé, Bronte realized, had been tepid at best. In the beginning when she'd told him there would be no children, Jonathan said he understood, was supportive, and then that, too, had changed.

What did that say about her ability to judge the character of another?

In the two years she'd been with him, Jonathan had never let her see his mercenary or philandering side.

Nico she'd only known for a matter of days.

How could she possibly trust him with her secrets?

What if he rejected her again?

How would she be able to handle that rejection?

The answer was that she wouldn't be able to handle it.

Not again.

No, she couldn't do it.

Rosie watched her closely.

"I hope you're not comparing Nico's behavior with you to Jonathan's? Because that's just insulting. How can you put every male in the same category?" Annoyance made Rosie's tone sharp and Bronte winced.

"I have no idea how Nico feels about me."

But she'd put good money on it that at the moment Nico Ferranti wished he'd never laid eyes on her. And even if he did have feelings for her, it wouldn't be fair to dump her issues on top of his own.

"There are times when I want to hit you over the head with a blunt instrument." Rosie banged her brow on the table, twice, and raised her head. "Nico treats you like a queen. And if Lucy Bartholomew believes he is and I quote, smitten, that's good enough for me. What do want the man to do, get down on one knee?"

The blood drained from Bronte's face.

Rosie swore in realization of what she'd just said.

Bronte closed her eyes.

No, she couldn't do it to him.

She couldn't do it to herself if he rejected her.

Nico deserved a future with a woman who could give him the family life he so desperately needed. He'd been so good with the little Italian boy in the cafe, she remembered with a pang.

The whole thing had been great while it lasted.

Eyes wide, Rosie took her hand.

"Bronte, you know I didn't mean it like that."

If there was one person on earth who was constant and never changed, it was Rosie.

Bronte reassured her friend. "I know you're only trying to help, but I can't do it. I need to deal with the future in my own way and in my own time."

His Smartphone pinged.

Sitting in the General Manager's office at Ludlow Hall, Nico scrolled down his messages.

Another email from Gabriel.

For years he had managed to conveniently push his father and half-brother to the back of his mind. But now first contact had been made. Nico still had plenty of uncertain feelings about the whole thing, but he'd finally accepted that a long overdue dialogue had begun.

The anger he'd embraced and kept close to him like a lover on the return journey, was not as bitter or intense this morning. Gabriel had made it clear that he'd approached Bronte in the first instance, and not given her any choice but to talk to him. When Nico felt able to speak to him, Gabriel would be available. But time was short, their father was fading fast.

There were so many questions Nico wished he could have asked his mother. She'd told him his father was a good man, but flawed. His father already had a wife and child and his mother had been too young to resist the first flush of passion and affection shown her by a man.

Never a robust woman, she had been plagued by ill health.

His grandfather's accusations about his father, that he was a criminal connected to organized crime were, Gabriel had made crystal clear, a lie. He might not be a saint, but their father was no crook.

Nico now wondered if anything his grandfather had said was true.

Bronte's words buzzed around his mind like mosquitoes.

She was right.

Unsaid words did breed anger, mistrust and pain.

Nico groaned into his hands.

And he had treated her in an appalling fashion.

He should have brought Bronte home instead of indulging himself and showing her a good time in Rome.

Bronte should never have become involved in his family affairs.

He had laid the blame, even taken his anger out on her.

That had been a mistake.

Perhaps meeting her in the first place had been a mistake?

His life up until then had been simple and uncomplicated before she entered it.

Nico dragged his hands through his hair.

He gave up.

Who the hell was he kidding?

He couldn't sleep if she wasn't in his bed.

When he closed his eyes she was there.

He could smell her, feel that smooth skin and hear those soft sighs as he loved her.

The memory of the taste of her drove him wild.

His heart thundered in his chest and he rubbed the spot with the flat of his hand. His stomach felt as if a hard fist had plunged into it. Perspiration beaded on his top lip.

He loved her.

A heady mix of panic, fury and delirious happiness surged through his system.

He stood, paced to the door of his suite and back again.

Dio mio, he was in *love* with her.

What was he going to do?

How could this have happened?

A man did not fall in love with a woman within days.

Did he?

He sank to the couch, stared unseeing at the wall.

The things he'd said to her, how he didn't do commitment, marriage or children, brought a flush to his cheeks.

He was a fool.

Frustrated annoyance brought him to his feet to pace.

How was he going to make her love him?

But then, when had he ever failed to get what he wanted or needed?

Words would be useless with Bronte, he realized as he continued to pace.

She'd never believe him, not after what Jonathan had done to her.

Nico knew he needed to *show* her he loved her rather than tell her.

Actions spoke louder and meant more, much more.

He'd find other premises for her business and he would live with her at The Dower House.

Nico picked up the phone.

Chapter Twenty Four

The tangle of nerves in Bronte's stomach tied themselves into a tight knot as the car Nico had sent for her joined the queue to drop her off at the entrance to Ludlow Hall.

She told herself it wasn't disappointment but relief she was feeling that he hadn't come in person to take her to the Ball.

There was plenty to be thankful for in her life.

The dinner in London last night with her father had been wonderful.

Of course, she could have done without the gossip columns this morning speculating on why Carl Terlezki was wining and dining a woman young enough to be his daughter. If they only knew. Her father's phone call this morning had reassured her and made her feel better. The truth would come out in due course, but not until Alexander had returned, met Carl and they came up with a plan on how to handle the truth coming out in the media.

Then she saw Nico waiting for her at the entrance to Ludlow Hall.

He looked fabulous in black Armani.

Her mouth dried with nerves and Bronte ordered herself to remain calm.

Nico opened the car door and took her hand.

His eyes, grey and intense, studied her features as if he hadn't seen her in a year rather than almost two days.

"*Grazie*, for coming. You look spectacular this evening."

His deep voice and his sinful Italian accent brought her out in goose bumps.

He brought her fingers to his lips and she felt the usual little hum in her system.

If the look in his eyes was anything to go by the Elie Saab gown was a hit.

Shame she could care less.

Well, at least he was being polite and for that Bronte was eternally grateful.

Perhaps they could remain friends?

He certainly looked dark and dangerous in his tuxedo.

The key to getting through the evening, she'd decided, was to play it cool. Keep the mood light and show him there were no hard feelings and agree to draw a line under the whole thing.

Pity she couldn't ignore the way his hand pressed on the small of her back and pulsed heat through her veins.

They walked into the ballroom and Nico kept his fingers on her elbow.

He snagged a couple of glasses of champagne from a passing waiter and handed her one.

"Thank you."

She kept her voice steady and the tone friendly, desperately telling herself she could do this.

Her eyes scanned the room.

The usual suspects, as she thought of them, were all here and dressed up like peacocks.

Among them were the great and the good of the county, heads of business, the local MP and his wife.

Rosie whirled past with a beaming young man.

She winked at Bronte and sent a very cool look to Nico.

A Nico who shuffled his feet and who cleared his throat at her side.

He took her glass, placed it on a table with his and turned to her.

The tune changed.

And in a smooth move, Nico slid Bronte into his arms, swaying in time to the music.

He studied her face.

His hand pressed on her lower back but she went stiff in his arms as she resisted his attempt to pull her close.

"We need to talk about what happened in Rome," he said to

the top of her head.

Her eyes flicked to his before she focused intently on his chin.

"There's nothing to talk about. You were quite right. Your private life has nothing to do with me."

The cool tone with the polite delivery told him he was not forgiven.

She held herself rigid in his arms.

"I want you in my life."

The words were said before he realized it and this time she met his gaze.

Her green eyes remained steady on his.

Nico thought he read regret and something else he couldn't quite define.

"You can't have everything you want."

Her eyes dropped to his chin.

"*Si,* I know this, but I am trying to apologize." Apologizing was not something that came easily to him. It was a unique feeling and not altogether pleasant. Neither was the feeling of desperation. Couldn't Bronte see he was serious? Confused and wrong footed, Nico tried again. "I am sorry, *cara mia*, for my behavior."

Bronte blinked twice and gave a little shrug of her slim shoulders.

"Apology accepted. But as you said, your life and what you do with it isn't any of my business."

He trailed a lazy finger down the silky skin of her neck.

She didn't shiver or tremble this time, he noticed with a small frown.

Her vivid green eyes were difficult to read tonight and although she smiled, it appeared remote.

"I see you've hit the headlines," he said now.

Her little jerk in his arms had him look at her carefully.

Heat flared in her cheeks.

A heat that intrigued him and worried him all at the same time.

"He's an old family friend," she said, eyes riveted to his chin.

She held herself immobile in his arms now.

Strain darkened those fabulous green eyes.

"I know," he said, trying to work out what the hell was wrong with her. "Alexander told me."

Now she appeared to be fascinated by his tie.

Anxiety warred with fear, a rare emotion for him.

Together, they marched up his spine.

They needed to clear the air, he told himself.

What he wanted to do, needed to do, was to kiss her senseless, but instinct warned him that it was neither the time nor the place.

The music finished and Bronte tugged her hand, but he held it firm as he escorted her to the edge of the dance floor and Rosie.

"Oh God, look who's here."

Nico caught Rosie's disgusted mutter to Bronte.

He turned as a tall fair haired man approached with his arm around a very pregnant blonde.

The atmosphere around them hummed with latent hostility and Bronte's nervous strain.

Her grip on his hand tightened convulsively and he looked at her.

Bronte's face was deathly pale now, but it was the expression in her eyes that ripped his heart in two. They were filled with a mix of despair, pain and longing. She blinked and the look had gone, but her grip almost stopped the circulation to his fingers.

"Bronte, how are you?" the man said.

Bronte's smile did not reach her eyes.

"Good evening, Jonathan, Annabel."

Her voice was too stiff, the tone too polite.

Jonathan beamed a smile in the general direction of the group and introduced his wife.

A woman who did not look particularly comfortable.

Jonathan moved towards Bronte with a calculating gleam in his pale blue eyes.

"May I have this dance? For old times' sake?"

Bronte hesitated, shrugged and moved towards the dance

floor, ignoring Jonathan's outstretched hand.

Standing there feeling helpless Nico fought the urge to plant a fist in Jonathan's smooth, handsome face.

Bronte narrowed her eyes at Jonathan's triumphant smile, but did not resist as he led her on to the floor.

His pregnant wife had caught her off balance and although she was all too aware of the speculative glances and murmured voices in the room, she chose to ignore them.

Two babies within eighteen months.

My, my, Jonathan was certainly a busy boy.

Although it occurred to her now that poor Annabel didn't look a happy bunny.

Bronte found she genuinely felt sorry for the girl.

"You're looking particularly gorgeous." Missing nothing, Jonathan's cold blue eyes slid over her dress.

Bronte wasn't in the mood for small talk.

"What do you want?"

The feel of his hand on her back did nothing for her, no chemistry, no shiver of awareness.

Nothing.

She noticed he had the grace to blush, even as his eyes flicked toward Nico.

A Nico who was watching them like a hawk.

"I hear you're selling The Dower House."

She blinked in surprise.

Her brows met as she leaned back to study his face.

"I don't know where you heard that piece of gossip. But I can tell you categorically it is not true."

"Come on, Bronte. You know in my business I hear about the decent properties coming onto the market first." His family owned an estate agents and auction house. He also had a cousin in the planning authority. Yes, she remembered Jonathan always kept his ear close to the ground.

"I don't know what you're talking about."

He flicked another, rather unpleasant, look towards Nico.

"You should speak to your new boyfriend."

"Excuse me?" Why had she never noticed his weak mouth

before? Or the sly look in his eyes? What on earth had she been thinking to even have considered marrying this creep? "You're talking in riddles this evening, Jonathan. I find it quite tedious."

He wasn't used to anyone, especially her, speaking to him in that tone.

By the clench of his jaw, she could tell he didn't like the change.

"He's been asking questions about planning permission for a helicopter landing pad to be built on Dower House land and changes to the house itself. He said it was hypothetical, since he doesn't own The Dower House, yet. Before you accept an offer, you should get independent valuations. I'd give you a good price for it. It's the perfect family home for us."

Bronte's pulse buzzed like angry bees in her ears.

What the hell was this?

She knew Jonathan was saying nothing but the truth.

The man always had his eye on the main chance.

But what on earth was Nico Ferranti doing asking questions to planners about *her* house?

Had Nico's apology this evening meant nothing?

Her tired brain was finding it hard to compute.

Nico knew she wasn't selling.

And he *still* wanted the house?

The sense of betrayal almost floored her.

And as for Jonathan, she wondered why the hell she was so shocked?

It was quite clear to her now that both men had always had their own agendas and were prepared to walk over her to achieve them.

The room tilted and then Bronte remembered to breathe.

Nausea hit her like a tsunami.

She needed to get out here.

Jonathan watched her reactions, his eyes reminded her of a coiled snake watching a timid mouse.

Utter fury hit Bronte so hard her hand made a fist.

Before she made a scene and actually struck him, Bronte pushed him away.

"Go to hell!"

She spun on her heel and almost ran from the room.

"Uh oh, looks like trouble."

Rosie moved to intercept Bronte but Nico put a hand on her arm.

"Let me."

Rosie looked at his hand and then up at him.

"Take care of her."

"I will."

Since Bronte had disappeared in that general direction, Nico headed for the ladies powder room. The ache in his heart as he'd watched her dancing with her ex-fiancé was nothing compared to the pain he felt at the absolute certainty Bronte was still in love with the man.

Her reaction when he arrived with his wife, and the upset now, proved it.

"Is Miss Ludlow in there?" He asked the attendant.

She shook her head.

"I think she left, sir," she said pointing towards the entrance.

Frowning, Nico picked up speed and exited in time to see the car she'd arrived in glide down the driveway.

Patting his pockets for his keys, Nico sprinted for his car.

Nico drew his car to a halt at the rear of the Dower House.

The light was on in the kitchen.

Fingertips tapping the steering wheel, for a moment he wondered if he was doing the right thing. Perhaps it would be better to let her lick her wounds in private? But then he told himself that was complete cowardice.

The point was that Bronte needed him, even if she did not know it.

After a couple of knocks, he turned the handle.

And as usual Bronte hadn't locked the door.

He entered.

To see her standing there, shaking as she sipped what appeared to be cognac, her eyes huge and dazed with shock, broke his heart.

"Bronte?"

He moved fast.

Gathering her close his hands ran up and down her back.

It took him a moment, but he realized something was off.

She held herself absolutely rigid in his arms.

He drew back to study her face.

It wasn't heartbreak Nico read, but pure undiluted rage.

He let his hands drop to his sides.

She turned, walked towards the sink and spun around to face him.

Her eyes shot scorching darts of emerald fury.

Bronte knocked back the rest cognac and threw the glass at him.

Nico ducked just in time as it smashed against the wall behind his head.

"You son-of-a-bitch," she snarled. "Bronte, do not interfere in my business," she mimicked his accent as she stalked towards him.

She looked murderous.

Nico shook his head, totally at a loss.

What the hell had *he* done?

"Did you, or did you not, query the local planning department about a landing strip on *my* land and structural changes to *my* house?" She held up a hand as he winced, his throat suddenly dry as his pulse kicked. "I'll take that as a yes, shall I?"

"I can explain."

"I'll just bet you can, you snake."

"You are upset. I could see how he hurt you, *cara mia*. Believe me you will get over him."

Her chin whipped up.

Stormy emerald eyes met his and narrowed into icy slits.

"How *he* hurt me? Compared to you, Jonathan is a rank amateur." She circled around him. "It doesn't matter a hot damn to you what my home means to me, does it?"

"Of course it does."

"When did you speak to the planning department?"

His pulse jerked simultaneously with the lurch in his gut.

Nico licked his bottom lip and had the dizzy sensation of standing on the edge of a precipice.

"Yesterday, but I can explain..."

She held up her hand like a traffic cop.

"Shut up! I do not want to hear it."

Desperate now, voice pleading, he tried again.

"Bronte, I care for you."

She whirled around and leaned on the sink and took a deep breath, her head bowed.

Keep calm, Nico told himself.

She was a reasonable woman.

Or she would be once she cooled down.

She turned to him her face bone white, anger leaking out of her like a deflated balloon.

"As a matter of interest, since you care for me. Where was my business and my employees supposed to go? Where was I going to live or had that thought not occurred to you?"

Hope sprang in his chest.

She was going to listen to him.

He kept his voice soft, the tone friendly.

"I have already found the perfect place for the business to relocate, just outside town, where..."

The look on her face stopped him in his tracks.

Eyes huge, Bronte merely shook her head and studied him with unconcealed amazement.

Nico immediately realized his mistake.

But if he could only get her to listen to him and his plans to live with her here in the Dower House.

He moved towards her.

"Stay back!" Chin high, she drew herself up to her full height, pure steel in those magnificent eyes. "You care for no one and nothing except yourself." She took a step forward and he stepped back. "Do you have *any* idea what you've done to me tonight? Jonathan made me an offer tonight. He told me this house would be the perfect place to bring up *his* family. Do you have any idea what that did to me?"

He was beginning to see.

A hot, hard lump lodged in his gut as she stepped forward again, eyes filled to the brim with pain and longing.

"You can live anywhere in the world. Why on earth do you have to live here?"

At last, she was going to listen to him.

"I need a base, a proper home. The Dower House would be perfect..." She flinched as if he'd slapped her and he hesitated. It is time I settled down with you, he desperately wanted to add. But now he spoke with his head instead of his heart. "I can see you are still in love with him."

For an instant her eyes widened in stunned surprise, before she sank into a chair.

Bronte frowned as she cleared her throat.

Then she studied a fingernail for an endless moment.

"What gave you the idea that I am still in love with Jonathan?" Her voice was hoarse, filled to the brim with pain.

She looked too pale, too fragile.

His heart wrenched in his chest.

"You almost broke my fingers when you saw him this evening."

She said nothing, just continued to stare at her fingernail.

He didn't miss the hectic pulse in her throat or the rapid blinking of her eyes.

Nico narrowed his own as he studied her.

In his business, timing was everything.

Running a frustrated hand through his hair, around his neck, he knew now for certain that Bronte was in love with another man.

She'd not denied it, which meant she needed time to heal.

The time had come for him to draw back, to re-group. They had a deep connection. He did not believe it was only a physical attraction on her part. Everything between them had happened too fast, burned too hot and too intense.

Patience, Nico told himself.

He would give her time to heal, and take her advice to see his father, get to know his brother.

Show her she was right.

But his battered heart waged a bitter war between fury and grief.

And Nico wondered if he would ever get over the events of this night.

Bronte sat, fingertips rubbing her forehead.

For the first time she looked totally defeated.

The need to pull her into his arms, offer her his heart, his life, made Nico light-headed.

Instead he pulled up a chair and sat opposite her.

Elbows on his knees, hands clasped, he leaned forward.

"Bronte. I have handled this whole thing very badly."

She licked her top lip as her eyes, empty now, met his.

"That is an understatement."

"I am leaving for Rome tomorrow, but I shall return in a couple of days."

She took a breath, nodded, as they rose in unison.

"Nico?" He turned to her. "I want you to leave me alone."

If he wanted her to trust him then they needed the truth between them.

"I cannot do that."

Chapter Twenty Five

"What do you mean you will not be available for the next two weeks?"

Bronte wore a black business suit and sat in front of Nico's desk with a spreadsheet of wedding functions between them.

He looked put out she thought, ruthlessly ignoring the pang in her heart. These days, he treated her as if she was a friend rather than an ex-lover. Don't go there, she ordered herself. But after four hellish weeks, she still missed him desperately.

He'd been the perfect gentleman at their twice weekly meetings, easy to work with and the consummate professional. He took frequent trips to Rome, usually over the weekend. The insight into how he ran his business had been illuminating, too. He ran a tight ship with capable people. In fact, he didn't really need to see her at all since his PA was super-efficient and could easily take the meetings, but he'd insisted.

Twice he'd invited her out to dinner with him and twice she'd said no. So he'd stopped asking and Bronte told herself she wasn't disappointed. He'd tried to talk to her about The Dower House, but she refused to discuss it with him.

It was all for the best.

Alexander was due back tomorrow and she expected Nico to move on.

"I'm taking a break from *Sweet Sensation* from this Friday," she told him. "Rosie has the team well-organized."

Nico gave her a level look, cocked his head as he studied her face.

"You look tired. A holiday will do you good."

She was about to say it wasn't exactly a holiday, but caught herself in time. They didn't talk about personal things these days.

Then her eye spotted the black photo frame to the right of the desk that held her drawing. He'd framed it? She picked it up with a hand that wasn't quite steady. In the bottom left hand corner it said - drawn by Bronte - and the date.

Her eyes met his.

Her chest felt tight with an emotion she didn't want or need.

"You framed it? But... why?"

She placed it carefully on the desk.

"It reminds me of one of the best days of my life."

His voice, soft and husky, sent shivers up her spine.

Bronte kept her eyes on his, fascinated by what she saw in them, for her.

Oh no.

She wasn't going to do this with him.

Not now.

On shaky legs she rose to leave.

Nico moved around the desk and took her hand for the first time since the scene in her kitchen on the night of the Ball.

He held her fingers in a comfortable, friendly manner and his eyes twinkled as heat soared into her cheeks along with a flood of awareness.

"Two weeks seems a long time for a workaholic like you. Where are you going?"

His thumb ran across her knuckles and her mind went blank.

Why wouldn't her brain function?

She blinked into his face which seemed too close all of a sudden.

His head moved closer and she leaned back as his eyes, dark and intent, held hers.

Saliva dried in her mouth and she licked her bottom lip.

The heat of his body, the unique scent of his skin mingled with his signature cologne and she almost purred.

He stared at her mouth as if he'd never seen it before.

Oh, God, he was going to kiss her.

She trembled and his eyes flew to hers.

"France. It's a busman's holiday." She had an eureka

moment. "You know, learning new techniques and ah... new ways of doing things. Got to keep one step ahead of the competition, new skills, etc," she babbled in desperation.

He stepped back and leaned against the desk, his expression quizzical.

She felt almost faint with relief.

"Where are you going in France?"

"Paris, it's the pastry capital of the world."

She shrugged into her coat, gathered up her belongings and moved at speed towards the door.

"Bronte."

His voice brought her out in goose bumps.

With her hand on the door handle, she turned.

"Yes?"

"I will miss you, *cara mia*."

His voice sounded wistful. Even as he kept his eyes on hers she read warmth mixed with a bone weary sadness. It brought her heart to her throat. For an instant she wanted to throw herself into his arms.

Then common sense prevailed.

She took a breath and blinked away the mist in front of her eyes.

"Goodbye, Nico."

He had missed something.

Something important.

The feeling refused to leave Nico as he watched her from the window get into her car and drive away.

Cristo, she was killing him. Seeing her only twice a week was killing him. She refused to let him apologize. He narrowed his eyes as her car disappeared down the long driveway. And she was too thin.

Again the feeling that something was wrong and he was missing a big part of the puzzle washed over him. Alexander was due back tomorrow and Nico would talk to him.

How the mighty have fallen, he mused, as anxiety ran up his spine. He knew his friend did not approve of him having a relationship with his sister, but Nico was not only a changed man. He was a desperate man. He would beg for Alexander's help if he had to.

With a heavy heart, Nico sat behind the desk and tapped his fingers on a pile of newspapers. A busman's holiday? Bronte? He did not believe it for a second. Plus, it was the first time she had mentioned it.

He flicked through the paper and on page four his eyes went wide.

Bronte Ludlow was shown in the arms of an *'Old friend of the Ludlow family'* wealthy financier, Carl Terlezki.

In one photo the happy couple were having what appeared to be an animated dinner conversation, Bronte's hand held by Carl's across the table. Her eyes were sparkling and her smile beamed out of the page. In another picture they were walking arm and arm down Oxford Street. The last one showed her being held close, her cheek on his chest as he stroked her hair. *Bastardo!* He simply could not believe what he was seeing. What was she doing with a man who was old enough to be her father? But what utterly destroyed Nico was the look of utter happiness on her face.

Shock roared through his system as he read the last sentence again and again.

Bronte Ludlow and financier Carl Terlezki were due to fly out to France for a two week holiday. The newspaper didn't exactly say they were in the middle of a hot affair, just that both looked very happy together.

And God dammit all to hell, they *did* look very happy together.

Bronte looked happy.

He couldn't deny it.

Sweat beaded Nico's forehead.

But... Surely the man was too old for her?

Due to his grand plan of taking it slow with Bronte was it possible that by doing nothing, Nico had let another man slide under his guard and capture Bronte's heart?

Had he lost her?

The memory of her phone call to 'Carol' when they were in Rome spun into his mind now. *Dio mio.* He'd put down her breathy low voice to nerves and being upset over Alexander's accident. Had Bronte been seeing Carl when Nico had been making love to her in Rome?

Nico shook his head, refusing to believe it.

But there had been nothing to stop her seeing Carl Terlezki, had there?

As far as Bronte Ludlow was concerned her personal relationship with Nico Ferranti was at an end.

Checking his watch, Nico knew there was no time to go after her now.

He had back to back appointments.

Tonight.

He would see her tonight and sort out the whole sorry mess for once and for all.

Chapter Twenty Six

"How did the meeting go?"

Rosie lifted her head from her work in progress, icing one tier of a three tier wedding cake. She held a spatula in one hand and a bowl of snowy icing in the other.

"Fine, but I am seriously pissed off," Bronte said in the voice of utter disgust. "Someone ran a key right down the side of my car in town and gouged 'bitch' on the bonnet. The garage has quoted me a fortune to fix it."

Rosie narrowed her eyes.

"Did you report it to the police?"

"Yep, I popped into the station, but I doubt they'll be much use."

"You never know, they might have caught something on CCTV. No wonder you look like dirty dish water."

Bronte tossed her best friend a look as she flopped into a chair.

"Gee, thanks for that."

She tried and failed to hide a yawn.

Her nerves were shot.

Every close contact with Nico left her reeling every single time.

It was as if he sucked the life blood and energy from her.

Rosie glared and glowered at the same time.

"You need a break. Ten hour days are ridiculous and you know it."

"Please, give it a rest."

"It's a displacement activity."

"Wow, you would give Dr. Phil a run for his money."

"Yeah, well, Dr. Phil would agree with me. At the rate you're going, we're going to need another freezer."

Rosie might be irritated now but she'd thank her one day

when there was an emergency to deal with. Perhaps, Bronte admitted, she had gone over the top a little, but the sense of satisfaction she gained knowing that different cake fillings were ready and waiting made it all worth it. Not to mention the variety of sponges. The coffee mocha with grated walnuts had been a triumph.

It gave her a warm glow every time an idea worked.

Bronte topped up her coffee from the pot, took a sip and made a face.

"Yuk. This coffee's off."

Rosie took the cup, sipped, tasted and sipped again.

"Taste's fine to me."

Bronte sniffed it, shuddered, rose and emptied it down the sink.

"Ugh, there's definitely something wrong with it."

She poured herself a glass of water and drank.

Rosie leaned back against the work surface and crossed her ankles.

"You okay? You look a little peaky." Her eyes went narrow and thoughtful as Bronte yawned again. "Your appetite is off and you've lost weight."

"I'm not sleeping. I don't know what's the matter with me."

"Alexander is back tomorrow and I'll be here, too, to make sure his meeting with Carl goes well. They'll like each other, try to stop worrying." Rosie took a sip of her coffee and grinned. "I'm surprised Nico didn't mention all the stuff in the gossip columns about you and your old sugar daddy, you slut. The phone has been ringing off the hook with people wanting all the goss."

Bronte stifled another yawn and shook her head, then wished she hadn't as the room spun.

"You would think they'd have something more important to write about. Poor Carl, he doesn't know whether to be furious or flattered. I've no idea how these people manage to find out stuff. You're right, I do need a holiday."

"Everything here will run like clockwork."

Rosie wrapped an arm around her.

Bronte let her head drop on her friend's shoulder.

"I'll be so glad when the most important men in my life meet and it's all over. I'm looking forward to the break."

Rosie dropped into a chair.

"Yeah, two weeks in France is a pretty good deal."

Her father had organized a week in Paris and a week at his home in Cap Ferret.

"Paris, I can't wait."

Rosie frowned, drumming her fingertip over her lips.

"You need to tell Nico how you feel."

"I don't want to hear it."

Shoulders stiff, ignoring the clutch in her stomach, Bronte sipped her water.

A heavy wave of nausea roiled up from her gut and over her cheeks, leaving her shivery and clammy.

A headache jabbed a punch behind her right eye.

"God, Bronte, you've turned grey."

With a roaring in her ears, her friend's voice seemed to fade into the distance.

Bronte found herself pushed into a chair with her head being thrust between her legs.

She took a few deep breaths and sat upright.

"Wow, a head rush."

She took another sip of water and closed her eyes.

"This is all my fault," Rosie told her.

"Excuse me?"

"If I hadn't been talked into forcing you out on that stupid blind date, none of this would have happened."

Bronte wasn't having any of it.

"You're being ridiculous. In many ways I don't regret a thing. I'm not responsible for Nico's behavior and neither are you."

"Men," Rosie said, looking very fierce. "Are the spawn of Satan."

Bronte caught her eye.

"Ain't that the truth?"

Later that evening, after a warm bath, pink-skinned and rosy-cheeked, Bronte felt more like herself.

The nap had helped enormously, too.

Dressed in pink flannel pj's with white bunnies and thick socks - a fun present from Rosie – she tied up her hair in its usual knot and padded into the kitchen in search of food.

How could a person have three freezers full and absolutely nothing to eat?

It was a mystery.

She surfed through the fridge, found a pizza past its sell by date and a dozen eggs.

Neither floated her boat.

The larder offered up oats, pasta, rice and various tins.

She turned up her nose, no wonder she wasn't hungry.

Then she found a tin of shortbread on the top shelf, a packet of salted peanuts and two bars of milk chocolate.

Strangely enough, the mix appealed to her.

On a wooden tray, she assembled the hoard and added in a bottle of Cumberland Ale.

Her taste buds appeared to have changed, too.

As a rule, she didn't drink beer.

Beer was her brother's favorite tipple, but wine didn't taste quite right at the moment.

With a biscuit between her teeth, the hair on the back of her neck rose as Bronte became aware of the presence of another right behind her.

Very slowly, she turned around.

Her brain did an emergency stop, as her eyes remained glued to his.

It took her a couple of heartbeats for her brain to actually believe what her eyes were seeing.

The sneer on his lips along with the slight tremble of his hands made her break out in a cold sweat as did the realization that hit her like a truck that she was in terrible, terrible trouble.

Wearing black jeans and a black designer puffa jacket over a sweater, he was a stocky big bear of a man with sandy hair that needed a wash and a swarthy complexion.

His skin appeared bloated and mottled.

A part of her brain that appeared to be working independently wondered if he'd been drinking or was on something, because his pupils were fully dilated.

"If you turn around and leave right now, I won't call the police," she told him, keeping her voice firm.

Anthony's cold eyes wandered from the top of her head to her feet and back again.

Perspiration beaded on his brow and his unshaven top lip.

Instinct, that had served women throughout time, told Bronte why he was here.

He was going to hurt her.

Like a rabbit caught in a trap, her pulse beat too hard and too fast.

She knew now who'd been phoning the house.

She knew who'd been leaving abusive comments on the website.

And she knew who'd damaged her car.

Bronte also knew that if she ran or showed fear, she'd be finished.

"No wonder Jonno dumped you, bitch. Do what you like, the back door was open and I'll say you let me in dressed in your pyjamas. It'll be your word against mine."

His over-excited voice was too high.

Now he licked his lips in a way that made her feel physically ill.

The room spun.

She took a sharp breath.

Think, think, think.

She shook her head, her eyes riveted on his.

"I don't know who Jonno is or what you're talking about."

Keep him talking.

Talk him down.

Get him to sit.

Run for the panic button at the door.

Get out.

"Your old fiancé, my mate Jonathan! He told me all about

you, what a pure bitch you are."

With an overdone bravado, which might have been comical under other circumstances, but wound the terror in her belly even tighter, Anthony swaggered over and picked up the bottle of ale.

His eyes slid over her as he sucked on the bottle.

"You owe me for running out on me. That room cost me and I didn't even get to enjoy it. They banned me from Ludlow Hall. Me, can you fucking believe it? And all because of that Italian you spread your legs for. He's not here now though, is he?"

Those beady eyes narrowed on her as he finished the bottle, broke wind and tossed it over his shoulder.

The glass bottle hit the stone floor and exploded like a gun shot.

Anger battled through panic that this revolting excuse for a man should enter *her* home and treat her like this.

"Get out!"

"Not before I get what I want."

"What do you want?"

Stupid.

She knew it was a stupid question.

But Bronte simply could not bring herself to show weakness.

Shrugging off his jacket, Anthony tossed it in the direction of a chair, all the while watching her like a starving wolf salivating over a fat and tasty lamb.

He grabbed his crotch, gave it an obscene jiggle.

And Bronte absolutely refused to let her mind go there.

"I want a piece of the action, Bronte baby. You know what your problem is? You can't keep a man, can you? Jonno, poor fucker, had to put up with you treating him like shit. Imagine telling your fiancé you fancied his friend? And when that friend takes you on a date, you get him hard and blow him off! Then the Italian lasted for what, a week? And now you've got yourself a stinking rich old sugar daddy?"

He barked a harsh laugh of disbelief.

"You fucking kill me, Bronte. But, you..." He pulled off his sweater, revealing a torso the consistency of fresh tripe and jabbed a finger at her. Bile rose into her throat and her heart beat even faster. "*You* need taught a lesson and I'm just the man to give you one. Take off the kiddie pyjamas. Let's see if you're a natural blonde. Or is the hair as fake as the goody-goody act?" With absolute clarity Bronte knew he was going to rape her.

A strange calmness washed through her.

Her mind seemed to split into two separate parts.

One part remained petrified, cowering in a corner in utter disbelief, while the other part of her brain looked at the situation objectively.

There was no question of giving-in in her mind.

No question.

She was going to fight.

Even though she knew that the advice given to women in her situation was to give in, get out of it alive and live to see another day.

And then it would be his word against hers?

Consensual sex?

No way.

If Anthony thought he could prove sex was consensual then it was up to her to make sure there would be plenty of evidence to the contrary.

But by God, she would put up a fight.

She was going to scratch and claw and bite.

Because even if she died, the world would know who killed her.

No way was she going to cower and whimper for him and give him even more power, more control.

No way.

But, oh God, she hadn't told Nico she loved him.

And now it was too late.

No.

She couldn't think like that.

Now Bronte lifted her chin and took a step towards the door leading to the main part of the house.

"Jonathan lied to you, Anthony. But you're too delusional to realize that aren't you? And you need to get high or drunk to get your rocks off. You're a pathetic excuse for a real man!"

The hot flash in his eye alerted her as he lunged towards her.

Bronte spun, at the same time grabbing the heavy fruit bowl from the table and threw it with all of her might.

Her aim was off, but luckily for her Anthony ducked.

The fruit bowl caught him on the temple.

And she raced out the kitchen, through the hall towards the front door.

His howl of outrage followed her.

The thud of heavy boots had her screaming at the top of her lungs as she slapped her hand on the alarm.

Shocked for a split second by the ear-piercing siren, her frantic fingers fumbled with the deadbolts at the top and bottom of the door.

Christ, why was it locked?

Then his hands were on her, tearing at her pyjamas.

He backhanded her across the face.

And Bronte Ludlow screamed and screamed and screamed as her nails tore into his hands, his face.

Then was a searing pain in her head.

She couldn't see.

She couldn't hear.

Panic and horror overwhelmed her.

His breath was panting in her ear.

Bronte's world went dark.

Chapter Twenty Seven

Nico couldn't believe it had been a whole month since he'd set foot in The Dower House.

The car entered Bronte's private road and he automatically drove to the rear of the property.

Would she be happy to see him?

Probably not, Nico decided, but he needed to swallow his damned pride and tell her how much he loved her.

If there was one thing he tried never to do, it was to live with regrets.

Thanks to Bronte, he'd found his family.

His brother was happily married to an American girl, Julie.

And he had two kids, Carmen who was five and Giancarlo who was six months.

Although his father was terminally ill, he'd rallied.

Thanks, Gabriel said, to Nico.

Perhaps Bronte would agree to meet them?

If they couldn't be lovers, perhaps she would agree to be friends?

The thought squeezed his lungs as he took a shuddering breath.

He switched off the engine and opened the door.

With his hand raised to knock the door, the scream of a woman terrified for her life pierced the still winter night.

Bronte!

He tried the handle.

The door was locked.

The house alarm screeching a high keening sound stunned him for a split second.

But he heaved a metal plant pot filled with happy pansies

through the door window.

All the while, his heart pounded in his ears as he groped through broken glass for the key in the lock.

Turning the key, he was through the door, racing towards desperate screams that stopped abruptly.

Tearing through the kitchen over broken glass, remains of the smashed fruit bowl and into the hall, all Nico saw was the man who straddled her, one hand squeezing her neck while the other dug hard fingers into a bare breast.

Her clothes torn and bloody.

And Bronte lay under him like a rag doll.

A howl of terrified rage roared from Nico's throat as he grabbed Anthony by the hair planting a heavy fist in his face.

Nico felt and heard cartilage break and didn't give a hot damn.

Blood spurting, profanities spewing from his lips, Anthony slipped, sliding through his own fluids in a vain attempt to clamber to his feet making ready to run.

Now the boy from Rome, a boy who'd survived in streets with no law, no justice, leaped through the veneer of civilised respectability to possess the man.

Nico simply drop-kicked the whimpering coward.

Then he placed his foot, his full weight, on the scum's thigh, grabbed his ankle and pulled.

Anthony's kneecap popped with a noise like a champagne cork.

The sobbing scream of agony was music to Nico's ears.

Anthony wouldn't be fucking going anywhere.

Nico spun around to Bronte and dropped to his knees.

A whine, like an animal in pain, escaped from his throat.

As he gathered her close, he reached for his cell phone.

The police and ambulance paramedics found Nico on his knees

rocking Bronte's limp body in his arms, bitter tears pouring down his face.

Chapter Twenty Eight

They wouldn't let him see her.

They'd told him nothing except she was alive.

She'd still been unconscious when they'd arrived at the hospital, so fragile, so pale and so damned vulnerable.

Nico paced to the door of the waiting room and back again.

How could anyone, any man, dream of hurting her?

He simply could not get his head around it.

For over three relentless hours he'd worn a path in the floor of the hospital waiting room while the police had taken his statement.

Anthony Lawrence Brown, to give the piece of shit his full name, had totally flipped, spewing enough bile about Bronte that the police would be charging him with assault and attempted rape. He'd confessed in front of witnesses. The police had had the presence of mind to take him to another hospital.

Nico could care less about the bastard.

The night had been a horror he knew he'd never forget.

Rosie was on her way and, since she'd phoned him, so was Carl Terlezki.

And if that wasn't proof of how much the man meant to Bronte, Nico didn't know what was.

It wasn't Bronte's fault that she couldn't love him.

It wasn't as if he'd given her much of a reason to love him.

He had handled their relationship so badly, so stupidly, he could not believe it.

Reflection had given Nico the luxury of time to realize that he only wanted what was best for her.

He'd thought he had plenty of time to win her back.

The truth of his situation was like a fist to the throat.

He'd wasted a whole month, held back by fear of failure.

To lose her now would kill a part of him and destroy him in ways he daren't contemplate.

The door to the waiting room flew open and Rosie's scared wide eyes scanned the room until they found him.

Rosie was closely followed by a too pale looking Carl Terlezki.

"How is she?" Rosie demanded and promptly burst into tears.

"They won't tell me..."

Nico's voice broke as Rosie hugged him very hard and he held on tight.

"Thank God you found her," Carl said in a voice that shook and extended his hand. "I will never be able to repay you."

Nico took his hand, realization dawning that the man loved Bronte desperately.

A tired looking young nurse appeared at the door.

"I'm looking for the family of Bronte Ludlow?"

Carl looked at Rosie.

Rosie gave him a gentle push towards the nurse.

And Nico thought his heart was being crushed in his chest.

Well, that said it all didn't it?

Defeated, Nico moved on unsteady legs to sit next to Rosie as the nurse asked Carl.

"And you are?"

Carl glanced at Rosie who gave him a nod of encouragement.

"Ah... I am her father."

"Great, come with me. She's been very distressed and is still little bit out of it, but the doctor will give you an update."

Stunned, Nico simply stared at the door after Carl and the nurse left.

Then he turned wide eyes to a Rosie who was watching him like a dark-eyed raptor.

He had the bizarre feeling he was living in a crazy parallel universe.

One minute his life was over, the next he had a glimmer of hope.

"Her *father*?"

Nico stared at Rosie.

She patted his knee.

"Yep, it's a long story. Thing is, Alexander hasn't met him yet. They'll only go public with it once Alexander agrees. The family's reputation will take a hit. And the press already have the bit between their teeth."

Nico held his head in his hands as everything Bronte had told him in Rome, something her mother should have told her and how words unspoken caused heartache washed through his mind.

"*Madre di Dio!*"

Rosie rubbed Nico's knee in a *there-there* gesture.

"I don't know what it is about men. But if anything can be fucked up, you'll do it every time."

In response, Nico gave a weary groan of heartfelt agreement.

Almost an hour later, Carl entered the waiting room with a decided glint in his eye, his mouth a tight white line.

Nico literally felt the saliva dry in his mouth as he stood to face Bronte's father for the first time.

In his Savile Row cashmere coat and handmade shoes, Bronte's father looked the impressive financier he was.

He had a reputation as a man who took no prisoners.

Now Nico felt the full force of an iron will.

He braced himself.

Carl stood in front of him, tall and still a dynamic man even though he was in his sixties.

He placed a deliberately heavy hand on Nico's shoulder.

"Son? Want a piece of advice?"

Nico knew when to fold.

He ran a hand over his jaw and met the man's beady eye.

"*Si*, I would be very grateful."

"Do you love my daughter?"

"*Si*, yes sir. I do."

"Then you walk right into that room and tell her."

Carl checked the time on his watch and turned to Rosie.

"I need to book into Ludlow Hall. You can keep me company for breakfast while you tell me every single thing you know about my daughter's ex-fiancé."

Rosie beamed up at him and took his arm.

"It will be my pleasure. I hope you're gonna kick ass."

"Honey, by the time I'm finished with him, he won't have an ass."

Nico followed the nurse to a private room.

Lying on the bed, curled up on her side with her back to him, the love of his life wore a cotton hospital gown the color of fresh garden mint.

The nurse trundled out an ECG machine and closed the door.

For a long moment, Nico simply stood there looking at her with words racing through his mind.

Deciding her father was right, Nico picked up a black plastic chair and carried it around to the other side of the bed.

Eyes stinging, his gaze lingered on the livid black and blue fingerprints on her neck and her split lip.

A fragile hand with bruised knuckles and torn and bloody fingernails clutched the remains of a tissue.

God bless her.

His baby had got her licks in and had fought like a warrior.

God, he adored her.

Even if she did look a mess.

Her nose and eyes were red and swollen.

"*Cara* ..."

Bronte opened her eyes and the single flick of fury in them stopped him dead.

Her utter loathing for him crystal clear.

"Shut up!" Her voice was raw as her eyes pooled and her lips trembled. "This is all your entire fault and so bloody *typical*!"

She spat the last word.

Nico winced as he sat on the chair pulling it close to her bed.

"But, Bronte, I... Ow!"

She punched him hard on the shoulder as tears tipped over.

"I don't want to love *you*. I didn't ask to love *you*. I don't even want to like *you*!"

Nico's response was to haul her into his arms

He didn't care if she was naked under the gown except for a pair of tiny panties.

And he totally ignored her yelp of outrage.

She punched him again.

And Nico took it like a man.

"It's so typical of you," she said again and spoke into his throat as he stroked her matted hair and begged her to shush. "No I won't bloody shush. I've read about men like you!"

His finger tipped up her chin and he studied her beautiful and bruised face.

"Men like me?"

Giving in to temptation, he kissed her.

She made a valiant attempt to thrust him away, but he held her close.

"Men with super sperm that can penetrate latex. You find them in romance novels. Trust me to find the genuine article."

His chest felt too tight as his lungs deflated.

He blinked at her.

"You mean?"

"I'm *pregnant*."

The last word was a long, heartfelt wail.

Nico shut his eyes and held her close as she sobbed her heart out into his chest.

And he bit his lip as he recalled one occasion when he'd made love to her without protection.

He pressed his cheek to her hair and simply rocked her back and forth.

And thanked God, Baby Jesus, Buddha and the Universe for bringing this woman into his life.

Once she'd cried herself out, he refused to release her even when she struggled.

"Let me go."

"Never."

He stared into her eyes and felt as if he could drown in their emerald depths.

Gathering his courage in both hands, he asked the question that would break his heart if she said no.

"Do you want a baby?"

Tears pooled again in her eyes as her breath hitched.

"I'm not supposed to be able to get pregnant. I have a medical condition, endometriosis and I was told I might never conceive. But trust you to ride roughshod over Mother Nature."

He bit his lip at the dazed expression on her face.

"Are you happy about the news or not?"

She punched him again.

"Of course I want our baby. You're the one who doesn't want a family, remember?"

"I want a family with you."

He kissed her and this time there was nothing soft about it.

It was a kiss of a man desperately in love with his woman, his mate.

Those eyes stared into his as if searching his very soul.

"You change your mind like you do your shirts. How do I know you won't change it again tomorrow or the next day or the next week?"

"You are my reason for living. I love you, Bronte. My heart, all that I am, is yours."

Tears swam in her eyes, but this time they were happy tears he was relieved to see.

"I love you so much, Nico, so much."

She heaved in a huge shuddering breath.

Enormous green eyes stared into his.

"But Nico, I'm a bastard."

His mouth plundered hers before he raised his head to grin into her face.

"That makes two of us, *cara.*"

Chapter Twenty Nine

Two months later.

With gentle open mouthed kisses on his wife's still flat stomach, Nico worked his way along her hip as Bronte gave a contented little sigh.

Lifting his head, he met her lazy smile with one of his own.

He pulled the duvet over them and felt her snuggle into his side.

He pressed his lips to her hair.

"Madame insists on supplying your wedding gown."

Bronte's head shot up and a sharp finger poked him in the chest.

"That woman is not coming within ten feet of me." She pressed her hand to her stomach, gave it a little pat. "Or my child."

With his tongue planted firmly in his cheek, Nico sighed.

"I only want you to look beautiful on our big day. She has selected four." His lips twitched as he saw her frown. Love swept over him as he buried his face in her neck and inhaled the pure essence of his wife. "Do it for me, *cara mia*, I do not wish to see you married in chef whites."

"We're already married. I don't see why we have to go through with another ceremony," she said in a sulky tone he was coming to adore.

"That was the civil ceremony, as you well know. Don't you want a party with friends and family?"

"We had friends and family."

Nico leaned on his elbow and stared down at her.

That stubborn, belligerent look he loved glared back at him.

The only time she ever gave him trouble was when it came to clothes. But they needed to do this for their families and then she would be his alone for a six week honeymoon.

He couldn't wait.

She narrowed her eyes and pouted as she gave in to his demands.

"Okay. If she pokes and prods, mutters and moans, I will not be held responsible for my actions."

They married on the beach at Cap Ferret at sunset, surrounded by the people who mattered most.

With Rosie as the maid of honor and a deliriously excited Carmen, Gabriel's five year old daughter as her flower girl, Bronte walked towards her husband dressed in an Elie Saab strapless gown of ivory silk. She carried a single blushing pink rose. Alexander held her hand in the crook of his arm. Carl had insisted her brother give her away. Bronte wore no shoes or jewellery other than her three carat diamond engagement ring.

Nico waited for her with his brother Gabriel, who winked at his daughter. His American wife, Julia, carried their dark-haired baby boy. The men wore cream tuxes with white shirts, no ties and Nico had refused to wear shoes, too.

He looked so handsome and so very happy, Bronte's heart caught in her throat.

Safe in the arms of her husband, Bronte watched the sunset and realized yes, dreams really do come true.

Epilogue

"Congratulations! Where is my godson?"

Rosie boogied into the hospital room holding a blue teddy bear with a helium balloon tied around its neck and an armful of cream roses.

She dumped everything on a table, danced to the sink to wash and dry her hands.

She turned to grin at Bronte in the bed and wiggled her fingers.

"Gimme."

Bronte sat in bed with a dark haired baby nestled in her arms and a beaming smile on her face.

Nico looked out of the window and caught his wife's eye over his shoulder.

"Oooooh, look at him, isn't he gorgeous?" Rosie took the baby carefully from Bronte, her eyes damp and misty. "Hello, Luca darling."

She touched his perfect tiny fingers.

"And meet Sophia." Nico turned round with another baby, smaller than her brother, but with a head of ash blonde hair.

Rosie's jaw hit the floor as Alexander arrived with a pink teddy and balloon.

"I don't believe it! How did you keep this a secret from me?"

Bronte pulled up her knees.

Three days after a caesarean delivery, she still felt fragile.

"Probably because we've been living at Lake Como and you've been running *Sweet Sensation*. Ooooh, don't make me laugh. It's the first time I've ever seen you speechless."

Rosie shook her head in mock disgust and beaned Alexander with a jaundiced eye.

"Let this be a lesson to you. Look what happens in this family when you have unprotected sex."

Rosie always had to have the last word.

The End

It Doesn't Stop Here

Please sign up to my New Release newsletter at:
http://smarturl.it/ccmcksign

From my newsletter you'll receive information on my new stories, deals and offers. Your contact details will not be shared with a third party and I promise not to spam your inbox.

Keep in Touch

CC MacKenzie is a USA Today Bestselling Author of contemporary and paranormal romance. She loves to hear from her readers; you can find her at:

Website
http://ccmackenzie.com/

Email:
ccmackenzie@ccmackenzie.com

Facebook
http://www.facebook.com/CCMzie

Twitter
@CCMacKenzie1

Hear CC MacKenzie's latest news.
Interact with her Readers.
And Please leave a review.

Thank You!

Other Books by CC MacKenzie

Available Now

LUDLOW HALL SERIES

A Stormy Spring - Book 2
Run Rosie Run - Book 3
The Trouble with Coco Monroe - Book 4
The Fall of Jacob Del Garda – Book 5
A Film Star, A Baby. and a Proposal – Book 6
A Christmas Story 1
Delicious and Deadly: Invitation to Eden Book 8
An Affair To Remember: A Ludlow Hall Christmas: Book 9

"A Daddy For Daisy" - Book 7 will be out in 2015

THE DESERT PRINCES SERIES

Desert Orchid – Book 1

First Chapter: 'A Stormy Spring'

A Ludlow Hall Romance: Book 2

Where were her panties?

On her hands and knees, and naked as the day she was born, Becca's fingers fluttered around the floor, under the bed and found a scrap of silk she realized was her bra. Further exploration found a single shoe. With hair streaming across her face she wondered where the hell was the other one?

A deep rumbling voice muttered words in Spanish and brought her head up with a jerk. Tucking a curl behind her ear, she peered through dawn's early light at the man the glossy magazines had crowned one of the world's most celebrated bachelors. He slept amid tousled white cotton sheets in a bed the size of a lake. Sheets she'd tangled and a bed she knew every single inch of.

What a night.

She ached in places she never even knew existed.

The things he'd done to her had been truly...

Becca froze as a muscled arm flopped over the side of the bed missing her by a whisker. She let out a shaky sigh in relief as he murmured again before pressing his face into the pillow.

The spiked heel of her designer shoe dug into her knee. How she managed to contain the hiss of agony she'd never know.

On shaky legs, dangling her shoes in one hand she got to her feet.

With short panting breaths, she tip-toed to the door and slid into the sitting-room of the luxurious hotel suite.

Her eyes widened as a table lamp shed an intimate glow on the evidence of the night before.

Amongst the debris, her dress lay in a heap of red silk. Along with his shirt and tie and hastily toed off socks and shoes. No sign of her panties.

She desperately tried to remember the sequence of last night's events.

Not a good idea.

Don't think.

Get out.

Struggling into her dress, Becca wondered what she'd been thinking. She never did things like this. Things like having a one night stand with a perfect stranger. And he was perfect all right, in every conceivable way. The society pages didn't do him justice. They couldn't begin to capture his height, his broad shouldered strength or the sensitivity of that amazing mouth.

One look was all it had taken, one dance, and she was the one who'd asked him to touch her, to kiss her, to...

Stop it.

Don't think about his mouth.

Frantic fingers zipped up her dress.

Shoving the bra into her bag, she thrust her feet into sky high heels.

Running away was sheer cowardice. She knew it, but it couldn't be helped.

The whole thing felt surreal.

She was way, way out of her depth. Perhaps she should leave him a note? Thanks for having me?

An erotic little shiver ran up her spine and she knew she'd never forget last night.

Her hand reached for the door handle.

"Going somewhere, Becca?"

The deep voice husky from sleep held the musical lilt of Spain. It vibrated up her spine and brought jumpy nerves to her throat. The gentle tone, filled with humor, stopped her from acting on her initial instinct and making a run for it.

She turned.

Eyes the color of dark chocolate slammed into hers. Once

RECKLESS NIGHTS IN ROME

again their impact left her reeling, off balance.

It was such a cliché but how on earth could one look across a crowded room have led to this?

He was naked except for black trousers, unbuttoned and unzipped. Her physical reaction, the shortness of breath as her heart ricocheted into her throat and the weakness in her legs couldn't be blamed on a couple of glasses of champagne. She was stone cold sober this morning.

Those immense shoulders leaned against the doorframe. She'd pressed her mouth against that marvelous chest, clutched those dark tousled locks as he'd kissed her intimately. Heat rushed into her cheeks. By his broad grin he'd read her mind.

Her brain soaked up the sight of him. He was ridiculously handsome with the light of fun along with a smoldering desire in his eyes as they stayed on hers.

Attack, Becca firmly believed, was the best line of defense.

She frowned. "Don't look at me like that."

Narrowing his eyes at the combative tone of her lovely voice, Lucas Del Garda recognized panic when he saw it and when he heard it.

Her hair, the color of burnt toffee, tumbled in slippery curls around slim shoulders.

Beautiful blue eyes glittered into his.

She hadn't sounded like that a few short hours ago with those high little moans panting in her throat as she'd begged him to take her. She'd been wild for him and he'd loved it. He had no idea how many times he'd made her come since he wasn't the sort of man who kept score. But she'd twisted and turned under him and almost burst his eardrums with her screams of completion.

If she thought he was prepared for her to leave without so much as a telephone number, then Becca was sorely mistaken. He had no idea of her surname, what she did or where she came from.

This had been a first for him. He never indulged in sex with a beautiful woman without covering the preliminaries.

Her eyes were spectacular, blindingly blue, as they stared into his he read embarrassment, despair and a mounting alarm that tickled his antennae. Hmm, it seemed Becca had regrets and wanted to escape. Interesting. Most women were more than happy to snuggle after sex. He wasn't a snuggler, never had been and usually managed to extricate himself without any trouble. But last night had been the first time he'd held a woman close. It felt natural with her. It felt right.

Lucas didn't analyze his feelings but accepted them for what they were. He'd known the instant she left his bed and listened to her hunting for her clothes. It had been wrong of him to play with her and he almost laughed as he remembered her little whimper of alarm.

Intrigued, he studied her. No, Becca did not look happy to see him.

For a moment he toyed with the idea of seducing her back to bed but those big eyes staring at him in silent appeal held him back.

He stepped towards her, zipped up his pants and sent her an intimate smile.

Much better to play it cool. Keep it friendly and relaxed.

"The least I can do after such a wonderful night is to offer you breakfast." He picked up the telephone and kept a sharp eye on her. A frown creased her smooth forehead as she moved towards the centre of the room.

He indicated the couch. "Please, Becca, sit down. We can be civilized about this."

Becca kept a wary eye on him as he ordered enough breakfast to feed a family of four.

Her stomach growled and she took a breath.

Okay, be an adult, you can do this. Eat, do small talk and then leave. No problem.

"Would you like to shower or have a bath?" His voice vibrated along her nerve ends. Deep, gravelly and sexy as hell, he could make a fortune as a voice over. She imagined him modeling Speedos lounging on a boat in the middle of the ocean.

Those dark sinful eyes curling the toes of every female who watched TV wishing she was there with him. Well, that's how advertising agencies sold expensive cologne for men. They appealed to the women in their lives. And Becca knew Lucas would appeal to any female with a pulse.

She blinked as he raised a dark brow and she realized she hadn't answered his question.

"Yes. Thank you."

He pointed her in the direction of another bedroom.

She wandered through and found an en-suite in black granite with a huge walk in shower.

Stripping down to her skin she wondered again where her panties had gone.

Becca piled her hair on top of her head, suddenly breathless as water shot from six different jets. The designer liquid soap smelt wonderful and she slathered it over her body, stifling a groan as the purely feminine part of her throbbed with desire and an aching need that scandalized her in its intensity.

What on earth was happening to her?

A gasp of shock escaped from her throat as large hands slid gently but possessively over her flat belly and small breasts. How did he know which parts of her were too tender this morning? His fingertips lingered with exquisite care on nipples so delicately sensitized to his touch they were hot-wired to that yearning pulse between her legs.

"If you want me to stop, *querida*, I will," Lucas whispered into her ear.

The man, Becca decided with a low moan, had magical fingers.

She knew she should tell him to stop, but heat scorched over her too sensitive skin wherever he touched her. Her breath caught as his tongue licked her throat and his arousal, thick and hard, pressed into the small of her back.

Lust detonated between her legs as he turned her in his arms, pressed her back against black granite and captured her mouth with his even as her nipples grazed his chest. She parted her lips to allow his thrusting tongue access. God, he tasted fantastic.

This time there was nothing gentle in the kiss. There was power, possession and a relentless hunger. That hunger called to her and she answered it with a desperation that verged on insanity.

Was she making those high, keening moans? Her ardor matched his, kiss for kiss, touch for touch.

When his fingers slipped between her legs, slid around that screaming little pearl of nerve ends, her legs gave way as the climax took her breath.

"Put your legs around my waist," he muttered in her ear, his voice was deep, the tone harsh as he caught her mouth with his and she did as he asked.

Then, thank God, he was inside her.

She clung to him, legs around his waist, and arms around his neck as he pumped his hips, thrusting into her, gasping desperate words in Spanish into her mouth. Together they soared higher and higher to a place she'd never known existed before last night. The muscles contracting her centre clutched him again and again. Then the world went black as her mind splintered into a thousand stars.

Their hearts hammering as one, Becca realized Lucas was bearing her weight as well as leaning a hand against the wall for support.

Their panting breaths mingled before he groaned into the soft spot under her ear. Pressing a soft kiss to his shoulder, she clung to him and blinked as the water, cool now, battered their skin.

Lucas flicked hair from his face and those dark eyes framed with wet lashes studied her carefully.

He grinned as a hot flush rose from her toes to flood her neck and cheeks.

"Now that is how I want you to look at me, *querida*, not like a scared little rabbit." Although his voice was soft, the tone was of a man used to command.

His fingertip stroked a burning path down the curve of her breast to a bullet hard nipple.

Then reality gave her a hard slap.

Becca caught herself and blinked furiously to hide the

emotions that flooded her throat and stung her eyes.

Blindly and on legs that were far from steady, she moved out of his arms, out of the shower. With a shudder she pulled on the complimentary thick white cotton bathrobe and wound a towel around her head.

Rolling up each sleeve, she refused to look at him as he dried himself.

A quick glance told her his eyes had tightened and his intense gaze made the nerves clutching her stomach grow claws.

She turned away from him.

A firm hand on her arm pulled her back.

Those eyes were not so gentle on her now, but edged with suspicion.

"I see we have a problem." Lucas gripped her other arm and gave her a non-too-gentle shake. "Are you in a relationship? or..." Those dark eyes searching hers narrowed into slits. "Are you married?"

Becca went very still, needles of tension prickling up her spine.

His eyes went ice over steel and she trembled.

"Answer me!" His voice was a whip lashing across raw emotions.

In her head the last ten hours had assumed a surreal quality, almost like an out of body experience. He shook her again and the cold reality of her situation gave her another slap. This time yesterday she hadn't set eyes on this man. The way she'd danced with him, kissed him, touched him, in the nightclub had shame burn a scorching path up her neck and into her cheeks.

The way she'd gone to his hotel without a second thought for her personal safety had common sense demand now what the hell had she been thinking.

She'd let a total stranger take liberties with her body. Do things to her; touch her in ways she'd never been touched before... even by... Guilt incinerated her cheeks.

Becca blinked up into a face she didn't recognize now. He looked too big, too wide, too male. His eyes were cold, hard and absolutely appalled.

How could she have been so stupid to put herself at risk and behave in a way that was so alien to her nature? Humiliation warred with self-reproach and utter fury.

The toxic mix of emotions burned in her throat and Becca hung on to anger like a lifeline.

How dare he treat her like this?

She pushed him, dismayed when he didn't budge.

Her legs might be trembling, but her chin came up.

"Let me go," she whispered.

Time seemed to stand still before he thrust her away as if she'd burned him. Becca staggered as he turned and stalked out of the bathroom. She nearly jumped out of her skin as the bedroom door slammed like a gunshot.

Scrubbing hot tears from her cheeks Becca wondered what on earth she was going to do.

She towel dried her hair before dragging a comb through it so hard it brought fresh tears to her eyes. No crying. It changed nothing.

For two years she'd held it together. Managed to lock grief into that dark place in her psyche. She'd thrown herself into working ten or even twelve hour days. But cracks were appearing in her facade when she least expected it. These days her behavior, her mood swings, were becoming more and more erratic. The pressure of delivering to strict creative deadlines again and again was getting to her. The feeling that she was like a hamster on a wheel, going nowhere fast, was taking its toll.

Last night had been her first night out since...

The agony in her heart was beyond pain and she ordered herself to focus on the moment and not to think about the past. The main thing was to get out of here in one piece and she still had to get past a very angry Lucas.

How could she tell a stranger something she still battled to come to terms with herself? She knew it simply wasn't logical to feel as if she'd betrayed Rick, but she couldn't help feeling terribly guilty.

Not only had she had sex with another man, but it been outside any experience she'd had with her late husband. Rick had been a careful, gentle lover. He'd cherished and loved her. What she'd experienced last night had been nothing but lust, the sexual act at its most primitive, most basic.

What did that say about her as a woman?

Grief, still horribly fresh, roared through her system. Closing her eyes tight, Becca fought for control as she steadied herself.

She desperately needed to find that dark place where she brooded in safe isolation.

The occasional shudder overtook her as she fumbled with the zip of her dress and thrust her feet into her shoes. She wound a cashmere pashmina the color of bone around her shoulders and picked up her bag, all the while chanting to herself to get out and away from this man.

With a deep inhale and exhale, she opened the door and stepped into the sitting room.

The scent of bacon and freshly ground coffee made her stomach heave.

Lucas was sitting at a desk writing on a sheet of hotel paper. He wore soft blue jeans and a black sweater. His feet were bare.

The logical unemotional part of her brain, the part that got her through every endless day, noticed the way his black hair clung to his skull and that he had the most beautiful hands.

He turned and saw her.

Becca kept her eyes on his chin.

The atmosphere was so icy she shivered.

"Rebecca, what?" The words, quietly spoken, vibrated with suppressed fury.

"I'm sorry?"

"Your surname."

"Wainwright," she whispered.

"That would be Mrs. Rebecca Wainwright?"

She nodded. It was the simple truth.

"Won't he be wondering where you are?"

The burn of utter grief in Becca's throat made speech impossible, so she merely gave a jerky shake of her head.

He folded the paper and placed it in an envelope. All the while those dark eyes stayed on her face.

"You are a piece of work, Mrs. Wainwright. I do not suppose I am the first to be taken in by those big eyes? Or do you have the usual sob story about how your husband does not understand you?"

Becca blinked and opened her mouth to tell him the truth then closed it. What had happened to her was none of this man's business.

Common sense told her she'd done nothing wrong, but her heart told her she'd betrayed Rick by acting like a common whore. She'd let Lucas Del Garda touch her in ways, kiss her in ways that had broken every link in the chain of her self control. Rick would never have bent her over the arm of a sofa, thrusting into her, rutting like an animal, so hard that his balls slapped against her sweet spot. Self-disgust burned her cheeks as she admitted to herself she'd loved every single second of the experience.

What she'd wanted, needed, had been a physical connection, intimacy, with another human being. She'd been starving for it, Becca realized now with the benefit of hindsight.

This man, who had swept her off her feet last night was physically overwhelming and an expert in seduction. He'd played her body like a violin, knowing precisely which strings to pluck to make her soar to his tune. And God, she'd soared to dizzying heights. Heights she'd never ever reached with the love of her life.

Her womb clutched again as she stood there just staring at Lucas and she wondered if she would ever be able to forgive herself for still having lingering erotic feelings of desire for a total stranger.

"I've never done anything like this before," she whispered.

The effect of his dark nerve-shredding stare was devastating.

The hold on her emotions became shiveringly unstable.

Heat scorched her cheeks as his gaze ran over her body possessively.

She caught a glimpse of the thundering pulse in the hollow of his throat before he swallowed and took a deep breath.

His hand fisted on the table.

"Can I call you?" The words were spoken so softly she strained to hear him.

The room was so quiet she might have heard a silkworm breathe.

Feelings all over the place with everything that had happened in the last few hours, initially her mind refused to compute.

Good God, he believed she was married and was willing to have an affair?

Disappointment with him warred with a righteous anger that she'd behaved like a wanton with a man who appeared to have no respect for women or the sanctity of marriage. Becca didn't take much notice of the tabloids, but it appeared they'd been spot on with this guy and he'd had the gall to say that she was a piece of work?

What kind of man was he?

She shook her head as the mounting fury with herself turned outwards. Anger felt a hell of a lot better than guilt.

Her throat was dust dry. "I don't think that would be a good idea."

His eyes were cool now and remained on her face as he stood and moved towards her.

For a moment she thought he was going to argue, but he handed her the envelope.

"If you ever change your mind."

Heart thundering in her ears, she stared at the envelope before dropping it at his feet.

Opening the door Becca looked back and tipped up her chin, finding it hard to focus through swimming emotions.

"Don't hold your breath. I'm not married." She blinked rapidly to clear her vision and saw his eyes narrow before she continued, "He died. And he was worth ten of you."

Made in the USA
San Bernardino, CA
23 July 2016